BLOOD OF THE SHARK

A ROMANCE OF EARLY HAWAII

I0629354

BY BEATRICE AYER PATTON

Drawings by Cornelia Macintyre Foley

PARADISE OF THE PACIFIC LTD.   HONOLULU, HAWAII

BLOOD OF THE SHARK

Copyright, 1936, by Beatrice Ayer Patton

FIRST EDITION, DECEMBER, 1936.
SECOND EDITION, FEBRUARY, 1937.
THIRD EDITION, MAY, 1946

All rights in this book are reserved. It may not be used for dramatic, motion or talking-picture purposes without written authorization from the holder of these rights. Nor may the text or part thereof be reproduced in any manner whatsoever other than in book reviews without permission in writing. For information address: Paradise of the Pacific, Ltd., 424 South Beretania Street, Honolulu, Territory of Hawaii, U.S.A.

Index

		PAGE
I.	THE RED SKIRT	1
II.	THE MESSAGE	12
III.	JOHN YOUNG	19
IV.	OLD ENGLAND	21
V.	THE WEDDING	35
VI.	WAR COUNCIL	46
VII.	THE OWL'S FEATHER	55
VIII.	LUCY	64
XI.	BRITISH CHIEF	72
X.	STONE HOUSE	82
XI.	DOMAIN	93
XII.	IS THE GROWTH STRONG?	100
XIII.	SHARK WEATHER	108
XIV.	LITTLE FIG	114
XV.	AHIA	119
XVI.	TATTOO	131
XVII.	CAST OFF!	139
XVIII.	CABALLERO	145
XIX.	MONTEREY	154
XX.	CASCARRON	158
XXI.	CROWN OF THORNS	163
XXII.	THE SEA PEOPLE	170
XXIII.	SENOR OSSA	181
XXIV.	FIESTA	188
XXV.	GRINGO	195
XXVI.	CHOLERA	201
XXVII.	POLOLU	208
XXVIII.	THE SKIPPERS' RACE	216
XXIX.	KEEP THE FLAG FLYING	228
XXX.	WHITE BLOOD	234
XXXI.	MARK	241
XXXII.	HALF GODS	247
XXXIII.	HALEMAUMAU	256
XXXIV.	THE NET	266
XXXV.	BLOOD OF THE SHARK	275
XXXVI.	ALOHA	286
XXXVII.	GLOSSARY	289

HOOKUPU

FOREWORD

HONOLULU has become the center of scientific research on the culture of the Hawaiians in particular and the Polynesians in general. To the average reader these scientific studies are abstractions. They describe in technical language the patterns of the customs and usages of native races but lack the individual life history which interests the public.

Fiction has to create an individual hero and heroine whose lives are affected by both their racial background and the impact of the usages and customs by which they are surrounded and through which they move.

From the native point of view, popular authors assemble a native background of coconut palms, pandanus trees, luau feasts, hula dances, and Hawaiian words, to form the canvas upon which pictures are painted with brushes and pigments that the authors brought with them from the lands from which they came. The picture remains English or American though painted in Hawaii.

Both the scientific writer and the popular author need the rare quality of sympathy to enable them to identify themselves with native life before they can paint word pictures that are worth while. Beatrice Ayer Patton possesses this quality to a remarkable degree. She loves the Hawaiians, and the Hawaiians with whom she comes in contact realize it. Her Hawaiian friends have therefore told her things not usually told to people of another race because they knew that such inner thoughts and ideas would meet with a sympathetic reception.

The very mention of the shark, the lizard, and the owl gives me a creepy sensation for they are the incarnations of family gods throughout Polynesia and in far south New Zealand. Through these mediums to deified ancestors gave signs and warnings to their living descend-

ants. *The Hawaiian informants of today have evidently come to think that these temporary mediums were originally actual ancestors and so come within the range of totemism. Whether they be right or wrong does not matter in a work of fiction. In "Blood of the Shark" the author has caught a vivid theme in ancient Hawaiian life and with mind and pen moving in sympathetic unison has produced a human document of absorbing interest.*

PETER H. BUCK.
(Te Rangi Hiroa.)

FOR ELEVEN CENTURIES the feet of progress have marched over the Hawaiian Islands. The first records tell of voyages from faraway Kahiki, steering their outrigger canoes by the stars across twenty-one hundred miles of open ocean. They found the smoking islands peopled with dwarfish, long-armed folk who ran and hid in caves away from the tall men and women of the sea.

Another migration followed and with it came Lono, the man god, who sailed away into the sun path promising that one day he would return.

Five hundred years later, two square-rigged ships anchored in Kealakekua Bay off the Island of Hawaii. To the natives they were floating magic islands, and the men who came ashore were gods. Lono, the man-god, teacher of the people, had redeemed his promise to return—and the English captain, James Cook, was led to the temple and dressed in the red tapa of the god. He took up his quarters in the shrine and christened the group of islands in honor of his patron, the Earl of Sandwich; but the natives finding that he was not God, killed him. His revenge was sure. Ship after ship followed in the discoverer's train, robbing the islands and sowing the seeds of death among their primitive people. The glamour of the white men was gone; but guns are better than spears, and drunkenness is the divine possession of a dying race.

Twelve years after Cook's death, Vancouver visited

the islands and befriended Kamehameha, the once ob-
scure chief who had made himself ruler of all Hawaii.
Children of Earth mated with children of Sea and Sky,
and Adam Gordon dreamt of a Little England.

Today, the grass houses have rotted away and no
one knows where the bones of the chiefs are hidden.
Cattle trample the temple floors, and the beat of the
tapa mallet is still, while the Children of Earth sit dreaming of helmets and feather cloaks, and a war god with
pearl-shell eyes.

CHAPTER I

The Red Skirt

IN THE YEAR 1793 Captain George Vancouver of the British navy brought the first cattle ever seen in the Hawaiian Islands as a gift to the king, Kamehameha. Five cows and two bulls were swum ashore at Kealakekua, driven inland, and turned over to the king's kinsman, Kaha, chief of the provinces of Kohala and Waimea, with a ten-year tabu against their slaughter. "Let them breed and prosper and fill the islands with meat that my friend may have beef for his ships and that my own people may never again know famine," were the king's words.

Chief Kaha sent back a runner to say that the cattle had arrived and to bid the king and the English captain and all his men to a great feast at Kawaihae, where the cattle rested in a stone-walled pen the chief had built for them. Then jugglers and dancers were summoned, ovens were crammed, and the English ships *Discovery* and *Chatham* set sail for Kawaihae to attend the banquet under the palm trees fringing the yellow beach.

The eyes of Kilohana, the chief's eldest daughter, swept up the long strip of ground laid deep in fern leaves and strewn with *poi*-filled calabashes, red crabs, and bananas from whose black cooked skins a sticky

1

fragrance oozed. Hawaiians in garlands and loincloths rubbed shoulders with ruddy Englishmen, and flower-decked women in skirts of sharply patterned tapa moved among the groups, pressing the men with food and drink, for it was against the Hawaiian law for the sexes to eat together. Servants with steaming platters pushed through the crowd, and men and women rose and wandered away from the feast with arms entwined and were replaced by newcomers, who tossed aside the rubbish left by the last guest and fell to all over again. At the far end of the spread under a canopy of palm fronds Kilohana's father and mother sat with the British captain between them. Kaha had thrown off his scarlet feather cloak and sweat streamed down his face and breast under the chief's necklace, whose ivory hook shook and bounced with his good-natured laughter. "This English brandy is a pleasant drink for all people," he boomed, and passed the bowl to his guest, who drank and passed it to Ahia; but the chiefess scowled and shook her head.

In all her fifteen years Kilohana had never seen her mother so grand. The feather wreaths that usually swung in bamboo tubes from the rooftree of the women's house fell so thick over her breast that they hid her chief's necklace, twice as big as that of her husband, and the wreaths on her shaved head fluttered as she fanned herself with the painted Chinese fan Vancouver had given her.

That shrivelled man in foreign dress on her father's

other side must be John Young. It was only a few years since Kamehameha had kidnapped him from a British ship, yet so close to the king was he that many of the chiefs believed him to be a witch. Kilohana shrugged. Vancouver's Englishmen all looked more like chiefs than did John Young. That stripling opposite, opening a mullet wrapped in leaves, might even be a king in his own country. How white his arm was under the blue sleeve! And his hair shone like the copper her father bought from the ships.

As though he felt Kilohana's eyes on him, the young officer looked up and their glances met.

She smiled an invitation, but he gave instant attention to the fish, slitting the belly with his clasp knife and loosening the backbone as he had seen the Hawaiians do. Suddenly the fish parted and half of it fell in the dirt.

Kilohana giggled. Then her attention was diverted. Someone had brushed her arm.

"You are as beautiful as snow on the mountain. Only the Sun himself may embrace you, while I must be content to woo the common morning-glory swaying in the wind!"

Kilohana felt the servant's baseborn eyes in her back, but she did not look around. It was easier to pretend that she did not hear than to answer. He set down a platter piled with smoking chunks of pig, hesitated, and stepped back into the crowd. Now that she was a woman and the ceremonies of the tabu had tightened about her, she could never again be like the wild morning-glory of the song. The wreath about her neck was made of the flowers of love; but her father was a great chief and her mother was of the rank of kings. "None but the Sun himself may embrace you. I wonder?" she said out loud.

"That is a pretty saying." The words were carefully Hawaiian.

She turned, and her shoulder brushed the blue jacket of the Englishman who had been sitting opposite. "It is very nearly true," she mused; then, in an altered voice, "Did you come to this side so that I could fix you another fish?"

He laughed. With her red satin shirt and those flowers like crimson thistles in her hair and on her breast, this girl was like some fire spirit. "Can't you think why I came? You're wearing Old England's favorite color."

"Olinikilani," she mimicked. "Is that his true name? Here in Hawaii we call him Vanacuva. He gave me this"—eager hands held out the red skirt and eager eyes sought his and turned away. Looking into blue eyes was like looking at the noonday sky. It hurt.

"Please, won't you dance for us? Those old women are horrible." He pointed to the *hula* dancers twisting and turning on their mat.

"Those are finest dancers in all Hawaii."

"Their legs are scaly."

"That is only from drinking *awa*. They dance best

when they're drunk." She glanced at her own smooth calves. In the women's house the *lomilomi* oiled her body every day. She pushed one foot toward him; it was brown, paler under the arch, with almond-shaped toenails. If he were to touch it now, she might dare to poke her finger into the tip of his chin, but he ignored her gesture. Perhaps he was unused to women.

A tiny lizard darted out from under the ferns and poised, blinking, on her knee.

With an exclamation of disgust the Englishman clapped his hand over it. She wrestled with his fingers. "Let go! Stop! You are the guest of the Awini clan. To us the lizard is sacred."

He laughed and raised his cupped hand, and, with a flirt of its tail, the lizard scampered off. "I don't understand."

"I have told you. Our line goes back unbroken to Kiha, the Great Lizard, Mother of Queens. She is our guardian. We are her children."   .

"Surely you're not trying to tell me that you are descended from a . . . lizard?"

"It is the proudest descent anyone can claim. Do you see those *kahilis?*" She pointed to the row of tall plumed staffs on the dais behind her father and mother. "Those are the standards of the Awini. They represent our ancestors who have become half gods: the red-tailed tropic bird, the rusty owl, the shark; and the mother of them all is Kiha the Lizard, the oldest, proudest line in all Hawaii. My own great grandmother was sired by a tropic bird and carried his rosy comb through life. I myself had a brother with a lizard's forked tongue and tail. He had no feet, and when he died, the gods took him."

"Still I don't understand. How can anyone so lovely——."

"You *must* understand. We Hawaiians are children of Earth. The birds and beasts are our brothers. In my veins flows the sap of all life." She leaned closer and in her eyes Adam Gordon saw twin, shadowy Adams looking back at him.

He heard himself ask a question—was he fey? "When you marry a . . . foreigner . . . must his children be . . . lizards . . . too?"

"We Awini do not mingle our blood with that of strangers."

"But men from the ships . . ."

"Wherever the ships touch Hawaii they leave a sickness behind!"

He turned away, mortified, suddenly busy with a chunk of cooling pork. When at last he looked up again she was gone but he stared at the place as though he still saw her. She was instinct, throbbing, with life, yet her eyes were secret . . . was she really an earth-child sprung from the dripping jungle and the burning core of the mountain? He pushed away the food. Whatever she was, he must find her. Without her there was no meaning in the day.

Kilohana stood at the edge of the crowd. The

Englishman evidently had not seen her leave and she was glad of it. Something about him had made her want to run away. Up there in the field above the coco palms, sunlight was glancing on the new stone wall of the cattle pen. What were the cattle up to, now that they were left to themselves?

The noises of the feast dwindled to a murmur as she swung up the narrow trail, humming to herself and tossing her red skirt up to catch the sunlight. It was like a skirt of fire. Fire! At the sudden thought her face tensed with that underlying dread which shadows all life in Hawaii and she glanced fearfully at Hualalai, reared against the sky. Heat quivered along its flanks and wisps of smoke hovered above the black streams that drooled from craters, like pockmarks, near the top. There was always danger of offending the gods: any hunchback on the road might be Kamohoalii, Lord of Steam; any red-eyed crone with ashy hair and claw hands might even be the dreadful Pele herself, journeying from her fire pit of Halemaumau where she lived with the bodies of her lovers. It was wrong even to think of fire if one could help it. Kilohana's lips moved in a half-uttered prayer. A voice like the braying of a shell trumpet answered her and she leapt under a bush and crouched there. Was it the voice of Pele, jealous of her fiery skirt?

The noise was repeated. It came from behind the stone wall and Kilohana crawled to it and peeped warily over the edge. Inside, the cattle were cropping and one of them kept lifting its muzzle and making the noise. The creature was calling her! Frightened no longer, she climbed the wall and jumped down inside. The cows hardly looked up and she approached them cautiously, holding her skirt in both hands to keep it away from the briars. She had never seen any animal larger than a wild boar and the small Brazilian cattle, runty and gaunt from their long sea voyage, seemed to her immense. In one corner a bull was backing while another walked towards him with lowered head. They locked horns, and Kilohana clapped her applause. They were like wrestlers at the *Makahiki* festival! At the unexpected sound they wrenched apart and the bull nearest her whirled, shut his eyes and charged.

Kilohana screamed. It was not far to the wall, but her skirt was a fetter holding her to every stick and briar and the bull's bellows were drawing nearer with every step. She had been too long in the women's house—her breath was gone. That drumming in her ears, was it the bull's feet coming on behind? She was sobbing, in a few more steps she must fall . . . the air was turning black.

Something struck her cheek and she tried to ward it off as she ran. A pebble hit her shoulder, and another, and she was running in a hail of pebbles, almost to the wall . . . she stumbled and clawed at the stones, as something seized her round the middle and swung her high. This must be death.

Kilohana opened her eyes and looked into the Englishman's. He was holding her and laughing, while the tears streamed down his cheeks and splashed on her naked shoulders. He flung a last handful of pebbles after the bull.

"You saved my life!" she panted.

He looked down at her, twisting in his arms. She was older than he had at first thought—old enough at any rate to keep away from bulls in that red skirt.

Her eyes filled and she held up the tattered shreds hanging from her waist. "Look! My beautiful *pa-u* ... spoiled ... "

He shook her in sudden anger. "You damned fool, going into a bull pen in that red skirt!"

Kilohana's eyes filled. Something she did not understand was making the Englishman angry. She pushed her face towards him, offering him her nose in the Polynesian kiss.

When at last he let her go, she studied his lips intently. What magic in them still held her? She was like water being drawn into the sun ... let him kiss her like this forever until all her being was drawn up into this godlike thing.

Slowly he freed her and she stood swaying. "No wonder our grandmothers believed that you were gods."

His arm went around her again. "And when you found that we were men?"

"We killed you." Her eyes were secret, Polynesian.

"Why?"

Kilohana did not answer. She was wondering why her heart thumped so under the Englishman's hand.

They walked down the hill without speaking. At the end of the path Kilohana took the wreath of *lehua* flowers from her neck and dropped it over Adam's head. "You have saved my life," she said. "I give it you." He hardly felt her lead him through the crowd past the dancing old women to the dais where her father and mother sat with the British captain between them.

Kilohana threw herself on her knees before them. "This man has saved my life," she cried. "I will have him for my husband!"

The dancers stopped turning and the crowd of feasters pressed closer. "Bulls were fighting thus!" she pushed her forehead against the Englishman's. "One chased me and he drove it away with stones. He saved my life, I tell you! But for him you would all be wailing for the dead!"

"It was nothing." Adam tried to free his hand, but the girl held it fast.

"You have saved my life. It is yours. I give it you."

The crowd yelled their applause, but Captain Vancouver was laughing as Adam had laughed up there in the field, wiping his eyes on his sleeve. He held up Kilohana's torn skirt. "It was this," he said, and the rest of his words were lost in laughter.

The girl stroked the soiled tatters, and her eyes sought Adam Gordon's. How could the skirt-of-fire

have anything to do with it? Why was his face so red
and why was he shifting from one foot to another as
though his hard boots hurt him? Why was he looking at
the Captain and laughing, and not at her?

The chief waved his arm for silence. "My daugh-
ter," he bellowed, "you have chosen well. Take this
Englishman for your husband and may the blue eyes of
England shine from the faces of the children of Kiha,
Mother of Queens!"

Adam's face grew purple and Vancouver beckoned
to him. "Take her as a reward of valor," he said in
English. "We sail for Keauhou in the morning."

CHAPTER II

The Message

THE FEAST WAS ENDED. The English ships were about to sail away and Kilohana sat with her mother on a slope overlooking the harbor watching the embarkation. Far below she could hear winches creaking while men like ants swarmed over the decks hoisting the last gifts on board from the canoes clustered around the water line. One of those men was Adam—strange that she could not pick him out from the others when she could feel him drawing the very heart clean out of her body.

"At last the English are going. Once more we can call our souls our own." Ahia's voice was rough with feeling and Kilohana looked warily at her mother. In all the hours they had been together the chiefess had not mentioned the events of yesterday, nor Kilohana's betrothal to the Englishman.

As if answering her thought, Ahia pointed to Kamehameha's temple on the flat land below. "Each stone of that temple was set in place by a vassal of the Awini clan. The priest who speaks from its oracle tower with the voices of the gods, is my brother. All Kohala and Waimea have belonged to us since the red-tailed tropic bird carried our ancestress to his nest in the cliffs and their child was Kelahuna of the Rosy Comb. Our line goes back unbroken to Kiha the First Mother. Kilohana, you shall not break the chain!"

The girl twisted her hands in her lap. "My father has promised me to the Englishman.'"

"Tchk!" Ahia spat into the wooden bowl beside her. "Your father is married to the new ways. Paiea and John Young have cheated him with their promise of cattle and the silly red coat they have given him. Better for us had the foreigners never come!"

Kilohana groaned. Her mother was of the old people. Even now when all Hawaii had been bidden to call their king Kamehameha, Ahia still spoke of him by his familiar name, Paiea. Her pride in the unknown kinsman who had earned the name of Conqueror was turned to spite for his foreign innovations, for the cloth jacket that he wore, but most of all for his advancement of the Englishman, John Young, over the chiefs of his own people.

The *Discovery* weighed anchor and a shout rose from the towing canoes as a puff of wind filled the topsails and the ship moved slowly ahead. Kilohana fingered her breast bone. Something was pulling at it, tugging at an invisible bond. Adam in his ship was pulling her out to sea. The wind blowing off the water filled her nostrils with the smell of hundreds of warm bodies— Adam's body. With eyes glued to the ship she rose and walked forward, a woman on a leash.

"Bring the *maneles* and carry us to the other side."

At Ahia's command four men lying on the ground picked
up the sandalwood litters and Ahia settled herself in
one and motioned to Kilohana to follow. The girl clutched her breast—the tugging was unbearable. Her eyes
strained over her shoulder, and she winked back the
tears better to see the ship as she climbed into the litter
and the bearers took up their stride.

At the summit of the ridge that divides Kawaihae
from Mahukona, Ahia ordered the men to halt. She
made a sweeping gesture toward the wild coast ahead.
"One day this will all be yours. From these valleys and
mountains have sprung the warriors of our clan. It is
to you, the eldest daughter, to strengthen our kindred
yet again." She pointed to a deep gorge far along the
coast, and inky blot in the blue cliffs. "In yonder valley
of Pololu stands the temple where I was born and where
I waited for the drums that heralded your birth. That
is the birthplace of our line. There the foreigner shall
never penetrate. From that valley your husband, my
sister's son, is even now speeding towards us."

Kilohana wrung her hands and looked back at the
ridge stretching like a wall against the sky. It seemed
to her that the litter was flying. On the plain below, the
foundations of an old camp showed like a checkerboard,
and the temple of Puuepa with its idol posts and tapa-
covered towers seemed to be coming up to meet them.
She closed her eyes against the sight. Once in Kohala,
she might never see her Englishman again. Then she
touched the front bearer's shoulder. He was Iwi, the

vassal, who at the cattle feast, had whispered the love chant in her ear.

He grinned back at her. "I have too much *aloha* for you Kilohana; I like to see you happy, to hear you laugh."

"How can I? I am to go to the marriage hut with another man," she whispered.

"I heard Ahia say that she had sent to Pololu for a husband for you. It is better that you wed with one of our own kin. But once you have borne his child"—Iwi's voice was so low that she could scarcely hear it—"You know the custom." According to usage, after the succession was assured a chiefess might choose her own lovers.

Kilohana was like to swoon. Once more she could feel Adam's mouth on hers, while his hard sailor hands held her as gently as a caught bird. Her voice shook. "The Englishman is mine and I am his. If you should bring him to me, someday, perhaps after I have borne his child . . . You too, know the custom, kinsman Iwi."

His face was ashen. "I understand. Tonight I go to Keauhou to bring him to you. Then—"

She pressed her hands to her burning cheeks. Iwi was the swiftest runner in her father's service. If he brought Adam back to her, she would gladly pay the forfeit—someday.

They were nearing the temple and the ground underfoot was strewn with shreds of tapa, bones and strings of spoilt *hala* nuts, and a nauseous yellow smoke was blowing toward them. The bearers set down the *maneles* as a huge man, dressed in the white tapa of the priesthood, walked down the incline that served as temple steps and raised his hand in greeting. "*Aloha.*"

"*Aloha* to you, kinsman Hewahewa," Ahia answered. "Has the young man come?"

"Not yet. Your sister's messenger is here saying that her son follows hard upon his heels, but, due to your hasty summons, he comes with empty hands."

Ahia snorted. "The gifts will come in due time. It is the husband I want."

The high priest bowed. In all his service in the great temple of the Awini he had never made ready so unseemly a marriage. "Your sister begs you to wait until we can gather the clan. There is much to be done."

"There is nothing to be done, except to consummate this marriage." She pushed Kilohana toward him. "Take her away and float her body in the water now, that she may be ready when the white scarf is looped about the marriage hut."

Hewahewa took the girl's hand. "Come Kilohana," he said kindly, "You know the ritual." Then to himself he murmured, "The old mud hen's feathers are as ruffled as though she herself were the bride."

Kilohana looked despairingly at her mother's back. Then her eyes sought Iwi's and flared with hope at their unspoken promise. The ceremonies upon which she was about to embark would take at least three days. In the temple bathhouse Hewahewa and the lesser priests would lay her in an ancient sacred canoe filled with water and march round her, chanting and prophesying what manner of child she would bear for the honor of the Awini. Her cousin Ono's teeth were whiter than the whale's tooth in his necklace and his hair was trimmed like a chief's helmet and scented with coconut and ginger; but she would never carry Ono's child in her body, for in two days the Englishman would claim her. She walked away with lightened tread.

Ahia watched her daughter enter the bath hut and settled herself in the litter with an order to take her to the women's quarters, a group of grass houses against the cliffs. At the entrance closed by crossed tabu staffs she dismounted and dismissed the men, who trotted away—all but Loki, Kilohana's second bearer. Ahia signed to him to speak, and, with his mouth to her ear, he whispered in the low urgent monotone of the eavesdropper.

At Ahia's muttered orders Loki dropped with his face in the dust.. "The names of the Awini are many. The power of the Awini is great," he fawned.

The chiefess sniffed and spat. "I rid myself of filth. This breeze has a ranting tongue; it carries News," she said loudly, and the other bearers standing within earshot wondered what news could have made their mistress look so black.

Iwi, the runner, wormed himself under the thatched

wall of the sleeping-house and crawled through the bushes to the Kona trail along the cliffs. Rain seemed to shut nim away from the world, and his thoughts were happy as he took up the easy jog of a long-distance runner. In three days at most he would return with Kilohana's English bridegroom. Then she would laugh and roll her eyes. There would be big doings in the marriage hut, and someday, when her baby was rolling beside her in the sand, he might even remind her of her promise.

Suddenly he was thrown to the ground. Something tight and heavy had wrapped itself around his legs in the dark, and Iwi, clutching at the bushes, felt the stone tied to a thong which robbers used to fell their victims. He caught at the cliff's edge but someone pushed him and, as he fell, he heard a laugh he knew.

The two murderers peered over the edge. "Iwi has taken my *piikoi* with him into the shark's belly," the first man grumbled; and Loki, Kilohana's second bearer, answered, "What do you care? Ahia will give us more than the price of a *piikoi* for this night's work."

CHAPTER III

John Young

JOHN YOUNG stared at the empty harbor of Kawaihae, shading his eyes with his hand. The English ships had sailed, and everything would be the same now until another ship came. Yet, he reflected, nothing could really ever be the same again, now that the cattle had come. A man could live for years on fish and poi and such slops, but it was beef that made a people great. He put his torn bit of British flag back in his pocket and said aloud, "The Lord is my Shepherd, I shall not want. He maketh . . . " he stopped, trying to remember, then shrugged and walked up the beach to his house, the only stone dwelling in all Hawaii, built by special permission of the king. He was proud of it, proud of the unglazed windows, and the man-size doorway; proud of the fine polished coffin swinging level with his head under the wide eaves. Every year since he had become the king's man he had bought a new coffin and hung it there. Everything in it was of the best, and one day John Young, the exile, should have a British funeral. As he crossed the threshold a man scrambled to his feet, and Young recognized Kaha, chief of Kohala and Waimea. They rubbed noses.

"*Aloha.* It is about the little daughter that I have

come. I am in trouble, Olohana."

Young smiled. His Hawaiian name, Allhands, amused him. "Well, what is it?"

"You know my wife. Last night she sent a messenger to fetch her sister's son from Pololu. She is *huhu* that I have promised Kilohana to the Englishman."

"What 'ave ye done about it?"

The chief looked uncomfortable. "What *can* I do? You know what she is. Yet I have given Kilohana to him before them all and a chief has but one word."

Young leaned forward eagerly, searching the chief's eyes with his grey ones. "Do ye fancy this Englishman for your son-in-law?"

"Why not? He is brave and strong, and he is Vancouver's friend. Every year more and more foreigners come to Hawaii and only Vancouver has brought us anything in return. If this man is my daughter's husband he will not let the others rob our forests of sandalwood and refuse to pay for our sweet mountain water."

"Have ye told Ahia this?"

Kaha shrugged.

"Then—," Young's voice was tense, "The ship is going to Keauhou. Follow it now in your war canoes filled with gifts and fetch him back."

Kaha put out his hand. "You are a good friend to my people, Olohana. I will go."

CHAPTER IV

Old England

A DAM GORDON was on watch, pacing the *Discovery's* deck with his hands behind him. So still was the night that he fancied he could distinguish the chants of the feasters ashore, where King Kamehameha was entertaining Captain Vancouver and his men. He could almost smell the steam from the ovens mixed with the scent of flowers and the reek of sweat . . . too bad the sham battle was over. Men had come back to the ship with stories of the savage king who caught and turned fifteen-foot wooden spears with his own hands. But there would still be time for sport when Adam's watch was over, for he would be free to go ashore at eight bells, midnight, when the Great Bear lay above the jagged peak to the north'ard. He leaned over the rail and shied a chip at something in the water which ducked and vanished in a ring of moonlit ripples. These natives would soon strip the ship if they could, hiding in the water for hours just to steal a nail or a pennyworth of copper sheathing. They were like ants bearing off infinitesimal prizes, columns of ants, columns of heads in the water —he threw another chip after the first and resumed his walk.

Adam Gordon had been in the Royal Navy since the

age of twelve. Born of an English father and an Irish mother, he had spent his childhood in Surrey with occasional visits to his mother's people. Mistress Gordon had been a pretty lady, and Adam remembered her rustling dress and slippery lap, and her round white arms holding him tight while he listened to stories of the Little People, and changelings, and a leprechaun in his wee green coat. Then there had been a darkened room and a blue-veined hand on the counterpane groping for his; a swaddled, mewing baby and Nurse sewing a black riband on his hat; the smell of wilting flowers; and once more sunlight in the empty rooms. He had hacked his wrist with a knife that day and had been whipped for it. Wasn't there trouble enough in the house already without a great boy of eight scarring himself for life? Adam never told anyone why he had done it. He could never forget his mother now.

Squire Gordon sent the eldest boy to school and the two girls, Adam and the baby were left to Nurse, until one winter's night the father seemed to see Adam for the first time. "Why you are grown a great boy! I must buy you a midshipman's berth," he declared, and soon after Adam joined the ranks of tough, homesick little boys who are England's second sons. For awhile his life was a combination of misery and exaltation, stomach-ache and adventure. Then, gradually, torturing memories of home faded to patterns and life at sea under the Union Jack became reality. He began to enjoy his rare leaves and felt no agony of parting when the time came to go back to his ship. The transplanting was complete. Only someday when he was old he would have a house like Windycross with a tall lady like the mother in the portrait on the stairs to greet his homecoming, and a little maid to sit on his knee while he sipped hot drink from a tall glass by the fire. He would have a setter dog, and a hunter with one white sock and a star on his forehead. But in the meantime, adventure was always just around the corner and Adam sought and found it in his own way. Proud of his skill as a woodsman, he explored mountains and forests, rejoicing in his young strength as others did in their conquests, for he loathed the order to woman ship and the greasy bodies and animal eyes of the females who swarmed on board.

Now, for the first time, the thought of a woman was troubling him. How the little girl had boasted of her relatives, the birds and the lizards, and how she had shocked him, Adam Gordon, brought up on the legend of the Swan Children of Lir! (But it would be entirely different, meeting one of them in the flesh.) She had pulsed under his hand like a caught bird. He closed his eyes and a picture forced itself against the lids; huddle of bloodstained red in the dirt, and a bull glaring at it with mean little eyes . . . strange how awkward the dead lie . . . well, he had saved her from that, at any rate. She would have gone home now with her father and that flat-nosed chiefess with the shaved head. She lived in Kohala, a violent unfriendly coast without a single anchorage. His fingers touched something waxy in his pocket, and he drew out a flower, crushed and brown. He raised it to his lips, then, embarrassed, dropped it over the ship's side and stared at the widening circle in the water. "Kilohana," he whispered. Once more she was pressed against him and he was kissing her mouth of love ... "In my veins runs the sap of all life." He gasped and gripped the rail as if to keep from jumping overboard. That which had happened to him so many times within the last few days was happening again. Must he go on like this forever, reliving his single moment of passion, whether he would or no? What barrier within him had prevented him from following the Captain's laughing counsel to take her? If he had, he might be free of her now. He looked down at his white knuckles and his hands relaxed on the rail, as with a single panting breath, he turned to face the relief. Adam's watch was ended.

He slipped down the rope ladder into the tender, and as he drew away from the *Discovery* with the choppy strokes of the blue-water sailor, the stay light, blinking orange among the stars, seemed to look down on him— England's eye watching over him.

The tender grated on the pebbles, and he jumped ashore and hauled it upon the beach. In the moonlight the shadows of the palm trunks made the sand look like a giant game board. What was it about these islands that made a man feel drunken? Even the stars swooped lower here.

He hurried past the group of feasters toward a field

where the sports were being held. The place was like a fair, crowded with performers and yelling bystanders, and Adam's attention was caught by a youth about his own age sitting cross-legged in the center of a circle of admirers. He was naked save for a tuft of owl feathers in his hair and was torturing a length of string into intricate cat's cradles. He signed to Adam to watch him, tossed the string figure into the air and caught it on his outspread fingers.

The Englishman clapped. "Bravo! *Maikai!*"

With a gesture of welcome the Hawaiian rose and drew Adam's hand through his arm while the crowd parted respectfully to let them through. His new friend led him to a pair of boxers, greased and glistening, who struck and parried with their fists. It was the first Hawaiian boxing Adam had ever seen, and he edged closer as the fists of one of the boxers flew up and his opponent's knuckles cracked him on the chin. The first man wavered and dropped and the crowd surged forward to the victor, who moved off, shouting his triumph.

Adam had been a pupil of Tom Cribb. He peeled off his jacket. "Come on," he yelled, and the surprised Hawaiian turned, faced him, and lashed out. Adam dodged and the crowd jeered while the Hawaiian drew back and Adam danced towards him behind questing fists. The Hawaiian made a jab at his eye, and Adam punched again as they locked and rocked back and forth. He felt for the man's ribs, but the enemy had his little finger, and naked toes were curling about his leg.

He hooked his boot in the Hawaiian's ankle, wrenched it toward him and shoved with all his might. They tell with Adam on top. He freed himself from his opponent's loosened hold while the crowd cheered, but the young chief said angrily, "The great boaster! Manu is a bad man, and twice your size."

Adam grinned. "That's why he fell so hard."

They walked on to a strip of mown grass where men and women were bowling with stone disks. Adam was good at bowls, but the stones had a different heft from the wooden English balls, and he lost. Then they joined a ring of Hawaiians sitting around five piles of tapa, and a man holding a wand struck one of the piles and scattered it. When it had been built up again, he proffered the wand to Adam, who took it, scattered a pile of tapa, and uncovered a white pebble.

"You have won," someone yelled. "Now take your prize!" The master of ceremonies pushed a girl towards him, barely grown and whose little breasts peeped from under a cascade of crimson *lehua* blossoms. He looked about for Huha but his new friend had vanished. What should he do with this girl? The smell of her flowers made him faint, and he did not want her—he had had enough of women at the cattle feast. "Will you show me your king, Kamehameha?" he invited.

She led him under the coconut trees to where, within a ring of torches, a knot of people stood watching the king and Captain Vancouver, seated on a mat on the ground with the king's draughtboard between them, lost to everything but the game. The captain's face relaxed as Kamehameha jumped the last white king, swept him off the board, and held out his hand to his guest.

Vancouver shook it heartily. "When I return to Hawaii you must teach me to play *konane* as you do."

The Conqueror's face was wistful. "This is only a game. If I could learn what *you* know my friend, Kamehameha's name would never die."

"It is late. I must get back to my ship. Good night." He blew his whistle and a sharp order answered from the waiting gig which slid alongside the rock landing.

Kamehameha buried his face in the calabash of English brandy at his elbow. Then—"Who will ride behind me on the *holua?*" he shouted.

Half a dozen voices answered, but Kamehameha seized Adam's arm. "You shall ride with me, Englishman," he cried, and Adam followed him. The path was steep and rough yet the servant dragging the long, narrow sled trotted ahead as fast as if they were on level ground. The slide, a smooth track scored in an old lava flow and made slippery by a covering of grass on which coconut oil had been poured, gleamed in the moonlight like running water. Kamehameha threw down his English jacket and stood in his loincloth stretching his arms towards the sky. Then, seizing the sled and shouting to Adam to follow, he stepped out on the greased track and flung himself on the forward part. Adam had barely time to grip the handholds behind Kamehameha before they were off, bumping, swerving, rocketing down the mountain. This was sport! They shot clear of the slide into the water and "Are you still there, Englishman?" the king bellowed. They swam to shore pushing the sled between them, and a servant caught it and dragged it back up the track while Adam followed, peeling off his wet clothes. At the top Kamehameha drank from the calabash of brandy and water. "This makes the heart strong and fearless," he suggested, proffering it to Adam, and Adam drank.

Hour after hour they coasted down the slide into the sea until the moon set and the stars paled and a light in the east showed that the quick tropic dawn was at hand. Then Kamehameha threw himself on the grass and for a while they lay on their backs, too tired to speak. At last the king put his hand on Adam's. "Englishman," he said gravely, "no Hawaiian has ever ridden my sled as fearlessly as you. From this day and while I live you are my *aikane*, my chosen friend." He took a knife from the sling under his arm and chipped at the black boulder beside him. In a few minutes he had cut two tiny human figures in the rock with a crescent and a circle between their outstretched hands. He finished the carving with a flourish. "There is the story that all the world may read it. King Kamehameha and his chosen friend have played together on the *holua* until the moon set and the sun rose."

The mountain frowning above them seemed to dissolve and the sea to change from black to lead and from lead to a shimmering rainbow; while in the east where the sun was about to rise, a tiny cloud like a blown feather was turning pink. "There is an ancient chant to express it," Kamehameha smiled. "The curtains of night are parted. The black peaks turn to violet. The east is painted in primrose—the ocean is furrowed with glory. It is the hour of Dawn." He broke off and pointed to the sea. "See those canoes rounding the point! If I mistake not, it is my kinsman Kaha at the head of his warriors. "Come, we must make ready for visitors at Keauhou."

"Stand there amongst my chiefs."

Adam Gordon took his place behind Kamehameha. The Conqueror was dressed in the blue cloth trousers Vancouver had given him, with the scarlet coat unbuttoned, showing his bare chest. He wore a brace of dueling pistols strapped about his middle and a wreath of yellow *mamo* feathers was pressed down on his clipped gray hair. "Friend, I will keep you here in Hawaii. I will marry you to a chiefess of the highest rank, and you shall never leave my court."

Adam tried to answer, but the king's attention had already been diverted to an official waiting between the tabu staffs at the entrance to the courtyard. At a sign from Kamehameha he came forward with lowered eyes. "Kaha, chief of Kohala and Waimea, comes bringing tribute and begs that he may be allowed to land."

"Bid him come."

As the messenger backed out, Kamehameha picked up the calabash beside him and gave it to an attendant. "This English brandy makes all men soft and tender of heart," he said sharply. "We will taste no more of it until we learn with what we have to deal." The messenger reappeared, followed by two adzemen in helmets and cloaks who laid their adzes at the king's feet and stepped back to make room for the next two carrying a hog slung on a pole. Next, a man with a roll of tapa spread it before the king and his fellow laid a cluster of bananas upon it. There was a short pause, and two giant spearmen entered, halted, and raised their wooden javelins in salute to their chief, Kaha, who passed between them and fell on his knees before the king. As he saw Adam, Kaha's eyes twinkled with recognition, but it was to Kamehameha that he spoke. "I bring *hookupu*, Lord and Kinsman."

"What brought you here, Kaha? Is all well with the cattle?"

"Aye, they have been turned loose that they may breed and people the islands with meat, but it is not about the cattle that I have come. I am here to fetch my daughter's promised husband."

The king's eyes followed the chief's to where Adam stood with Huha's arm across his shoulders. "I do not understand."

"Before all the world I bestowed my daughter Kilohana on this Englishman. He accepted her. The bride is waiting. The marriage hut is ready to receive them."

Adam sprang forward. "I cannot leave my ship! I will not."

The King raised his eyebrows. "So!" he exclaimed. "Order my racing canoe." He held out his hand to Adam. "Come." The order brooked no appeal, and he led the way to the landing place, where they waited in silence while a single canoe put out ahead to prepare Vancouver for his royal visitor. Then the rowers shoved the king's own *kioloa* into the water and leapt aboard and Kamehameha and Adam followed.

What was to pay? Surely the Captain would refuse to meet the demands of this native tyrant. He would never consent to leave Adam behind. A breeze, poignant with the scent of ginger, stirred his hair, and his nostrils dilated. Kilohana had smelled like that. Was he drunk, or what, to think of Kilohana now? He must think of his future . . . drowning men must feel like this when the waves fold them in. He sat quiet, staring at his hands.

Kamehameha had been on board the *Discovery* only on ceremonial visits, but his instant decision to nail the British captain on his own ground was an indication of that rare quality which had earned him the name of Conqueror. Decent foreigners were needed in Hawaii to curb the white-skinned outlaws beginning to settle there, and so far Kamehameha had only Young and Davis to deal with them. Here was another good man already promised to his clanswoman. Adam Gordon should not escape.

The rowers shipped their paddles and Kamehameha clambered up the rope ladder with Adam at his heels. They were ushered into the captain's cabin and Vancouver rubbed noses with the king while he looked around for his followers.

For answer the Conqueror pointed to Adam. "I am alone. It is with this man only that I have to do. I wish to give him the building of my royal ship, the *Beretania.*"

Vancouver frowned. His own ship's carpenter had already laid the *Britannia's* keel. "John Young can easily train your native workmen to finish the *Britannia.*"

"This man can do more. He can build other ships. Besides, there is something else."

With deep attention the Englishman heard Kamehameha's story. This mighty savage was eager for civilization. England's gifts of tools and seeds and cattle for the revictualling of British ships was not enough. He turned to the young officer standing at attention. "England can become a great sea empire through men like you. Her sons will one day girdle the world. The king has asked England's protection for Hawaii. Shall I give it him by leaving you here?"

Adam's face went white, but Vancouver ignored his beseeching eyes. "You are a younger son. You can never inherit. If I were your age—Gordon, can't you hear Fortune knocking at your door?" He turned to the king to give the youngster time to make his decision. "Your men, Young and Davis, would be landless men in England. Adam Gordon is a chief's son," he said sternly.

Kamehameha nodded. "I understand. His betrothed is my own clanswoman. I have already given him the rank of tabu chief."

Adam stared at the two men bandying with his fate: one spare and clean-cut as a head on a Roman coin, the other primitive, heavy as a mountain. Memories stabbed him: a bay mare with a hunting flask strapped to her saddle; the chase through the soaking mist; English laughter; the scent of fresh cut hay in the sun; the smell of tar, whale oil and bilge water that is the sweat of a ship filled his nostrils, clamoring for remembrance. Then a face pushed between. "My life is yours, I give it you." She had throbbed under his hand like a caught bird. Behind her swept the mountains dotted with forests melting into blue-white peaks—an uncharted kingdom.

"You will stay behind?"

Oak cabin walls blotted out the vision. "Sir," Adam struggled to keep his voice steady. "My life—"

"Your life will be of greater service to England here than as one of the ruck of ship's officers. A man of your kidney can build a little England of his own wherever he bides." He took a flag from his sea chest and spread it on the table. "This is England's *kahili*, Union Jack. Adam Gordon shall be England's man and yours." He folded the flag and gave it to the king, then turned to Adam. "When I come back to Hawaii I shall expect to find you a great man," he said kindly. "England will not set you adrift. We shall keep your name on the Navy rolls."

Adam wrung the captain's proffered hand. Then, without speaking, he turned and walked out of the cabin.

CHAPTER V

The Wedding

KILOHANA was cooped up in the tabu house. She made some peepholes in the straw walls and held whispered conversations through them with her sister, Alapai, who vibrated with news of the gathering clan. The bridegroom had arrived and had borne himself right chiefly toward their mother. No, he was not as beautiful as the English sailor, but—and the little sister sighed— he would be a mighty chief one day and she would gladly marry him if only she could be free to walk the hills and to swim in the surf once more.

"Who is carrying the litters now?" Kilohana tried to conceal the eagerness in her voice, but Alapai, bursting with wedding gossip, did not remember. Did her sister know that Ono, the bridegroom, had come to Mahukona unattended? And such had been his haste that he had jumped across the gulch at Pailualama, using the leaf of a palm frond as a sail!

The bride flattened her nose against the wall and looked towards Makukona. Where was Iwi? Had he reached Keauhou only to find that the *Discovery* had sailed away with her Englishman on board? Through her peephole she could see people running toward the beach, but an angle of the hut hid the landing place from her sight. "Who come, Alapai?" she whispered in an odd tremble, but her little sister was already running with the crowd.

From the women's house at the foot of the cliffs lumbered the mother, Ahia. She had seen her husband's canoes shooting through the reef channel and hurried down to greet him, but she stopped midway and screamed as the chief leapt ashore followed by a man in the uniform of the British navy.

Kaha indicated his companion with a triumphant gesture. "I have brought her husband home to Kilohana," he shouted.

The chiefess spat and ground in the spittle with her bare heel. "May the bones of the foreigners rot away joint by little joint," she muttered. "May the Great Worm eat their loins." She watched her husband and the Englishman walk through the chattering throng to the temple. Surely Kaha would not profane it by taking the foreigner within? They were joined by the high priest, who spoke earnestly to Kaha.

The chief strode angrily toward his wife. "What is this talk of a marriage to your kinsman? Have I not given our daughter to a man of my choosing?"

Ahia drew herself up. "Kilohana's husband, my sister's son, comes to the marriage hut even now."

Kaha scrowled, "There stands Kilohana's husband. It is Kamehameha's order that she marry this Englishman at once."

Ahia glared. "The glorious kindred of the Awini is

interwoven like the strands of a fine mat," she said hoarsely. "These foreigners shall not—"

The high priest thrust himself between the combatants. "Paiea has spoken. Paiea shall be obeyed." His voice was stern as he used his brother Kamehameha's little name. The Conqueror's mandate allowed no opposition. "For years the foreigner has broken our sacred tabus and has loaded our sandalwood forests into his ships and gone away, leaving the seeds of death behind. We Hawaiians cannot fight them alone. Paiea chose Isaac Davis and John Young to help her people. Now he has chosen this man. And what has happened before will happen again. Are the children of Davis and Young English? This man's skin is fair and his eyes are blue. But once he is wed to Kilohana his children will sing the name chant of our Awini clan and the lizard, the rusty owl and the shark will all be numbered among their ancestors as they are among yours and mine, and Paiea's too. This foreigner will not let vandals despoil him of his own. Come, the girl is waiting."

The chiefess glowered. "Not long ago Paiea was only a minor chief. Now, when he beckons we run. My belly is full."

The high priest's face worked with his intense feeling. "The old times are changing, kinswoman. One day even the old gods will lie on the rubbish heap."

Ahia slapped her hands together. She was desperate. "What can I do? The clan is gathering. The bridegroom, my nephew, is even now in the men's house. I myself sent for him."

"We have two marriageable daughters, Ahia," her husband reminded her.

The priest's relief was evident. "Two daughters and a husband apiece. I wager the young chieftain will not begrude the change. Shall I order a second marriage hut built besides the first?"

Ahia bowed her head.

During the argument, Adam stood apart studying the people among whom he had cast his life. The chief was kindly, intelligent, and shrewd, but the face of his prospective mother-in-law was more savage than the carved idol faces leering at him from the temple wall. And his bride . . . that little girl in the torn skirt who had tried to rub noses with him, was waiting. With a sudden impulse he peeled off his jacket and folded it inside out. The brass buttons stamped with the GR and crown were out of place here.

The Hawaiians stopped talking and the high priest held out his hand to the Englishman.

"I shall need a friend like you." Adam was a tall man, but as he took Hewahewa's hand, his eyes were on a level with the priest's massive shoulders. These natives could carry their three hundred pounds with a dignity that was god-like!

Hewahewa touched Adam's cheek with his nose. "I am the King's brother. Kamehameha's friend is mine." He turned to Ahia and her husband. "Are we ready?"

Ahia swallowed a stormy sob. Then, because her

outraged feelings would not permit her to speak directly to Adam, she addressed the priest. "He must promise me the first born."

Adam dropped his eyes.

"Promise," the priest urged.

For a second the Englishman was silent. The first born! Passion surged over him as he thought of Kilohana waiting in the hut. "I promise."

Adam hardly knew what happened after that. There was a feast with dancers and drums and plenty of *awa* to drink. Kilohana and her little sister in new red skirts sat between him and the other bridegroom, whose head was shaved to look like a helmet and whose body glistened with oil. Then each pair was covered with a sacred tapa and bundled into a tiny hut while an infernal chanting and shouting and beating of drums went on outside.

When they came out it was dusk and Alapai was kneeling before a crone who was sawing at her long hair with a shell. The dark strands lay around her on the ground and she was crying.

Kilohana's lower lip went out. "Say goodbye to my hair," she whispered, "I am married now."

Adam twisted his wife's black mane into a rope and wound it round his wrist. "Never! I shall keep you like this always, Kilohana Gordon." He seized her and carried her out of the enclosure. Perhaps he could outrun the drums. The drums were driving him mad. At the edge of the cliff he set her down. "Come, run away with me," he panted, and Kilohana answered, "To the end of the world!" She ran behind him over the rough cliff trail as though her bare feet were shod.

The moon rose over Kohala mountain, streaking the sea with sudden silver and making black pools of shadow in the rocks, and Kilohana seized her husband's hand and pointed. On the black at the water's edge people were dancing a slow solemn figure marked by the staccato of a single drum. She craned her neck to look, then shrank into the shadow and her hold on his hand tightened. He felt her body tremble against him as he watched the dancers bowing, waving their hands and singing a low throbbing monotone. The chant stopped and a white figure detached itself from the others and threw something into the water which sank without a splash. A sigh came from the watchers on shore as a fin cut across the moonpath, vanished, and the song began again, growing into a chantey as they heaved on the taut line. Foot by foot they drew the monster shark in to the rocks, where he lay belly up in the starlight and the priest raised his spear. Kilohana hid her eyes, but Adam strained at the dark, trying to see. These people had drawn a twenty-foot shark from the sea with a barbless ivory hook and killed him with a wooden spear. "How did they do it?" he whispered, fascinated.

"It was the singing," she explained in her soft guttural. "The King of Beasts has made our marriage sacrifice."

Adam heard himself laugh as he ran along the cliff path. Could they never get out of sight and sound of this heathen savagery? "The foxes have holes, the birds of the air have nests!" In the tangled forest above them there must be some refuge, some fern-lined hollow where the wild boar hid his mate! He picked her up in his arms and charged away from the trail.

It was the hour of dawn. Sunlight filtering through the leaves touched Adam's eyelids and he smiled in his sleep, opened his eyes and sat up. Save for the dark patch on the grass where he had lain, dew quivered and twinkled everywhere. He was dripping with dew. He must have slept all night in this little dell and it was high time he was getting back to the ship. Still half asleep, he reached for his shoes and his hand brushed Kilohana.

In a flash he remembered. Yesterday had been his wedding day and his girl asleep beside him was his wife. He must have tucked his shirt around her that way sometime in the night. He touched her gently where a sunfinger turned her brown breast to gold. Strange that she did not fly awake, strange that anyone so alive could be so quiet, almost as if . . . his eyes narrowed. For the first time since he had known her, Adam studied his wife. From her widow's peak and her proud chin to her high arched foot with its almond-shaped toenails, Kilohana was wholly noble. His lips brushed her hair, but he did not finish the kiss. Instead, he picked up one of the red flowers of her scattered wreath and crushed it to his mouth. It smelled of Kilohana. He would not wake her yet. Adam had a way with wild things.

He tiptoed across the grass to where a brook bubbled between rock walls, washed his face and combed his hair with his fingers. Bees droned overhead, pushing themselves into the wine-red blossoms drooping at the tip of a stalk of green bananas, and Adam snatched down a handful of fruit. He would cook his own wedding breakfast and he and Kilohana would eat their first meal together here in the forest—but the bananas were too green. If there were only breadfruit here, he could cook a breakfast fit for a duke. Adam was proud of his skill as a woodsman. He set up some dry twigs in the form of a steeple, struck flint and steel together, cupped the spark in his hands and blew on it until a wisp of smoke wound upward and lost itself in the branches of a tree like a sort of tropical sycamore. A twig cracked, and Adam looked up. Something with long arms and a face hidden in a matted beard was watching him from the other side of the dell. Adam sprang at it, but the shaggy thing pointed to Kilohana and vanished in the woods. He rubbed his eyes. There were no wild men such as he had just seen, in Hawaii. He stole across the grass and looked at his sleeping wife. At her feet lay two breadfruits. He picked one up gingerly. "Zounds!"

Kilohana opened her eyes, and her arms went round him. "I dreamt that a god took me, a fair god with hair like sunbeams and eyes like the sky at noon." She laughed—a low contented ripple that seemed part of the woodland noises.

For an instant Adam forgot everything. Then—
"Did that creature frighten you? That wild man who
left those?" he pointed to the breadfruits. Without their
evidence he could hardly believe what he had seen.

Kilohana crept onto his lap. How sweet Adam was!
How different he smelled. But why was he so unyield-
ing? Her quick wit sensed something amiss. "Is anything wrong?"

"A shaggy man came out of the forest and left these."

Her eyes were thoughtful. "My wedding gift."

"Then you know him?"

Kilohana shook her head. "Was he all stooped with
long hanging arms and crooked legs? Did he blink as if
the sun hurt his eyes?"

Adam held her at arm's length. "Then you *do* know
him?"

She put her mouth to his ear. "He is the *Menehune*
King. No one has ever seen him."

"Who?" Adam was whispering too.

Kilohana nodded vigorously. "*Menehunes* live in
caverns. That's why they blink so; the daylight hurts
their eyes. They are the Little People who work in the
night. They were kings here long ago, before the Hawaiians came."

The Little People! So his mother had called the
fairies.

Kilohana nodded again. "All they ask is to be let
alone."

"That will be easy if he lets *me* alone. I never saw

a man I cared for less." He slit the breadfruit, laid it on the fire, and a smell arose like that of sweet potatoes cooking. That he should be getting breakfast for two in a forest glen with a naked wife watching his operations seemed perfectly natural. Life was like that. He speared the breadfruit, slid a banana leaf under it and offered it to Kilohana. Then, at her sudden nearness, food was forgotten. He had never known that loving a woman could be like this.

Kilohana was the first to free herself. She pointed to the breadfruit sizzling in the ashes. "Eat."

Adam laughed. "Ladies first."

Kilohana shook her head, "Tabu."

"You mean you won't eat with me?"

"I cannot."

Adam was nonplussed. He sliced off a bit with his knife and pressed it against her pursed lips. "Come," he teased.

She pushed his hand away. "I cannot break my tabus, Adam," she begged. "I might bring a curse on us both."

Adam ate his half of the meal sulkily. He wiped his hands on the grass and picked up his shirt, but it was soaked with dew, and as he put his head into it, it wrapped itself around him. He clawed at it furiously and burst through the neck hole like a jack in the box.

Kilohana laughed. Then at sight of his angry face she turned and ran away up the stream bed.

Adam shoved his shirttail into his belt and took after

her. He would show this wild thing who was master here!

The gorge was narrow and slippery. Fine spray spattered him from the rocks overhead and he stumbled and fell over the rotten banana trunks spanning the brook. Then all at once the walls broke away and he was out of the gorge standing ankle-deep in moss. Before him lay a still brown pool and on the edge of it sat his wife staring at her image in the water. "Kilohana!"

Like an otter she slipped into the pool, which closed over her without a ripple.

He plunged after her and came up sputtering icy water. Where was she? Had she drowned herself, afraid of his anger? He sucked in his breath and dived into the brown shadows. Something was lurking behind a boulder and he grabbed at it as it shot past. Over and under she went, Adam pursuing, catching her a dozen times only to have her slip through his hands like a fish. He was getting tired, but she showed no sign of giving up. Then, suddenly, she sank like lead and lay still on the bottom. Adam waited—would she never rise? As if he had lost volition, he sank slowly down beside her. Instantly she was off again, to the surface this time, but Adam had her by the hair and they clambered out of the pool together. He shook her. "What are you, a fish?"

Kilohana giggled. "I wonder! Don't you know I am of the blood of the shark?"

CHAPTER VI

War Council

KING KAMEHAMEHA was walking on Waikiki strand. Before him trotted a servant calling *"Noho! Noho!"* a signal to all people to withdraw from the Presence, and behind walked the spittoon bearer, the *kahili* bearer, and the *lomilomi*, carrying their implements of office. The king walked with head thrust forward and underlip protruded, thoughtfully scanning his war canoes drawn up so close along the beach that a man might step from one to another without touching the ground. Every landing place from here to Waimanalo sheltered his war canoes and flew his warning—shreds of red tapa fluttering from branches stuck in the water. The whole eastern end of the island of Oahu was under war tabu, and Kamehameha had put it there. "All Hawaii, Hawaii *Nei.*" The words tasted sweet. It had been an easy matter to land at the lonely hamlet of Waimanalo, and his men had raised a shrine while he directed the unloading of two brass carronades. The incurious fishermen who inhabited the place had even helped him and his foreign companions lay the short, heavy pipes on sleds and drag them up the paved trail to the top of the pass. Then the sea was dotted with war boats landing at Hanauma and Kahala, and wherever the spearmen ran out to fend them off, the foreign chiefs watching from the cliffs blew into their hollow pipes and *pu!* the spearmen fell, torn open, although no hand had touched them. Kamehameha laughed aloud at the memory. So Cook had frightened the people at an earlier time. Now is was his turn. No spearman could rally against the guns. The old king of Oahu and his ally, Kaiana, were fools. Kaiana, who had stolen the King's beloved Kaahumanu from under his very nose and kept her for one whole year, was now openly arrayed with his enemies. Well, even handsome Kaiana would not stand against the guns. His eyes sought Leahi's headless cone, thrusting out of the sea. John Young said that there were pebbles in it worth even more than sandalwood to the traders, and there were pearls too, in a long winding harbor to the westward. These English knew so much; he had done well to take them into his service. The jealous chiefs would never dare show their feelings while Kamehameha lived. He sat down on an overturned canoe and clapped his hands. "Fetch me Kekualapa and Kekupohi."

The servant ran off, and returned with two scarlet jackets made in the English fashion. Kamehameha stroked them fondly. Then—"Bring me my feather cloak." He spread the yellow mantle over his knees, covering the foreign coats and flowing onto the sand at his feet, and traced the red and black figures with his forefinger, talking to himself. "This was made for me by my own people, the Awini, before I was born. On it is every point of land which I must conquer. Leahi—"

he raised his eyes to the dead crater of Diamond Head,
"When we look ahead, the way is long." He roused
from his reverie. "Summon my brother the high priest,
my Englishmen, and my high chiefs to the council hall!"

He walked away, thinking of the young Englishman,
who had made his first camp at Waikiki near the royal
one until his wife Kilohana had found a valley stretching back into the mountains. "I am sick for the dark
gorges of Kohala. The wife of the Englishman is still
the child of the Awini, and it is near my time. We will
build our huts in Manoa valley, Adama." So their servants had raised a fence and cleared the ground within
it, and the cluster of grass houses due a chief of rank had
sprung up almost overnight. Soon the valley was filled
with other chiefs' compounds swarming with Kamehameha's people, and in these new surroundings Kilohana
settled down to the occupations that she had always
known. Like Rachel of old, she had brought her household gods to this strange camp; a carved wooden figure
with human hair and a wreath of owl feathers on its
neck, and a smooth egg-shaped stone which she declared
was the goddess of maternity.

Adam was eating supper when the king's message
came. He sucked the *poi* from his fingers and looked
about for Kilohana. He knew other Hawaiian wives
who ate with their foreign husbands, and it irritated him
to have her still observe the eating tabu, but when he
spoke of it she only laughed. "Adama," she said, wagging his chin, "one day you will be the captain of a

great ship and we shall sail away to your home in Beretania. Then I shall eat with you in the captain's cabin,
but here in Hawaii those women who do not keep the
tabus are people of no consequence."

He had never spoken of it again.

"Kilohana, I am summoned to Waikiki to the council," he called.

She stooped through the low doorway and dropped
on her knees beside him. "This means war. *Aloha* go
with you, Adama," she said with her arms around his
neck.

He took his coat from the peg and kissed her hurriedly. Her brown face was stretched and puffy under
the eyes and her tapa skirt cruelly outlined her protrud-
ing belly. She seized his shoulders and turned him
squarely to her. "If we wait, I will fight by your side
like a true wife, but we shall not wait. I feel the war is
now. Adama, promise me that you will not take another
wife among your captives.'"

Adam held her at arm's length. "No, I don't want
another wife, one is plenty," he muttered, and slammed
out of the hut. The God-damned savage.

Adam had been expecting this. All winter the army
had been held in leash, and now the air of the camp was
thick with rumor. The allied chiefs were gathering in
the mountains, but they could never drive out the land-
greedy men of Hawaii. Kamehameha would see to that.
He walked down the valley with frankly British tread,
past the compounds of other chiefs, past the peering

idol posts of the temple between whose leering faces he could see the new shrine of Ku-Who-Snatches-The-Lands, Kamehameha's personal war god. In the muggy air, the place smelt of spoilt flowers and carrion. The priests must be sacrificing again. True the sacrifices were mostly pig, but this smelt more like—one could never tell. A rum old idol, Kukailimoku! A man might almost fancy that the pearl-shell eyes rolled under his red helmet. Kilohana swore that he gnashed his shark's teeth when the sacrifice was set before him.

"*Aloha.*" The high priest strode down the temple incline and fell into step beside Adam. They walked on together and other chiefs joined them, all bound for the council. At the gate of the royal stockade a sentry raised his javelin in salute and they passed into the long thatched hall flooded with torchlight that searched out, here a gleaming body, there the polished shaft of a spear, and glanced on the flashing eyes and teeth of a half circle of men standing at a respectful distance from the king, who lay on a pile of mats with his two queens beside him. The regular swaying of the *kahilis* overhead scarcely seemed to stir the steam that rose from their bodies, yet that fat chief from the torrid Puna district was shivering. Adam smiled as the man drew his mantle close about his hips, for he knew that, but for Kamehameha's presence, it would cover his shoulders. These subject chiefs swallowed many a bitter draught.

The king raised his hand for silence. "I have called you to a council of war," he announced. "King Kalani-

kupule and the traitor Kaiana are gathering their forces
in Nuuanu valley and are planning to fall on us in our
camps. At daybreak we will march against these rebels
and destroy them before they set foot out of Nuuanu.
If we can force them up the gorge between the thighs of
the mountains—chieftains of Hawaii, I have stood on
those cliffs and have seen taro fields and fish ponds
spread out before me two thousand feet below. They are
ours! The time is now!" The chiefs shouted their applause. "This bowl into which I spit is inlaid with the
teeth of my fallen enemies. Kaiana, my one-time friend,
I swear that your bloodstained teeth shall rim it first of
all. Woe to the traitor, Kaiana!"

The chiefs thumped their spears on the ground in
token of approval. Once they had envied the proud
knight. "Woe to Kaiana," they muttetred, glancing sidewise at Queen Kaahumanu.

"Let your attack be as stealthy as that of a robber
among the *hau* trees," the king finished, and signed to
them to go, and the chiefs filed by in review. "Keeaumoku!"

As his name was called, Kamehameha's giant father-
in-law stepped out of line. Over his loincloth was strapped a navy cutlass and his body, seamed with newly
healed red welts and whitened scars, gave evidence of
the courage in his face.

"Hewahewa, Huha, Ono, Davis, Young, Gordon."
They lined up beside the king, and the lesser chiefs
passed silently out of the hall. When the last one had

gone, Kamehameha spoke again, "Before the curtains of another night have drawn together, this island will be ours. Hewahewa, you are the battle guardian of the War God, and fight by my side. Davis and Young, you command my two cannon and ten muskets. You, Adam Gordon, follow me close with six muskets, my bodyguard." Adam saluted.

"Ono!" Adam's brother-in-law stepped forward. "You are the youngest of my warriors. You may be among the bravest. You will stay behind the army here at Waikiki. If these patriots of Oahu"—he spat contemptuously—"attack the fleet, defend it. If you fail, burn every canoe."

Ono's eyes rolled. He and two hundred liegemen to save the mightiest fleet his little world had ever known! Twelve of the canoes had been levied from his own valley of Polou. "I will defend the canoes until I drink of the bitter waters," he vowed.

"Keeaumoku, old friend, I give you no orders."

A slow smile widened the warrior's mouth. "Wherever the fight is thickest, there will I hurl my spear."

"Huha!"

All eyes turned to the young chief.

"You are my champion at the forefront of the battle. Child of the Awini, you shall lead my warriors into the fight, and shall pass first into the Land of Shadows."

The young chief bowed so low that the tuft of owl feathers in his hair brushed the king's knee, but no flicker of his stolid features showed that he knew the order to be that of death with honor.

Queen Kaahumanu raised herself on one elbow. "What of me?" she drawled.

The king tweaked her ear affectionately. "What indeed? Tomorrow one man shall die for every shark's tooth in that glove on your sweet hand." He turned to Queen Keopuolani, including her forcibly in the conversation. "Sister, are *you* ready for tomorrow?"

Keopuolani was the mother of Kamehameha's only son, yet the king loved only the barren Kaahumanu. Jealously and contempt soured her voice—"Look to your own spear, my Lord, I am ready." She rose and stalked out of the hall as if to forestall her dismissal, and the chiefs followed her.

Outside, the mist was so thick that the fronds of the palm trees seemed to Adam to float above their boles in the fog, and he himself to be walking in a white space where sound did not penetrate; yet footsteps hurrying past him in the mist showed that already the camp was moving. He strode up the valley, exultant. The muskets with their homemade store balls and patches lay ready to hand under the eaves of his house. Plans studied months ago were dropping into place.

He crept into the sleeping-hut and lay down beside Kilohana who stirred and drew his arm around her. In the dark intimacy of night she smelt like flowers.

"I have come to say good-bye," he whispered.

Instantly she was aware of him. She padded to the shrine, and lifted the wreath of owl feathers from the neck of her wooden god. "Adama, you are a chief above all others. This is the war talisman of the Awini. Take it with you," she begged.

He stuffed it into his pocket, "May your goddess of maternity be with you," he answered, and kissed her mouth, eager to be gone.

CHAPTER VII

The Owl's Feather

DAWN BROKE, changing the color of the fog from black to pearl, and in the mist the army was moving forward. To Adam, it looked an undisciplined horde, yet he knew that every headman was in place, down to the captains of the four-times-four. The chiefs seemed to be everywhere, brave targets in scarlet and yellow, and beside the marched their standard-bearers carrying family gods battered in many an ancient clan war. One-eyed Opihi, hero of Koloa, stalked head and shoulders above his mob of slingwomen, and close by him limped Kanehu, the canoe bearer, dragging his twisted leg and flanked by seven sons with battle saws. Chiefesses wound so thick with tapa that they looked like bundles, hailed greased youths with fans and war clubs weaving in and out of the throng, and servants with packets of food strapped to their shoulders straggled everywhere. So far it was more like a fair than a fight.

A ripple, like wind passing over long grass, stirred the crowd, and helmets were doffed and cloaks dropped as the Conqueror appeared among them, his head high under the red feather casque, the points of his short cape barely reaching his thighs. Beside him walked the high priest carrying the war god, and behind him the two

queens with the king's spear-bearer between them. Isaac
Davis, John Young and Adam Gordon followed with
their detachments of carronades and musketeers, a mix-
ture of Hawaiians and white flotsam who had somehow
drifted into the king's service.

Canoes ferried them across the Kewalo stream to the
swamps, scalloped with fish ponds and crusted with salt
pans, that lay between Waikiki and the village of Honolulu. With the main body still at their backs, the men
swarmed forward on either side like the fingers of a hand.
They worked inland up the valley of Nuuanu toward
the enemy camp, marching through patches of sweet
potato and squares of taro dyked with mud. Now and
then they passed a shelter under a breadfruit tree—
somebody's mountain house. No detail of the valley
escaped Adam, though that part of him sorting and
docketing his impressions seemed entirely disembodied.
He could hear himself giving orders: "Work along behind that screen of bushes. In this fog we cannot tell
when we may meet the enemy. (That little house has
just been burned . . . what creature is that stirring in the
doorway? I am marching into a great battle, fighting
with six guns against ten thousand spears.) Careful,
men, prime your muskets and load now, and keep moving. Keep the King in sight. See! He is climbing that
hill to the right. To the right, men, and be quick about
it! Keep the King in sight." The fellow at the left stumbled, picked himself up. "See that you haven't dropped
any of your equipment, Uli. (I am going into a fight,

now in a few minutes I shall be fighting.) "He quickened his pace to a run, trying to catch Kamehameha scrambling up the hill ahead where some men stood shouting and pointing across the valley. As the king reached the top he yelled, and Adam looked back. Below him marched Kamehameha's army picked out in glittering mist, and across the stream dividing the valley like a sword, the crests and trunks of a mighty host were advancing with their legs hidden in the fog. There was a second of quiet as the two armies discovered each other. Then the uproar drowned out the noise of shuffling feet.

"Champion, champion," the king roared above the tumult, and Huha knelt before him. Save for the tuft of owl feathers behind his ear, the young chieftain was naked and his head and body shone hairless and oily as that of a greased pig. He carried a long spear.

The king put his hand on the shaven head. "Kinsman, yours is a glorious fate."

The champion rose and his eyes sought Adam's in farewell while his lips framed the word *"Aloha."*

From the enemy side another man, also oiled and shaven and carrying a spear, advanced to meet him, and the champions faced one another across the narrow stream. The enemy's words rang clear. "What branded slave sired Paiea, you King?" and Huha answered, "Mudsill, no worm of Oahu was worthy to be the steps of Kamehameha's house!"

Adam dodged, as a spear hurled from behind whizzed past his ear and struck the enemy champion to the ground. Spears were flying around Huha now, and he caught and threw them back at his assailants. Then one pierced his eye, and in an instant he was at the bottom of a pile of fighting men.

The king made a trumpet of his hand, "Loose all the guns and every man for himself," he roared, and ran downhill into the melee.

Adam and his men kept close behind, but in the fog each man was soon fighting his enemy alone. Yells, groans, popping of musketry, and thud of falling men echoed back from the rock of the walls of the valley until Adam felt as though he were fighting in some monstrous building, and he shot and primed as he ran, avoiding the crumpled bodies underfoot. A *hau* thicket loomed through the fog and he looked under it. There was no one there. The barrel of his musket was hot and this would be a good place to clean it. He crept under the tree, fitted a rag into the tip of the ramrod and began to pass it up and down through the muzzle. There was an outcry near by—someone wailing for the dead—and a little procession came into sight—two men carrying another between them, and a woman sobbing and wringing her hands. The dying chief's bearers had wrapped his cloak about him, but it had loosened, and now it dragged on the ground and the man's entrails dripped from his open belly onto it, leaving slimy patches on the scarlet feathers. Adam craned his neck. He knew this man whose half-closed eyes seemed to hold some secret and whose bearded lips still twitched. He was Kaiana, the rebel who had once been Kamehameha's friend. The spirit of the fight was dead, wrapped in a feather cloak. The enemy's back was broken. He rammed a charge into his gun, and ran on up the valley. He must find Kamehameha and tell him that Kaiana was dead. Beside him alien men were running too, dropping their weapons in flight while the name, "Kaiana," flitted before them in the mist like an evil spell. The Oahuans were stampeding up the gorge toward the ridge which must be their last stand. The underbrush was almost impassable and he stumbled and fell in a network of branches. As he picked himself up, a man from behind plunged past him into a sort of tunnel through the brush and he followed, keeping the footwise enemy in sight. "You damn native, show me the way through this maze," he muttered. He could just see the man's feet ahead as he wormed along. Then they flashed out of sight around a bend and he stopped to listen. Someone was following him! A man leapt on his back and Adam felt a sharp twinge in his shoulder as they rolled over and over in the narrow tunnel. He felt for the knife in the arm-sling inside his shirt and plunged it to the hilt. The Hawaiian's hold relaxed, and Adam slipped the knife back into its sheath. How wet his shirt was! How hot it was in all that muck of *hau!* He straightened, but the bushes were above his head, and there was nothing for it but to wriggle through. He did not know that he had stumbled into the lair of the robbers who for centuries had made Nuuanu valley infamous. He felt only relief that he was alone, and scrambled on with his eyes fixed on the far end of the tunnel. Suddenly he saw a leg flash past the opening, then another, and he was out of the thicket running uphill with a mob. The cliffs were closing in, for he could hear waterfalls splashing on both sides of the valley, but he could see nothing in the drizzle except men stampeding past. He could hear them panting as they rushed by.

His foot caught in something soft and he kicked at it and fell sprawling and clutching at the red feather cloak that had tripped him. It gave way in his hands and uncovered a woman's body skewered to the ground like a butterfly on a pin. It was still warm, and close around it lay others in huddled attitudes of death, with their red and yellow cloaks trampled in the mud. "The last stand," thought Adam, and pushed on, scarcely wondering at the amazons who had fought and fallen side by side. A sudden blast of wind caught his hat and whirled it out of sight as he rushed on with the mob pouring up the valley toward a spot of light.

Something clawed at his face, and an owl swerved and disappeared in the fog. He plunged sideways and struck out with his gun to steady himself, but the gun dropped out of sight and he threw himself backward. He was standing on the edge of a precipice. For one instant he saw Oahu beneath him spread out like a map, its plumy forests and dark squares of taro stretching away to the walled fish ponds scalloping the shore, while out in the sea a rock, crowned with a single palm tree, made a vivid dot on the water. Behind him to the right men were swarming up the pass, tottering on the ridge and dropping over the precipice, pushed by the clamoring horde behind. Then the drizzle closed in and the world became once more a welter of sound. The quick tropic dark was upon him. He crawled slowly backward, feeling for a toe-hold on the rocky shelf, and his foot touched something soft that groaned. There was a low growl, and a man's voice said, "Hush, Towzer."

That an Englishman and his dog should be huddled together on a ledge of Nuuanu Cliff in the midst of a great rout did not seem strange to Adam. Life was like that. He felt for his knife. "Who are you?" he asked in English.

"No matter," the words were indistinct. "I'm done for. Will yer take my dog? I don't want them damn natives to eat him." His hand moved feebly and the dog licked it with long steady strokes.

Adam knelt down beside the wounded man, evidently a deserter from some ship.

"Thank 'ee, sir. 'E's different to them stinkin' native dogs, Towzer is." He reached for the dog's paw and gave it to Adam. "This 'ere's your master now, Towzer. It's too late . . . too dark . . ."

Adam dozed a little as he crouched beside the dying sailor. When the rough breathing was still, he whispered, "Come, Towzer," and started down the ledge again, but his shoulder was so stiff and sore he could hardly move, and he was shivering in his sticky shirt. He ran his fingers inside the armhole and a warm trickle answered the pressure. He must have been wounded back there in the *hau* forest. Lucky his legs were all right—he must keep moving—must keep going—must find Kamehameha to tell him . . . what was it he wanted to tell Kamehameha? And why was he so dizzy? The whole place was whirling. He seized a bush, which came up in his hand, and clawed at Towzer's rough coat as they rolled backwards together in a spatter of pebbles.

"Have you fallen from the sky, Adama?" The high priest was leaning over him. The giant body in its white robe seemed to Adam to weave in and out between the mist wraiths—shooting longer and higher until it grew to the monstrous god-head grinning down at him. "Does he really gnash his teeth at the smell of blood?" Adam mumbled.

Hewahewa leaned the idol against the rock.

"Your spirit wanders, Englishman. You are hurt." His voice seemed to come from far off, and he tore open Adam's bloody shirt and felt him with practised hands. He pulled something from Adam's pocket and held it up. "What's this?"

"Kilohana gave it to me."

"It is the war talisman of the Awini," the priest said reverently, as he returned it. "The rusty owl will warn his children of danger." (The rusty owl beating his wings against the wind!)

"I must find Kamehameha. There was something I had to tell him. I have seen Kaiana dead, and men drop-

ping over the cliff like sand. I have so much to tell
him—"

"What, that the island of Oahu is ours and the bones
of the enemy lie rotting at the foot of Nuuanu Cliff,
while the death wail rises over the body of Kaiana? He
has seen it all and he is alone in the tabu place, praying."

Chapter VIII

Lucy

IN ADAM'S compound Kilohana's women were busy heating stones for her feet and stomach, and moving the sleeping mats from the women's house to the courtyard and back again, for their mistress could not rest. Even her favorite work of printing tapa could not keep her quiet. She had barely time to spread the dye on the carved stick and press it to the white sheet in front of her before something made her stand up, and the stick moved in her hand and blurred the fine new surface. Suddenly she groaned. A claw was twisting her vitals.

The watching nurse looked at her sharply. "That was a birth pang," she said, and led Kilohana to a log in the corner of the yard. "Put your hands on it, so. When the pain comes, pull."

Kilohana seized the log and pulled with all her might, as, with a grunt of compassion, the old nurse wiped her sweating head with the corner of her skirt. People were beginning to straggle into the courtyard, attracted by the groans. Where was Adama? Kilohana's lips framed the question as her eyes searched each new face. There was a battle going on somewhere and Adam was fighting. That was why her baby was being born here on this strange island, without any drums. She dug her fingernails into the log and panted because the nurse said it would ease the pain. Surely there must be someone here who could find Adama to tell him how it was with her! But this clawing inside—she could not think for pain.

The nurse bent over her. "The child is about to be born," she declared. "The priest is here."

The crowd parted for an ancient holy man carrying a board and a bamboo knife. He squatted beside Kilohana and passed his shriveled fingers through her hair.

She closed her eyes. She was falling, dropping into unconsciousness. Her hands lay limp along the log. Then the strong pain jerked her back and she screamed, "Save me! I am bursting open!" Then silence and a voice saying, "Sneeze, living heart. It is a girl."

Kilohana opened her eyes and felt the bark with her aching hands. There was no more screaming now, only the sound of many people breathing, and a steady rasping noise as of something being sawed with a dull knife. The priest was kneeling behind her, bent over something on a mat on the grtound. His white robe was spotted and his hands and arms were slimy with blood. Across the little board beside him lay a long grey cord whose ragged end still dripped. Her eyes closed. Where was Adama? It was too much effort to ask. She slept, with the question throbbing like a drumbeat through her exhaustion.

When she woke, she was lying on her mats in the tabu house. A torch flung fantastic flares and shadows about the little room. The old nurse put a calabash to her lips, and she drained it and slept again. Dawn stole through the chinks in the braided wall and the nurse snipped the blazing nuts from the torch into a little bowl. A finger of sunlight felt its way across the floor and touched Kilohana's sleeping face and the nurse pulled down a tapa curtain, shrouding the little room in dusk again. All day she watched beside the sleeping mother, and at nightfall lit the torch for another vigil.

Kilohana stirred and opened her eyes. That sound of a puppy nuzzling its mother that had been running through her dream was still in the room, and it came from under the coverlet where something warm and soft was nestled. Her hand stole under the baby's naked body. "It is Adama's child. Adama's and mine," she said aloud, wondering.

In a far corner of the room a shadow moved, as Adam heard his name. He had sat there, propped against the wall, ever since his men had brought him home the night before. They had found him lying with his feet in a stream, dressed his wound, and carried him back, and he had crawled into the tabu house to be near Kilohana. The nurse had waved him away, but he angrily bade her be quiet—he was master here. He looked at his wife's pinched face with the baby's black head beside it—his baby. Across the white bedcover a procession of black scratches seemed to walk, fading, growing, disappearing, and growing again—his father's angular handwriting. "You are not married according to British law," the letter said, and something more about boys being boys. Adam's mouth hardened. His father had never been out of England since his grand tour of the spas as a young rake, and to him this marriage was no more than an amorous episode. He dozed again and the shadows in the corners took on strange shapes—a clutching hand, owls flying in his face; and he moaned as once more he struggled up the path with the shouting dream warriors, saw them totter on the · edge of the cliff, and drop out of sight. "Adama's child and mine." The words roused him, and he crawled across the floor and took his wife's groping hand.

"Our child," she whispered to him. "Someday she will be a woman, and a great chief will come from Beretania to marry her and take her away in his ship."

He chuckled. Kilohana always had such droll fancies.

The nurse interrupted. "This child shall wed with no foreigner! At your marriage feast she was promised to your mother, Ahia. I am to take her home."

Across his wife's body Adam looked into the little face under its fuzz of hair, and sudden anger possessed him. The child was his. "A forced promise is no promise at all," he said roughly. "We will not part with the child. Now get out."

With an evil look, the woman slipped behind the door curtain.

Kilohana stroked his shoulder, silent over his mandate. Her hand brushed a bandage and he winced. "Are you hurt?"

He made light of his injury, yet spoke vehemently of the battle. "Kaiana was killed, and his army stampeded up the valley. Our men pushed them over Nuuanu Cliff."

She made less of the fighting than of his wound. "Are you badly hurt?"

"No, only weak from bleeding."

"And did *you* push the enemy over the *pali*, Beloved?"

He put his cheek to hers. "No, indeed. I lost my way in the fog and got on the ridge above them, but I saw them fall, thousands of them, slipping over the cliff like sand. Phew! that forest below stinks."

She clutched his hand. "You too, might have slipped over . . . like sand."

"I nearly did. An owl saved me. He must have been blinded by the fog, for he flew right in my face, and, when I looked down, there was nothing below me but the wind."

"An owl? A rusty owl? The half-god of our Awini clan? No, he was not blinded by the fog." Her voice shook. "How is it with Huha, the King's champion?"

Adam did not answer. He was thinking of the mound of bodies by Nuuanu stream.

She pushed back her hair and looked into his eyes. "Huha, the owl, will care for his own. Huha himself warned you. He has become a god," she said, and wept for the dead champion, that laughing kinsman who had worn the tuft of owl feathers.

Adam was silent. In this topsy-turvy world, anything might be true. The Holy Ghost and the Dove, his friend's soul and the tutelary owl. It was a matter of hemispheres, of white race and brown, of Christian faith and heathen tradition.

A dog's wet nose poked itself into Adam's hand and he patted it soothingly. "Charge, Towzer."

Kilohana drew her baby close. "What is that great creature?"

"That's Towzer. He's an English sheep dog. His master was killed and he followed me home," he answered, rolling the skin of the dog's neck between his fingers.

Kilohana had never seen a dog larger than the small, pointed-eared table delicacy of her people, but she stroked Towzer's muzzle fearlessly. Why not, if he was Adama's dog? The baby began to whimper. "Touza, Touza," she wheedled, "You are too big. You must not frighten the little chiefess here, since Adama wants to keep her."

Adam was curious at the willingness with which Hawaiian mothers gave away their children. "Don't *you* want her?"

"If you do," she answered gaily. "But if we keep this little one, we shall have to give Ahia the next, and I feel that this one is going to be like Ahia—*paakiki.*"

Adam stood up with his nerves suddenly on edge. The air in the hut made him sick. "She is not the least like Ahia! She is an English baby and her name is Lucy, after my mother. Come, Towzer."

Outside, with the wind blowing and the trade clouds scurrying over the mountain ridges, he felt better and walked down the path toward Diamond Head. It reminded him of Gibraltar—strange in how many places he could remember the moonlight; he was still only twenty-one. A native slipped into the bushes to let him pass. Did these people never sleep? Below him, surf pounded on the rocks and Diamond Head loomed larger and nearer until it seemed to fill the sky. Suddenly, he all but fell over a man sitting propped against a boulder who greeted him with the Hawaiian *"Aloha."* Adam hesitated, then sat down beside John Young.

His countryman spoke with racial intimacy. "I came out here to get away from these damned Kanakas. Man, but it were a great battle, though! They're feckless people, fightin' wi' stocks and stones agin' oor guns."

Adam answered irrelevantly, "Kilohana's baby was born during the battle." Unconsciously he repeated his wife's description of their child. "She is like Ahia—*paakiki*, but I have named her Lucy."

John Young chuckled. "A fair English name, but they'll call her Luki, and she'll be a native baby in spite of you."

"I have named her Lucy, and I'm going to have her christened if ever another navy chaplain comes to this God-forsaken island," Adam retorted.

"Ye fancy ye can have an English baby by a native woman? Not in Hawaii!"

Adam's face paled. He could never tell John Young his dream of a Little England. The fellow had gone native.

The ex-boatswain stared at him. "Ye're a gentleman born," he said compassionately. "It might be possible for you, but remember this, keep her away from her people. Keep her away from the priests, and from her mother most of all."

The moon had set when John Young rose and took Adam's hand. "Ye've made your choice, Adam Gordon. Never look back. These islands are the nearest any living man can come to Paradise."

Adam wiped his hand on his trouser leg. The old man's palm was scaly. He had been drinking *awa*. Then abruptly, without another word to his self-appointed adviser, Adam walked away, back up the path whence he had come.

CHAPTER IX

British Chief

THE WARRIORS were straggling back from battle, carrying their spoils. On the heaps of captured weapons in their compounds captive women crouched, wringing their hands in silence because the Conqueror had forbidden the customary wailing for the dead. Slaves trying to conceal their branded foreheads lurked in the byways, and medicine men walked the lanes practicing their calling. There was still scattered fighting on the island, and King Kamehameha ordered his giant father-in-law, Keeaumoku, to run down the unconquered chiefs and Oahu's fugitive king, Kalanikupule. Only when this royal quarry was taken would the conquest of the island be absolute.

But the Conqueror was impatient to explore his new domain, and one morning he and Adam sat out incognito in the king's red racing canoe, daubed with black and rigged with a canvas sail of Adam's making. Kamehameha's spear and Adam's fowling piece lay side by side on the leaf-wrapped packets of dried *poi*, which are the mainstay of all native travelers. They paddled into the bay of Honolulu, avoiding the hamlet. "This sheltered haven is the perfect water on which to launch a fleet of ships," Kamehameha declared. "They could nestle inside this point as safely as the red-tailed tropic birds hide in the crags of Kohala."

At the head of the tidewater where the Kalihi stream flows out between glossy-leaved *kamani* trees, they hid the canoe in the undergrowth, slung their weapons on their shoulders, and started inland.

"We will keep out of sight of the temple," Kamehameha declared. "Moanalua is the runaway king's own shrine. Tck! I could burn it to the ground, but that would only scatter his followers. I must find some other way." They tramped on up the valley, following the stream, and the dwellings grew scarcer, the taro fields farther apart, and the valley more cupped between the hills. At a rocky basin they stopped to swim, plunging down the waterfall into the icy pool, and when they were tired they rested by a *hala* tree hanging over the water. Kamehameha threaded a handful of nuts on a morning-glory stem. "We have not had a *lei* to our necks since we left the camp," he said, tossing the golden garland over Adam's head.

The air was heavy with the scent of ginger flowers, like butterflies in the thick green leaves that edged the pool, and Adam picked one and slipped it into his pocket. Kilohana loved ginger flowers. If she were here now her tapered fingers would be stringing a *lei*.

Kamehameha twisted up his loincloth. "Don your pantaloons and your hard boots, my friend. We are going to climb the ridge. From there we can see half my kingdom." He was off up the slope, scampering like a boy. Save for the splashing of the waterfall, the valley was empty of sound and the cloud shadows drifting over the short grass seemed the only living presence. Ahead, the ridge scalloped bare outcroppings against the sky, and they stopped to look back. Far below, a harbor wound to the sea, and to the north a forest-covered plain stretched to the base of a blue mountain range. Sandal-wood! "Mine," he said aloud, "mine." Then, turning to the young Britisher, "Build my ships at Honolulu! You shall hold the land from Honolulu to Waipahu and be chief over many lords. You shall build a stone house like John Young's—a home." He pronounced it home-ay, changing the word from an English to a Hawaiian one.

Home! A sudden storm of feeling robbed Adam of speech, and when at last he found his tongue the words were meager. "I should like to build schooners. Ships are all very well in the trades, but this new fore-and-aft rig will sail straight into the wind's eye." Why did he want to blubber? He had not cried since the day when, a lad on his first voyage, he had seen the English coast fade and dissolve into the North Sea.

"Who goes there?" Kamehameha pointed at a figure in a woman's skirt, crawling down the ridge, picking its way like one wounded. At the sound of Kamehameha's voice it faltered, then let itself down by the hands and limped along the base of the rocks.

"Kalanikupule!" With a bound the king was after the fugitive, who stumbled and fell, with Kamehameha's foot on his neck. "You worm disguised as woman, will you beg for mercy?"

A cunning look crept into the red-rimmed eyes and the runaway dropped his skirt. "Let me stand up and rub noses with you as King to King."

Kamehameha lifted his foot. "As King to King," he repeated.

With a desperate lunge, the Oahuan wrapped his arms and legs around Kamehameha and Adam heard the sound of ripping flesh. He shoved a charge home and lifted his fowling piece to his shoulder, but, with a cry of "Leave him to me," Kamehameha tore himself free and swung his enemy above his head.

Kalanikupule screamed, and Adam heard the snap of a back breaking as the fugitive crashed to the ground.

The Conqueror picked up the limp right hand and examined it with an exclamation of disgust. Across the palm stretched a piece of leather in which was set a double row of shark's teeth. "That was to rip my belly," he said, wiping the blood from his arm.

There was a battle cry overhead and someone called, "Hey you, down there, which way did he run?" as Keeaumoku, followed by a band of warriors, jumped the ridge and landed in their midst.

"This man-woman runs no more, Keeaumoku, I have robbed you of your prey. Whittle his thigh bone into a shark hook and hammer his teeth into my spittoon!"

Keeaumoku's face was grim. "Master, what are *you* doing here? We have traced this traitor for days, and thought we had lost him."

Kamehameha kicked the huddled body. "Take him to his own temple at Moanalua and fetch my brother Hewahewa there to make the sacrifice. I will follow soon." He watched the warriors tie the dead king's body with vines, sling it between them and start down the trail. "The rebels will trouble us no more. Let us sleep awhile." He lay down and in a few minutes was snoring.

Adam sat with his back to a rock and watched the moon rise. It was cold, and clouds like ships running for port hurried past the ridges. The grass around him looked grey and the sea, miles away, was the color of lead. A dwarf *lehua* tree growing in a crack in the rocks creaked in the wind. He shivered and dropped into an uneasy doze.

"Come." Kamehameha was standing over him. He must have slept some time, for the moon was high.

They walked down the trail past the waterfall, crushing the ginger flowers underfoot. A faint mist rose from the earth, and the air seemed to grow heavier—Adam could even fancy that it throbbed with a living pulse. They had nearly reached Moanalua when the king dropped, put his ear to the ground, and turned a savage face to Adam. "The drums!" He broke into a run. Adam, too, heard the drums now, and ahead, fire was reflected on the sky. Outside the temple walls a silent crowd waited. "Englishman, you may not enter here." The mob fell on their faces as Kamehameha stepped over them and disappeared through the temple gate, and Adam saw the

crowd rise and heard it yell as the shell trumpets blared
the consummation of the sacrifice. Then he started down
the trail. He would camp at Kalihi tonight, and tomorrow he would show Kilohana his domain. He found the
canoe where he had hidden it in the *kamani* trees, and
crept under it to sleep.

All night Adam's thoughts were in a turmoil, a pano-
rama in which he danced grotesquely before his own
mind's eye as chief over many lords, a British officer
aide to a savage king in a feather cloak; and through it
all a procession of faces marched; the war god, Kukailimoku, Captain Vancouver, Kilohana with a wreath of
white ginger in her hair.

He woke with the sun and ate his breakfast of dried
taro and bananas hurriedly, eager to take the road. The
orgies at the temple might last for days and at the end of
them the king would go back to Waikiki in triumph, in
his war canoe manned by eighty men. He shoved the
kioloa into the water. It was a good day's paddle to
Waikiki against the wind through the domain the king
had just given him. This winding waterway and all the
land around it was his, even the temple and its tributary
village. There were other villages too, scattered along the
coast, and beyond them were sandalwood forests in
which wild pigs rooted. Even that little brown bird eye-
ing him from its branch was his . . . with a squeak and
a whir of its tiny wings it rose and vanished. "Come
back, Elepaio, who knows but I may be your cousin
now?" he called, and laughed at his own joke.

Even the tide seemed to favor him, setting the canoe toward Honolulu point. Outside the reef a school of flying fish flew up and one dropped into the canoe. He threw it back into the water for luck and one of Kilohana's proverbs flashed through his mind, "Even the seaweed stands up to do him honor." At sundown he paddled into Waikiki to find a deserted village. There were no fires anywhere, and the familiar clucking of fowls and barking of dogs was absent; the temple seemed abandoned. At the gate of his own compound he called to Kilohana.

She ran to meet him with her finger on her lips. "Hush, we are under a silence tabu! They have slain the king of this island and everyone has gone to the sacrifices at Moanalua. Even the pigs and dogs are hidden under calabashes."

He brushed her news aside. "I know, I was with him. Kamehameha killed him singlehanded. Oh, Kilohana he has ordered me to build him a whole fleet," he finished breathlessly. The spoken word sounded even grander than he had imagined.

"Then you are a Captain, like Vanacuva?"

"Not yet, but I am to build the fleet and lord it over some of your chiefs."

She pulled him down on the mat beside the baby. "Then we can go home to Hawaii? This little chiefess longs for her native island, and my double canoe has been stocked and ready to put out these three weeks."

Adam shook his head impatiently. "I am not talking

about *Beretania*. Someone else will have to finish that vessel. You and I are staying here. The King wants his fleet built where he can watch the ship's knees seasoning and learn how treenails are driven." She opened her mouth to answer, but he put his hand over it. "Won't you understand, Kilohana? Honolulu is the finest harbor in the Sandwich Islands. I will build the ships and launch them here, and Kamehameha has given me land, and permission to build a stone house—an English house, Kilohana, a home." He lingered on the word lovingly. "You damned vixen!" Her teeth snapped shut, empty, as he snatched his hand away.

She glanced back at him. "I have left my people to follow you! Here on a strange island I have borne my child alone, like a slave. Now . . ."

Adam rubbed the red mark on his hand, "Very well, take your child and go, but don't come back."

With a look that reminded him of her mother, Kilohana rose and went into the hut.

The baby left on the slippery matting began to cry, and Adam stared at the dark door-hole where his wife had disappeared. She would certainly be back in a minute. Surely she must hear her brat howling like a deserted cub! Where was she? Where were those other women who were always crowding around when they were not wanted? The baby was kicking—perhaps it had colic. He poked at it. How soft its skin was, like a new leaf. Its fist closed on his finger and it stopped crying, then began again, insistent, hungry. He tried to loosen the tiny clutch, but it hung to him, crying, and he passed his free hand under its back and picked it up. The little thing felt cold. He held it tighter and it nuzzled his breast. How did they soothe babies, anyway? He pushed his little finger between its lips and the cries turned to loud smacks. It fitted into his arm as though it had always lain there, and he began to rock it gently. "Rock-a-bye baby on the tree top . . ." With the welling tide of memories, the crooned notes grew louder. Adam was a little boy again, in the nursery at Windycross, on his mother's lap before the sea-coal fire. "Father's a nobleman, Mother's a queen, Betty's a lady and wears a gold ring, and Adam"—Adam was a little boy again, Adam was a soldier drumming for the king. The last note spun out in silence and the hills behind him seemed to whisper the echo. Then, as if he were another singing, his voice deepened and his lips shaped the words of an old lament:

   "Oh, quiet rest the darkling veils of sorrow,
   Oh, softly sleep the stormy hills of pain,
   The way they go who have no more tomorrow,
   And turn not back to look upon their land again!
   But, Oh, to wait and feel the wind a-blowing
   Across the sea from that too distant shore,
   To know the pain, the bitter pain, of going
   From that dear land of dreams that I shall see no
       more."

The hills flung back the notes as if a dozen voices

answered him, and he looked up. Across the courtyard Kilohana was coming to him on her knees. Tears were coursing down her cheeks and she made a gesture of supplication such as one makes at the temple shrine. "I have heard the glory of sunrise," she said in a still voice. "Do with me as you like, Adama, I am only the child of the Awini."

And Adam, the exile, put his arms around her and sobbed against her breast. He could not know that this was the first singing Kilohana had ever heard.

CHAPTER X

Stone House

STONE HOUSE was finished. It stood in a cluster of tributary huts on the point overlooking Honolulu Harbor, and between it and the water a giant *hau* tree sprawled. Adam had lifted the tangled branches over a framework like that of an English arbor; for the lemon-colored blossoms, that, in falling, turned to orange and then to bronze, reminded him of beech leaves in autumn. Kilohana said they were feathers dropped from a chief's cloak. On the point stood the flagpole where Adam's British flag waved its welcoming challenge to every incoming vessel, and beyond it the land ended abruptly in the reef whose shaggy shoulders seemed to rise and fall with every streaming sea. On the ocean side, surf riders coasted ashore on rollers that had gathered in California or Mexico, and Adam often joined their sport; but his real world lay on the harbor side. He stood under the arbor now looking out at the dock of sawed-off palm stems, the long spar shed, and the cradle beside it holding a new-laid keel. Three little vessels, the work of five years, lay moored off the dock. He had had to build the yard and train the workmen before he could build ships, but the next years would show more. Vancouver was dead and could never see this Little England that Adam had built for himself on a dot in the Pacific Ocean, and with his death had come the final loosening of Adam's ties with home. The rare letters, rarer since his marriage, nearly always referred to other letters which had never come. He had even heard of his eldest sister's child before the letter describing her wedding reached him, smelling of whale fat and almost undecipherable from its three-year cruise in a sailor's dunnage bag. His brother Hugh was already in the House of Commons, and his sister Rose kept house for his father and the baby whom he remembered as a spoiled little boy of six. Adam could hardly envisage the changes of these last years at home. It was easier to give himself to things as they were, for he was not only an important chief under the king, but his trusted friend and an independent shipbuilder as well. The Conqueror was even talking of sending him to California to buy a full-rigged ship for sale by the Spanish government there.

"When we look ahead, the way is long." Adam spoke the native proverb aloud and Kilohana, sitting on the ground near by, looked up at him and smiled. Like all men who live surrounded by inferiors, Adam was becoming a silent man. He stared at the *Lucy's* spars, rising naked between the two other hulls. The *Lucy* was his own vessel, a topsail schooner of twenty tons, and everything that had gone into her so far as was Hawaiian-made: *olona* rope, red native paint, even the hogs' grease smearing the bottom—Adam's own substitute for tallow; but her sails would be of good China canvas which Adam had bought from the captain of the *Butterworth*, bound for San Francisco, in exchange for a shipload of hogs, coconuts, and fresh water. The men had finished loading that noon and the brig was waiting to sail on the fair tide. Adam was always glad when a vessel left port; he hated to see the native women swarming out to the ship like rats, and he had forbidden Kilohana to walk abroad when there was a ship in harbor. He turned now to look at her, sitting cross-legged on the ground with her back against his chair. His "sailor's housewife" was spread out beside her and she was trying to sew, biting her tongue and making little faces whenever she pricked herself with the needle. In a patch of sunlight beyond, Towzer, the sheep dog, lay asleep with Lucy curled up beside him. A fly buzzed past his ear and he barked softly in his dreams. Adam's eyes rested contentedly on the picture. Kilohana was lovely even in that calico *pa-u* she was wearing, but the money in his belt was more than enough to buy her the finest gown a Chinaman could make; and he had seen it, white silk embroidered all over with little pink flowers; something a man might buy for his sister, or for his sweetheart at Home. The captain of the *Butterworth* had promised to sell it to Adam if his woman could be induced to part with it. With a silent chuckle he picked up his braided native hat and started for the dock to meet the brig's tender.

Captain Brown scrambled up the dock ladder. Over his arm hung the prize Adam coveted, and he counted three English sovereigns into the captain's hand and ran back toward the arbor, clutching the dress. "Look Kilohana, see what I've brought you!" He thrust it into her hands.

"What is it?"

"It's a gown such as English ladies wear. My sisters wear gowns like this."

She rubbed the soft folds against her cheek. "Is it for me?"

Adam kissed her. "Let me put it on you!"

He slipped the dress over her head and she ran to the calabash of water which served her as a mirror and looked eagerly at her reflection, but as she turned and caught the look of dismay on Adam's face, her smile died. The dress was too tight and the skirt hardly covered her bare calves. "Do I not please you?"

"No, you look outlandish."

"What is wrong? Are you angry with me, Adama?" Her eyes filled and she stroked the dress lovingly with her brown hands.

"That woman on the ship looked—"

"I understand. I have seen her." Kilohana gathered up her hair and held it coiled with one hand, while she sidled up to him in perfect imitation of the bawdy woman's walk.

With a tweak, he pulled the coil loose and her hair tumbled down over the little embroidered flowers. "Wear it that way," he laughed. "You are still the Awinis' child." He put his arm around her and led her to the water's edge where they stood silent, watching the sun drop in a tawny sky. Between them and the purple mountains to the west lay harbors, islands, forests— his own uncharted kingdom. Unconsciously he drew her close. Kilohana was his, like the land. A short wave wet their feet. The tide was turning.

"Hark!" She raised a listening face. .

Adam's ears were not so keen as hers, but in a moment he, too, heard shuffling steps and they faced about. The high priest was coming through the arbor, dressed in his ceremonial robe and leaning on a staff, and behind him loitered a crowd of servants who tagged the heels of any newcomer.

"I have come to say farewell." Hewahewa looked like a man dying of fever. His eyes seemed to stare through Adam into the shadows behind him as he repeated the word, "Farewell."

Adam took his friend's hand. Hewahewa's appearance shocked him. "Are you leaving the court?" he asked, puzzled, and the Hawaiian's head drooped in assent. Adam pointed to the *Lucy*, her red hull still gay in the fading light. "Come with me in the *Lucy!* We are making our trial trip as soon as we can bend on the sails."

Hewahewa drooped lower. "You have not left your shipyard for so long that you are ignorant of what has happened to me, my friend. Where I must go, no ship can carry me."

Kilohana slipped her hand through the wasted arm.

"If it is the coughing sickness, you will get well in Kohala. No one ever spits blood there."

Hewahewa beckoned to his servant, who offered him a wooden bowl into which he spat. "Look!" he pointed. "I spit no blood. This is not the coughing sickness."

The servant backed away trembling, for the high priest's last spittoon-bearer had been strangled.

Kilohana's face was troubled. "Tell us," she said gently, "but first lie down and rest." She led him under the arbor and spread her own mat for him, then sighed to her household to be gone, and one by one the watching faces drifted away.

The priest lay down with his head propped on one hand and Kilohana squatted beside him, while the silence waiting in the dark corners of the arbor closed in about them.

Watching the faces of his wife and Hewahewa, Adam felt like a man bewitched. The silence was like the noise in a cotton mill, clanging and seething with the regular rhythm of a beating heart. Why didn't they speak?

A palm frond rattled to the ground, and Hewahewa raised his eyes. "I have to tell you that which must be whispered, not spoken." His voice was almost inaudible and Adam and Kilohana hitched nearer. "You remember the night, Adama, when my brother alone captured the fugitive king of Oahu? It was I who sacrificed him at Moanalua and gave the Conqueror the dead man's eye to swallow. I alone stripped his bones and made them into arrows for shooting mice. So be it with all traitors!" he ground his teeth. "For this, I have been betrayed. My faithless servants have given some part of me to the enemy—my hair, the paring of a fingernail, my spittle. Enemy priests are praying me to death and I am wasting, dissolving . . . " he sobbed openly, like a child.

Kilohana covered her face with her hands. "*Auwe, auwe,*" she murmured between her fingers. Hewahewa had long been her friend.

Incredulously Adam studied the two Hawaiians. He had heard, in these wild islands, of folk being prayed to death by some sorcerer who could possess himself of even the basest excrement of his enemy's body; of the slow wasting of the victim; the Great Worm at the vitals; the maggots in the brain; but that this could happen to a man like Hewahewa was unthinkable. "What makes you think you're being prayed to death?" he demanded.

Hewahewa held out his shrunken hands. "Behold, ever since word came to me that I must die, my flesh creeps away. I eat, and vomit. I am starving to death. I love you, Adama, so I have come to bid you farewell before the black tapa covers me forever."

Adam scrutinized his friend. He had seen Hewahewa brave out a hurricane in a leaky dugout canoe and stand, an unperturbed and shining target, guarding his brother's war god in the thick of a great battle. This man, who had never known fear, was dying of fright. "Have you sought the murderer?"

"It is no use. My augurs have scattered their nuts and gourds to the four winds, and the pigs I offer tell nothing," the priest answered brokenly.

Kilohana rocked back and forth on her heels, wailing softly.

"Stop that!" Her moaning ceased, and Adam realized that he had spoken. The hairs on his neck were bristling.

"Can you save him, Adama?" she whispered between her fingers.

"Can *I* save him?" Adam clenched his teeth. There had been a witchwife in a low thatched cottage, dangling a waxen image over a peat-clod fire. "As the flame melts Thee, so shall She waste and waste away . . . " Adam must have made some sound, for the witch's eyes rose to his in the window and he fled, falling and picking himself up and falling again, but never stopping until he reached his own nursery. There was witchcraft to be reckoned with, even at Home.

"*Can* you, Adama?" her voice was insistent.

Adam had been reared in the Church of England. There must be something in religion to fight this sort of thing, yet why was it that, when he needed so to think, his mind would only catch at thoughts like straws in the wind? "As fire drives out fire, so pity pity"—what was he saying? The thing sounded like an incantation! He stopped, as the meaning of the words sank into his consciousness—fire against fire. "Put on the whole armor of God." "Deliver us from evil." Ah, that was more like it! That was from the Prayer Book. He spoke with effort, searching for the right word. "Hewahewa, do you believe in God?"

Hewahewa repeated the Hawaiian formula in a sing-song voice: "I believe in red-eyed Ku, in Kane, Lord and Giver of Life, in Lono the Man-god and in Kanaloa the Fallen."

"My God is above all those."

The Hawaiian covered his face. "None dare name Him. He is the Unnamable One, whose glory is reflected on the clouds."

"I dare! I pray only to Him." Adam's voice was stern.

The Hawaiian shuddered. This foreigner invoked the God above all gods, the Life-Taker, known only to the inner circle of priests.

"My God is all-powerful. These heathen gods have no power against Him. He will not let the death spell catch you, Hewahewa."

The priest raised lifeless eyes. "How can I approach Him? He is too far away. He will not hear."

Adam did not answer. He was no person to call on God, yet as an Englishman . . . What would the Captain do if *he* were here? In Vancouver's sea philosophy, there had been a cure for every ill. What was it he always said when the *Discovery's* barber-surgeon came to him for advice? "Brace him up, man! Make him believe you are helping him, and he will get well of himself," the Captain had said. Adam stared into the Hawaiian's beseeching eyes. "Brace up!" he said in English.

He walked away from them into Stone House, and there was a flash as he struck flint and steel together and lit the stone lamp on the table. What to do? He reached for the cocunut dipper, plunged it into the calabash of water beside the lamp and drank thirstily. He would have to do something. His wife and his friend expected it because he was white. He closed his eyes and his lips moved soundlessly. Then, very carefully, he dipped up some water and carried it out of the house. Fire against fire. He knelt down and held the cup to Hewahewa's cracked lips. "Drink, and spill no precious drop."

When he had finished, Adam covered his face with his hands. "God forgive me," he muttered in English. "Thou canst heal even with water, if it be Thy will." The moment of exaltation had passed. What right had these natives to invest him with such power? "Now then, brace up!" he ordered roughly.

Slowly the priest sat up and drew his mantle about his shoulders. "A miracle has been performed," he said reverently. "I fear death no longer. Io is above all gods."

Adam turned away from his wife's worshiping eyes. Somehow he felt a cheat, as, like an actor in a dream, he helped Hewahewa to his feet and guided him through the arbor down the path to the landing place where his double canoe lay waiting.

"Will your God avenge me on my murderers?" Hewahewa's voice shook with hatred.

Adam stared at him, disgusted. Was this the way

God must feel toward importunate mortals?

The Hawaiian shook his arm. "Will He, I say?"

For answer, Adam burst out laughing, but there was no merriment behind it. He was still laughing when the canoe had shrunk to a speck in the moonlight. A wave, alive with phosphorescent fire, struck his feet— Hewahewa's stern wave splashing its farewell challenge. He turned homeward to Stone House, gaunt and black among the moon-drenched huts. Cat's-paws, harbingers of wind, were ruffling the water, and in the moonpath flung like a silver bar across the harbor mouth, the *Butterworth* was sliding out to sea.

CHAPTER XI

Domain

MOONLIGHT pouring into the window holes touched
Kilohana's face, and, as if in answer to a call, she
sat up beside her sleeping husband and sniffed the damp
night smells. Inside the house, everything was black and
silver where the light picked out the patterns of the
braided floor mats and burnished the calabashes on their
stand and Adam's homemade chair. No one but an
Englishman could sleep on such a night! She slid out
of bed and tiptoed to the door. Out on the reef, a torch
fisherman was walking with his flare above his head and
the reflection blazed back at him from the pools in the
liver-colored rocks. It was a night for sweet scents, for
love, and wet lips clinging to one another in the sea. She
closed the door softly and stood drenched with moonlight, one with the Hawaiian night. This time tomorrow
she would be far away from Stone House and the shipyard and the foreign captains who smiled at her while
they talked with Adama, for tomorrow he and she were
going together to explore the furthest reaches of the land
Kamehameha had given him. Since he had been building ships, Adama was different. Except to give orders,
he hardly spoke to anyone any more. Now he was going
away to California to buy a big ship for Kamehameha.

Men behaved like that, sometimes, when they were going away. Sometimes they went off and never came back. She begged him to take her with him, but he only laughed at her. "What could you do in California? You must stay here and take care of Lucy," he said, and the subject was closed.

Kilohana sulked for days afterwards. Why must he love the child above everything? Luki was like any other child. There were plenty of servants to look after her. If she were an *ehu*, fair with blue eyes, it would be different, but Lucy had no look of Adama.

Then, suddenly, as if in answer to her longing to be with him, Adam had decided to explore his land and to take her on the journey. She lay down and pressed her face in the grass. Kilohana and the land—together they would hold his love. Everything came from the earth— rocks, trees, even people. One day everything would go back to the earth. Why must Adama torture the stones into houses, and saw the trees into planks for his ships? One could feel so much nearer life in a grass shelter and a dugout canoe.

A fine mist began to scatter liquid moonshine. Tiny drops coated Kilohana's body and stood in her hair like frost. Perhaps they filtered down from that moon rainbow arching the sky. The goddess Hina's husband had built it to bring her back to earth when her moon lover snatched her away. Hot tides of love surged in Kilohana and she opened the door of Stone House. She heard Adam murmur and saw him stir and feel for her in his sleep. Quietly, she tiptoed across the room and slipped into bed to wait for daylight. Soon they would be away from this shut-in world of houses and people, sleeping on a bed of sea-lavender under the stars.

Day broke, orange and crimson. The five rowers were already up to their waists in water, steadying the canoes, and Adam was calling.

Kilohana scrutinized herself in the water mirror. Her wreath, thick as a woman's finger, of closely set yellow feathers gave her a chiefly look, and her hips and stomach, under the tightly wound pink tapa, were as slim as a young dancer's. She ran out of the house. Adam was kneeling before Lucy, who was putting a *lei* on his hat, and as Kilohana joined them he pointed proudly to the wreath of knotted grass stems decorated with a withered *hau* blossom. The child clung to his leg. "Take me with you!"

There was a commotion in the house and Lani, Adam's bodyservant, burst out, dragging a man by the ear. He threw him on the sand. "There, eavesdropper and thief! The whole world knows that my master's house is tabu. Lord, what must I do with this filth?"

The intruder wormed along the ground. "Kilohana knows me, she will speak for me," he whined.

Lani seized the man's hair and bent his head backward, while Kilohana studied his face. He bore the tattoo marks of the Awini. "Who are you, what do you want here?" she demanded.

"Only food and shelter, mistress. Surely the Awini

will not refuse her own!"

"Give him something to eat, he belongs to my mother's house," she said impatiently, and turned eagerly to her husband. "See, Adama, the sun is already throwing his leg over the mountain. Let us be gone."

The little crowd of watchers on shore waved and shouted as Adam jumped to the bow paddle, and his wife curled herself among the stores on the bottom.

The sheep dog swam after them. "Go home, Towzer, go home to Lucy! Take care of her."

As if he understood Adam's charge, Towzer swam back and crawled up on the beach to Lucy, who screamed her delight while he shook himself, dousing her fat little body with spray. *"Aloha, aloha,"* she called, and buried her hands in his coat, and Adam shouted back, *"aloha!"*

Kilohana touched his arm. "We are crossing the reef," she said breathlessly.

They paddled up the coast to the westward and reached the mouth of Pearl Harbor at sunset. A walled fish pond thrust into the water on the land side, and an old man fixing the water gate wiped his hands on his loincloth and peered at them with dim eyes. The place was evidently a shrine of some sort, and Kilohana gathered a handful of leaves, and laid them on the wall beside some other offerings. It seemed to her that Adam was embarrassed. The land was his. Why did he not tell this aged one that here was the new lord? Perhaps he was waiting for her to speak. She touched the old man's nose with her own. "We would sleep here tonight."

He led them to a grass hut overlooking the fish pond, broke open some coconuts and set a calabash half full of lumpy *poi* on the grass, calling to Adam to come and eat. The woman could eat later, alone.

Kilohana's nose wrinkled with disdain. "Have you no fish to offer with these broken meats?" she demanded, pointing to the fish pond.

He waded into the water, and the fish boiled around his legs as he caught them in his hands and bit them on the neck to kill them.

"See the fish boiling, Adama? That means a great chief comes. Who is he, I wonder?" she teased.

The keeper of the pond threw a fish over the outside wall, and they heard the snap of jaws and saw the flash of a belly in the water. "Did you see that big shark? This must be his pond, and the priest his servant," she cried, as the old man joined them with his catch.

Adam did not relish the taste of raw fish, but he dipped bits into the common *poi* bowl and swallowed them. "Are you the priest of this place?" he asked.

His host nodded. "I am the priest of the Little Red Shark of Puuloa. Who has not heard of his fame?"

Kilohana clapped her hands. "Is this his shrine? Was it he who caught the mullet from your hands?"

"Only he."

"Did you hear that?" she cried. "Now I know why the fish boiled so. I thought it was for you, Adama, but the Little Red Shark is king here."

Adam made no comment, but her enthusiasm was

undiminished. "Even in distant Kohala we know his story. Listen." She sat down with her back against a tree. "Once upon a time, there lived, in the waters of Puuloa, a Little Red Shark. One by one he fought all the sharks in that part of the sea until at last the Great White Shark of Waikele grew jealous of his victories and went to see him. 'I am King of these waters,' he declared. 'You must do me honor.' The Red Shark laughed. 'Catch me!' he bubbled, and dodged away. The White Shark gave chase and they swam back and forth until the water was lashed and streaked with foam and the big waves slapped the shore. At last the Red Shark turned at bay and waited for his enemy, who swooped at him with his mouth wide open, and the Red Shark dived straight into his stomach. Then the Little Red Shark began to swell. The White Shark swam furiously up and down. He tried to belch. He stood still in the water. Other sharks swam slowly to the scene of the fight, and the round squid peered up out of their holes to see why the King of Waikele stood so still. He was swelling visibly. His eyes rolled and bulged. An explosion sounded and the water clouded. When it cleared, the onlookers saw the Little Red Shark of Puuloa, swimming about merrily, chasing his tail, and all about him in the sea lay his enemy, in strips. Ever since that day the Little Red Shark has been King in his home waters of Puuloa."

Kilohana's soft voice ceased, and Adam's eyes, which had been following the windings of the harbor, came back to her.

He pulled his wife to her feet. "Let us walk a little."

Kilohana dropped her skirt on the sand. "See those drowned stars looking up through the water," she said. "Watch me scatter them!"

Adam caught at her and missed her, and she plunged in. "Come back! Have you forgotten the shark?"

"He will not hurt me! I am of the blood of the shark," she called over her brown shoulder.

As she swam away, something glittered beneath her in the water—did Adama see it? Was he wondering if it was the white belly of a shark? She laughed and swam on, flush with the ripples, one arm flashing clear with every stroke, her hair clouding the water like floating seaweed. Here, in the sea, no Englishman could catch her unless she willed.

Chapter XII

Is the Growth Strong?

ADAM was up before dawn. He helped the priest uncover his smoking oven and spread the food on banana leaves under the breadfruit tree, and, as they worked together, the old man's tongue was loosened. Few travelers passed this way, but he had heard of the great battle of Nuuanu—was it true that men had dropped over the cliff like mullets flying over a dam? And did the foreigner know whether Chief Opunui had perished in the fight? He was the lord of this place, called Opunui because of his great belly and his loincloth as long as a woman's skirt.

Adam's announcement that he was the new lord was received with apathy. Chiefs died and others came to take the poor man's utmost tithe—they were all alike. Did the new chief know that another foreigner lived on an island in the harbor? Whether he was also a chief the old man could not say. He was more like a priest· in his knowledge of poultices and healing draughts.

Adam ate his morning meal with his host, and went to wake Kilohana. She lay with her cheek on her hand, half covered by her *pa-u,* and sunlight, filtering through the straw walls, spattered her body with little stars. He knelt and kissed her hair. "Taro! Breadfruit! Fish!"

he announced.

Her arms stole round his neck. "No shark?" she whispered teasingly. "None of my kindred?"

He shook himself free. "Never speak to me of sharks again," he ordered.

Soon they were paddling up the smooth harbor and Kilohana exclaimed at the greenness of the hills—so unlike her own scarred Kohala, greener even than Honolulu. But for the twin black cinder cones, the fire goddess Pele might never have visited this part of Oahu.

Adam made no reply. His eyes were on the island ahead, where a white man in shirt and trousers like his own was waving from the beach, and he gave the order to land. In a few minutes he was shaking hands with the hermit of the island.

"I am Marin. The natives call me Doctor," he explained in Hawaiian, adding the universal greeting, "All that I have is yours" and led his visitors up the beach to his shack, smothered in banana trees, with an orange tree in bloom beside the door. "I brought that seed from California. It is the only orange tree on the island," he told them. Across a clearing stood a row of trees bandaged like wounded men. "These are my graftings. On this fig both black and white fruit will ripen."

Kilohana examined the grafted tree while he explained the process. "Is the growth strong?"

He nodded. "Where the graft takes, it is stronger than an ungrafted one."

Kilohana clapped her hands. "That is you and I, Adama! The dark and the fair, and one life for both!"

Adam chuckled—Kilohana always had such droll fancies. He explained that he was the new overlord and the Spaniard, anxious to please, offered to pay any tithe from his precious garden provided he might only be allowed to live and cultivate in peace. The ancient tithe had been hogs and taro, for the last chief had cared for nothing else, not even pearls. He fished in his pocket and brought out a pearl. He had more in the house, found in thin brown shells on the beach, but they were of no use, for traders never came to this lonely place. Perhaps the new lord would like the tithe paid in pearls?

Adam rolled it on his palm to catch the light. "Kilohana, look here!"

She was standing by the orange tree with her eyes closed.

"Kilohana, see what I have! Would you like to own this?"

She poked obediently at the pearl. It was white, like a cooked fisheye. Then, without answering, she buried her face in the orange blossoms.

Adam laughed low and deep. His wife's sense of values was amazing. "You may pay your tithe half in pearls, half in—oranges," he said, substituting the word he had intended.

The Spaniard understood. "There will be orange blossoms, too, for love," he said softly, with his eyes on Kilohana, standing drunken among the white flowers.

They talked late that night, and Marin told Adam many things about his new possessions: villages, fish ponds, and, in one of the cinder craters above the harbor, a salt lake and salt pans worked by the natives. And Kilohana, stringing an orange flower garland, drank in the talk with eager ears.

In the morning, Marin piled their canoe with fresh food and bade them farewell, and as they paddled away Kilohana spoke proudly to her husband. This vast harbor country, bigger than all Kohala, belonged to him. The fish ponds and salt tithes alone would make him rich, and those unexplored forests rolling away to the blue mountains were sandalwood! Did he realize how rich he was? They steered across a wide channel to the village of salt workers at the base of the twin cinder cones, and the inhabitants ran out to meet them, pointing to the trail and offering themselves as guides.

Kilohana waved them back. She would see the salt pans with Adam alone, and they left the villagers plying their canoemen with questions.

The hill was hard climbing, cloaked with morning-glory vines and dotted with *ti* and *hala* shrubs that barely concealed the dry lava streams winding down from the dead crater, and red dust devils swirled around them and made them sneeze. They found the salt pans, mud-dyked squares lined with *ti* leaves on which gleamed a frost-like coating. A sleeping native lay across the trail and Kilohana touched him with her foot. "Wake up and salute your Chief! The Master wishes to see the salt!"

He sat up, rubbing his eyes, then, seeing the strangers, dropped on his face in the dirt. "I am the guardian of the salt. Your Lordships can see that it is fair and ready to count." He led the way to a hut in the shadow of a big boulder. The hut was windowless, but through the door they could see heaps of chunky green packets, some of them so old that salt had poured out between the cracked leaves and lay on the ground in little melting heaps.

Kilohana put her mouth to Adam's ear. "You must collect your tithes. These people are robbing you. You must appoint a bailiff."

Adam whistled. His gentle wife was demanding a bailiff.

"I know my people, Adama. You are a foreigner and ignorant of the law," she insisted.

Adam was embarrassed. He was a shipbuilder, not a landlord. "You tell them about the—dues, Kilohana."

She called the guard and pointed to the piled-up packets. "This is your new Chief's law. You will bring the ancient tithe of salt to Stone House at Honolulu. Every village in this district will bring its tithe there, whether fish or hogs, taro, feathers or bananas. The Chief does not eat dog. Now go! Tell your village runner to carry the Chief's word!" As she watched the salt-guard's retreating back she touched her neck, as though fingering a chief's necklace like her mother's, of human hair, mounted with an ivory hook. No doubt the guard must think Kilohana his chief and the foreign man merely her plaything, but Adama should never know that.

Adam had pictured himself as lord of the land, owning the country and hunting over it, never as a rapacious landlord exacting tribute; but Kilohana understood her people. Let her deal with them! Streaming with sweat and sinking ankle-deep in cinders at every step, he followed her to the top. The crater was crusted with grey salt, and in it was a lake so still that their dirt-streaked faces stared back at them without a ripple.

"Now I know why Pele left this island. It was because my ancestor, Moo, the lizard, drove her out and filled up her crater with water."

Adam walked on, pretending not to hear, but she caught him by the shoulders and shook him, half in anger. "Why not? It happened long ago, in the Twilight of Antiquity. How else can you explain it?" she demanded triumphantly.

Halfway down the trail they met the returning guard, who fell on his face, and Kilohana ordered him to walk behind. The village seemed deserted. "They are hiding in the houses," Kilohana told him. "They are showing you the respect due a tabu chief."

She called to one of the canoemen, an Awini. "Do you see that trail up the black hill? At the top of it is a house filled with salt. You will stay here to guard it. The village folk will bring you food. Take your place in the canoe," she ordered the sullen ex-guard. As they pushed off, natives poured out of the grass houses and followed the new guard up the hill.

They paddled westward, skirting a long peninsula, and Kilohana amused herself by letting down a fishing line improvised from a morning glory vine and weighted with a shell. She could hardly throw it overboard before she drew it in with a crab clinging to the lure, and they were soon crawling all over the bottom of the canoe— purple crabs with spidery legs, and pink, orange-spotted ones. "You shall have a feast tonight, Adama," she said. "This is the Lagoon of the Crabs."

He voiced the question which had been shaping in his mind. "How can you know so much about all these places? You and I are both strangers here."

"I wonder," Kilohana answered dreamily. "My people have lived on these eight islands ever since they came here from Kahiki. I am no stranger."

Adam made no comment. He was thinking of Kilohana's ancestors, sea kings paddling their canoes over twenty-one hundred miles of open ocean, steering by the Pleiades for the smoking islands of the north.

They camped at the tip of the peninsula and the canoemen dug an oven, built a fire in it, and laid Kilohana's crabs on the red coals. Then, when everyone had eaten, they scraped out the fire and covered in the food Marin had given them. The cooked food would last them many days.

With the dark, ragged black clouds began to spread, and squalls ruffled the lagoon. When the storm broke, Adam and Kilohana crept under the overturned canoe and lay pressed against one another and Adam slept, heedless of the wind thrashing in the banana trees and of the crash and rattle of falling palm fronds. To him these storms were not, as they were to Kilohana, a familiar terror of childhood.

When they crawled out from their shelter at daybreak the weather had cleared somewhat, but the wind was still howling and the harbor was mottled with foam.

Kilohana shivered in her wet clothes. The men were opening the oven and the steam from the bananas, tabu to women, made her mouth water. "Bring me some hot taro, Adama?" she begged.

He answered impatiently. "When will you quit these heathenish eating notions?"

"When I go with you to California in your ship. Here in Hawaii, taro is good enough for a woman!"

They carried the canoe across the neck to where a wide lagoon stretched westward. Adam was impatient to cross it, but Kilohana pointed to the frothing, yellow water. "This is shark weather," she objected.

The men also seemed unwilling, waiting for her to give the word to launch, but she only walked up and down, studying the sky and the sea and shaking her wet hair.

Chapter XIII

Shark Weather

IT WAS ADAM who gave the order. The men laid hold of the canoe and tried to shove it into the water, but as fast as they floated it the waves swung it broadside and wet the stores in the bottom.

Kilohana protested. "It is an omen! The sea does not want us!"

He turned on her furiously. Would she even claim knowledge of the sea, his special province? The sea was human, was it? And it had feelings? Well, he was human too, not a fly caught in a web of heathen superstition! He would show her. "The devil it doesn't want us! Shove off!" He jumped on board and seized the steering paddle.

The Hawaiians gave a running push and followed.

Out in the chop, the wind was high and the shallow water of the lagoon was piling up. Contrary squalls hit the canoe from all sides, yet the men paddled steadily, bending their backs to the spattering rain and the waves slopping over the gunwales.

Kilohana began to bail. She looked at Adam, steering for a narrow bight between two hills, and her lips moved as she scraped up the water in a calabash and dumped it over the side. These sudden gusts pouring out of the valleys were treacherous, and the lagoon was too shallow to navigate in a choppy sea. The outrigger lashings were loose—they must have caught on something when the canoe was being dragged through the woods. The crosspieces were working! There was a rip and a tear, and a wave lifted the canoe and flung it down with the broken outrigger trailing on the quarter. Kilohana held her breath. Without the outrigger the canoe would capsize—a man's weight shifting ever so little would capsize it now, yet Adam in his anger did not appear to notice the danger. She dropped her bailer, and, with a rope in her teeth, felt for the one crosspiece whose lashings still held and wormed her way along it towards the outrigger. The men paddled grimly, trying to counterbalance her weight and still keep steerageway. If only a Hawaiian were steering! Why had Adam taken the steering paddle? She could almost touch the point of the outrigger now. If she could crawl out far enough to get a rope around the other end and draw it inboard ... There was a crack of splintering wood, and Kilohana pitched into the sea. She came to the surface as the canoe turned turtle, and the men disappeared and bobbed up again, six of them, swimming with their hands on the overturned canoe. She could see Adam's fair head and hear him shout, though she could not distinguish the words. She waved, and saw him wave back as the water broke over her ... no use trying to signal again in this sea. She struck out for the canoe, swimming with her head under water to offer the least possible resistance to the waves. The wind was drifting the canoe away from her, but she was slowly gaining. She rolled on her side to gulp air and saw Adam's yelling face of horror, as something brushed her and a shark swept past toward him whose warning had been for her. With a leap that lifted her out of the water, she threw herself on him and pushed him under, feeling for the hunting knife in the pit of his arm, and faced the shark, aiming her knife at its one vulnerable spot between the snout and the eye. It turned on its back to bite, and Kilohana drove the knife home. Its jaws snapped feebly. For an instant, she seemed to embrace the shark. Then they drifted apart and Kilohana lay still, face down in the foam.

Adam pushed the dead shark aside, and Kilohana's body swerved and dipped past him, following the carcass. He dived, and swam up between the two. Her hand was in the shark's open mouth, caught on the back-turned teeth like wool on a hatchel, and he forced the jaws open and pulled it loose. Her eyes opened and closed again as the dead shark rolled out of sight under the muddy water.

The canoemen swam up and towed Kilohana by turns, keeping up a splashing and hoarse shouting lest other sharks be attracted by the blood. Sometimes the wind from behind pushed them towards the lee shore, then a land squall caught the waves ahead and the swimmers butted into them. Only the Hawaiians were helping Kilohana now. She had revived enough to swim a

little, but Adam was moving heavily and did not appear
to sense the Hawaiian's firm shoulder under his, nor
to see the brown arm stroking beside his own. The Hawaiian stood up. "Master! Let your feet down, you
can touch bottom."

Hardly conscious, Adam clung to him. Then he
rallied himself and walked ashore.

Kilohana lay across Adam's lap, asleep. His shirt
was spread over her and he was feeding a fire with little
sticks, moving carefully so as not to waken her. Her
injured hand, bundled in leaves, had stopped twitching,
and her breathing was tranquil. She opened her eyes
and touched his thigh with her lips. It was hers. Adam's
whole life was hers, for, in saving him from the shark,
she had given him life. "It's good to feel your strong
legs under my back," she said contentedly. "I know a
man in Kohala who escaped from a shark, but he does
not walk any more. His legs are in ribbons."

"I saw a man once—a handful of jellied bones and
a belt—cut from a dead shark's stomach. The sailors
tied the leg-bones in knots. You would have given your
own life for mine. Am I worth that to you?"

"You *are* my life."

He kissed her torn hand. "Is your hand very bad?"

"No, much better. In ancient times, the god Kane
healed Lono with these same *popolo* leaves."

Adam smiled. Kilohana was herself again, with her

talk of heathen gods. "Did Kane teach you where to strike the shark?"

She shuddered. "Who knows? I saw shark go for you, and I struck. That was all. A thousand generations of sea fights shaped my aim . . . The hands of my fore-fathers, struggling in the sea, covered mine. I am of the blood . . . of kins."

He kissed her mouth and laid her back across his knees, as his men crashed through the undergrowth.

"The canoe has washed ashore over there," the leader shouted. "It will be as good as new with another outrigger!" They knelt round the fire, opening the big leaves they carried, which were filled with mussels and sea urchins. These they laid on the ashes, while one man spitted a sea slug on a stick and held it over the coals.

"Is there water here?" Kilohana asked faintly.

The man pointed to the woods. "In there, a cold spring." He disappeared, and came back with water in a taro leaf. "The food is first for the Chiefess who has slain the King of Beasts," he said humbly to Adam.

The men slipped away. They could find more food and build another fire elsewhere.

Outside the ring of firelight, it was so dark that the torn white flowers of a *naupaka* bush seemed floating in the night like phantom stars.

As the shells in the ashes opened, Adam drew them out and fed her the morsels. He smashed a sea urchin with a knob of coral and offered her the pulp, but she shut her lips, and he popped it into his own famished mouth. With the firelight playing on his naked shoulders and flickering in his hair, he was godlike—God of Fire, God of Love. There would never be room for any other god in her heart, save only Adam. There was magic in firelight. If she should conceive a child tonight . . . she lay still, waiting.

A stick parted and fell into the coals. As if the sound had awakened him, he leaned over and hid his head in her breast. "I love you."

Kilohana's arms went round him. The child would be fair, with blue eyes.

CHAPTER XIV

Little Fig

A DAM was exultant. The very air seemed to sing as he bent to his paddle, dipping in the sunlit waves. Behind him wound his harbor, great enough to shelter a navy, and all around him the ocean swelled and curled, while the canoe danced on it like a living creature. He threw back his head and sang:

"A-hunting we will go!
A-hunting we will go!
Tantivy, tantivy, tantivy,
A-hunting we will go!"

"Tativi, tativi, tativi," Kilohana echoed from the bottom of the canoe.

He waved his paddle. "Sing, all of you!" he shouted to the men, and their childlike voices echoed his deep one, timed to the sweep of their bronze bodies. "Tativi, tativi, tativi, A hunitiwi-wigo!"

They were nearing the end of the return journey. Stone House loomed in sight, then the schooners, bobbing in the water in front of the spar shed, and people on the beach. He could see Makoa, the one-legged spar finisher, giving orders, and Lani, coming out of the house. The canoe grated on the pebbles and the men leapt into the water.

"*Aloha*, Master . . ." Lani hung back.

"*Aloha!*" Adam whistled for his dog. "Here, Towzer!"

Lani blocked the path, with his eyes on his master. "The dog, Towsa—we could not save him."

"What's that?"

The servant hung his head. "Towsa attacked a thief —who killed him. We tried to keep the body, but, Master, you were away too long. We had to bury it yesterday."

Adam was perplexed. He had never yet been troubled by thieves. No doubt his dog had been stolen and the frightened servant was explaining the loss as best he could. The man would have to prove his words. "Where is the grave?"

Lani pointed to a new cairn of stones. "There. We made a little shrine at the top. Master, I have caught the thief."

Adam pushed the man aside. His dog was dead. What did he care for sneak thieves?

Kilohana touched his arm. "Let him explain. Speak, Lani!"

Lani gulped, and looked furtively at his mistress. "He is the one who came here the day you went away. He covered the child's head with a tapa and was making off with her when Towsa caught him. He ripped the dog's belly open with this." Lani pulled a dagger set with shark's teeth from his loincloth.

Kilohana drew a sharp breath. "It is well with the

child?" she asked, and Lani nodded. On the instant her face was disfigured with fury. "Where is the kidnapper?"

Lani led them to a cellar, hollowed in the ground behind Stone House. On the wooden hatchway which served as door a boulder had been rolled, and Adam looked through the air hole at the thief lying on the ground. Blood was still oozing from a long gash in his stomach. "What do you know of this?" he demanded of his bodyservant.

Lani's round eyes searched Kilohana's face. "He is an Awini," he mumbled. Now that he had shown the master his prisoner, he seemed anxious to leave the subject, and pointed to Stone House. "The child is asleep— inside."

The familiar room was just as they had left it: the raised bed place, the chair and table with its draughtboard and stone lamp ready for lighting; and on her little bed in the corner lay Lucy, crooning a child's tuneless song. Adam picked her up and examined her. The child had come to no harm.

Kilohana watched him with veiled eyes. "I understand," she said, half aloud.

He turned on her. "What's that?"

She answered slowly. "Our firstborn was promised to my mother on our wedding day. We have not kept our word."

"You mean that your mother . . . "

Kilohana nodded. "She has waited five years. There

is no one to be chief when she dies. My sister Alapai is barren." Adam clutched his child. But for her creamy skin, she was a small edition of her mother, and she would look all too much at home in Ahia's sodden grass house, reeking with mildew and alive with vermin; she would take all too easily to her grandmother's schooling in the odious way of a Hawaiian chief. And she was to have been spirited away during his absence from home . . . how could Ahia, on another island, two hundred miles away, know his plans? Suddenly suspicious, he glared at his wife. Her eyes were like her mother's.

"I demand an explanation!"

She shrugged, and he seized her with his free arm and turned her round squarely. "Do you hear me?" he shouted.

Kilohana snickered. "What makes your face so red, Adama? What are you *huhu* about? Isn't the thief caught? And you are holding Luki in your arms. Suppose she *had* been taken? After all, she is part Hawaiian, you know. She would have had the same rearing I' had myself, and—" she laughed outright, "we are not old! We can still have more children!"

"I will not have any child of mine kidnapped to be reared by your mother! Did you know of this plan to steal Lucy? Answer me!"

She grew suddenly grave. "Certainly not! But I can guess how it happened. The thief is the son of Luki's nurse." She paused as the door burst open and a distraught woman ran into the room and clasped her knees.

The household crowded after her. "Mercy, Mistress, have mercy!"

Kiolhana's eyes were stony. "There is no mercy for an unfaithful servant."

The nurse beat her head on the floor. "Your daughter would have been reared a tabu chief! It is not my fault that my son was sent to fetch her away!"

"Bind her and throw her in with her son," Kilohana ordered. "The Awini may rule in Kohala, but not in Honolulu! Here, Adama is Chief!"

They dragged her out of the room, and Kilohana slipped her *lei* of fragrant *hala* nuts over the child's head. "Your warm baby smell will make their perfume doubly sweet, little Fig," she murmured, and buried her nose in Lucy's neck.

Adam's sudden suspicions vanished. His Hawaiian mate was faithful. For love of him she had planted her feet firmly against the undertow of her race that strained and tugged, undermining her loyalty to him at every step. He could only guess at the secret plottings of her priesthood. What did he know of the thoughts behind the eyes of even his own workmen? Without him, the undertow would sweep away both mother and child.

He would not leave them now, even on King's business. "Wherever I go, you two go with me," he promised. He put his arm around Kilohana and held her, clasped with the child—flesh of his flesh.

Chapter XV

Ahia

IT WAS A NIGHT of driving rain in Kohala, and in Ahia's grass house the chiefess and her youngest daughter, Alapai, sat playing draughts by torchlight. In the corners, servants sprawled over dice and cat's cradles; women chewed mouthfuls of *awa* pulp and spat it into a bowl to make drink for the masters, and at intervals someone made the round of the torches, snipping off the spent candlenuts. Then the steadied flame lit up the faces of the chief and his son-in-law, snoring in the bed place, and glinted in the eyes of the two women bent above the draughtboard, one with the heavy jowl and pendulous breasts of middle age, the other still wistful and unrounded. Alapai resembled her elder sister, Kilohana, as the shadow does the substance.

Ahia swept a handful of pieces into her lap. "Your wits are wandering, Alapai! I have won again."

The young woman looked at her mother with lacklustre eyes. Would the old sow never stop playing? "I was listening to the rain. It has an evil sound."

There was the rattle and clatter of a falling tree outside.

Ahia snorted. "Tcha! This water will undermine us all. For ten times four days the valley has been a run-

ning river. Between the flood and the earthquakes, the
whole coast of Kohala is crumbling into the sea! Hark
to the thunder! On such a night Paiea was born."

"Tell me the story of the Conqueror's birth," Alapai
said listlessly. She had already lost a feather *lei* and
two *pa-us* to her mother and Ahia's tale would stop the
play for awhile.

The chiefess settled herself against a post, and a
black and white piglet, which had been asleep at her
feet, crawled into her lap and nestled there. " 'Twas
November, the month of portent. Rain fell and thunder
roared and shook the earth as it does tonight." She
paused, while the flimsy grass house trembled as though
shaken by an angry hand. "It was a night of battle in
heaven and on earth, and, while the lightning ripped
the bellies of the clouds, Paiea was born. Who sired
him? It was enough for the queen's husband to learn
the prophecies, and he ordered that her love child should
never see the light. But the mother was of our clan,
and a kinsman spirited away the babe and took refuge
from the storm in a hut where my mother sat suckling a
girl child and making a feather cloak for the unborn
Conqueror of Kings. Her kinsman thrust the babe under
a heap of feathers and ran out of the hut just as the
royal messenger opened the other door. He asked if a
man had been seen carrying an infant. Then, without
waiting for my mother's answer, he seized her baby and
dashed its head against the doorpost, thinking that he
had killed the love child of whom it had been foretold:

'He shall eat the eyes of the Kings.' Paiea took my sister's place at the breast. Sometimes I wonder if—"

She did not finish her story, for the door flew open and some of the torches went out in the gust of wind and rain.

A man crawled acrss the threshold to Ahia's feet.

"Hiku," the chiefess asked in her deep voice, "where is Kilohana's child?"

The man groaned, "Mercy! Have mercy!"

Ahia stamped her foot. "What have you done with Kilohana's child?"

"Mistress, I could not steal her. The father is a sorcerer! He has tamed the ghost dog of Kanikaa and made it his familiar spirit. See, Mistress, the wound will not heal! I was bewitched and thrown into prison, but in the night I made a hole in the wall, and a tramp ship brought me here."

"Then you have not got the child?"

"Mistress, the Englishman would have thrown me to the sharks!" He was crying with terror.

Ahia clapped her hands. "A fit ending for such a craven, whether it be in the maw of Niuhi of Oahu or of Ukanipo of Hawaii! Bind this man! The chiefs shall make shark-bait of him the first fine day."

There was a sudden deafening report, and the room rocked while drops showered from the roof. Servants rushed to steady the swaying torches and the sleeping chiefs woke and felt for their spears, as the crash echoed up the valley and died in long reverberations.

"Another mountain fallen," Kaha exclaimed. His eyes fell on the bound man on the floor. He was vomiting, vomit like the mud from a volcano. "What's this?" he demanded.

Ahia laughed. "Only a slave, bewitched by our foreigner, your daughter's husband. Let him die outside."

The servants dragged him out, and Ahia turned back to the draughtboard. "Our game was interrupted," she said to her daughter. "I will play all my winnings against your new *manele*."

Alapai's eyes were glued to the black pool spreading at her feet.

"Come, has the foreign spell bewitched you, too?" Ahia asked impatiently.

Kaha turned on his wife. "Let the child alone, and cease your talk of spells! On a night like this, evil is everywhere!"

Alapai shuddered. The slime was creeping toward her, and she seemed powerless to move. Then a servant mopped up the stain, and she brushed her hand across her eyes like one waking from a trance. A tremor shook the grass house, and Alapai shivered violently. "Even the earth trembles at the sight," she muttered.

Her young husband offered her a coconut shell full of *awa*. "You are cold! Drink this."

Kaha reached for the *poi* bowl. "Come, son-in-law," he said affably. "Let us eat and sleep again."

Alapai leaned over her mother at the draughtboard.

She was already reeling from the *awa.* "Let us rest awhile," she entreated, "I am so tired of play." She walked dizzily to the bed and sank down on it.

Kaha wiped his hands on his loincloth. "Go you and keep her warm," he advised his son-in-law, and sat down opposite his wife. "Your winnings against my fine new sleeping mat," he said, and placed his share of pieces on the board.

Luck was against Ahia now, and her trophies shifted one by one to him. At last she threw up her hands. "Curse these foreigners! I cannot play for thinking of Kilohana's child. Why did I send that filthy slave to fetch her, even though he was the nurse's son? I should have gone myself!"

"You should have let the matter alone as I told you," Kaha answered. " You have heard that Kilohana keeps the tabus and is rearing the child well."

"Married to that foreigner, she will not keep the tabus long, and when the child is older I shall not want her, with her spoiled foreign ways." Ahia looked suddenly aged and shrunken. "One daughter has forsworn us and the other is barren. Who will be chief when I am gone?"

Kaha pulled her over to the bed. "Come, Ahia! Once you are snoring, I warrant even the house tumbling about your ears will not waken you!"

One by one the torches guttered out, and servants and masters slept. The wind, shrieking up the valley, hissed and whispered in the thatch where a cricket cheeped above the drumming rain. Grey light began to seep through the chinks—dawn, making the storm more terrible and the scene within more real—the servants huddled in the corners, Ahia and Kaha snoring on their backs, and, in her young husband's arms, Alapai whimpering in the clutches of an evil dream.

Ono's hold on her tightened. "Be quiet, Alapai," he mumbled.

She answered with a scream. "Help! I have swallowed a knife."

Ono shook her gently. "Go to sleep. What phantoms are troubling you?"

She sat up, grimacing. "Something has happened to my body."

"Lie down. You are cold all over."

Alapai obeyed him and he put his arms around her, but pushed her away again, disgusted. "What are you doing?"

"The knife in my belly . . . " she retched.

Ono tapped his father-in-law's shoulder. "Something is wrong with Alapai."

The chief rubbed his eyes. "Is it the cramp? Do you want the *lomi-lomi*?" He walked across the room and waked one of the sleepers on the floor. "Alapai is sick."

The masseuse picked up a round stone and rolled it back and forth over the sick woman's stomach, urging her to lie still, but Alapai could not lie still.

Ahia yawned and sat up. She had been dreaming

of earthquakes. What was the *lomi-lomi* doing, shaking the bed and giving her bad dreams? She opened her mouth to scold, but a scream from Alapai cut her short. She was calling for water now, and Ono was holding a gourd to her chattering teeth. "What's the matter?"

Her husband shook his head. "She woke up like this. She thinks she has swallowed a knife."

Ahia felt her daughter's body. It was burning and the sweat was pouring off it, yet the girl was shivering. "It is some evil spell. We must call a medicine priest."

The young husband rose. "I will fetch one. No priest would venture out in this storm unless he were forced."

Ahia sat down beside the bed. It would be a long wait for the priest and her eyes roved restlessly, trying to look at anything rather than at Alapai, yet always drawn back to the slobbering lips and doglike eyes of the stricken girl. Victims of witchcraft seldom recovered, and, with innate fatalism, she felt that her child was as good as dead already. In such cases, one could only assuage one's grief with revenge. She smoothed the girl's thigh where dark spots were appearing under the skin, and her eyes overflowed as though she would wash the spots away with her tears.

Kaha touched his wife's shoulder. "The medicine priest will soon be here to comfort us."

For answer, Ahia gave him such a look that he turned away and hid his face in his hands.

They did not speak again as they sat beside Alapai,

giving her water, wiping her dribbling mouth and doing
the hundred useless little things with which watchers
by a sickbed seek comfort for the dying and for themselves. When their glances met they looked away,
frightened of what each one read in the other's eyes.
Would the priest never come?

At last there was a rattle at the door. A waiting
woman ran to unfasten it, and Ahia's son-in-law pushed
in an old man whose tapa covering was lashed to strips
by the wind. From his arm swung a calabash holding
his implements of office.

Ahia pointed to her daughter. "There is no time
to lose."

The priest looked intently at the girl, then went into
the corner to offer his prayer and unpack his remedies,
and the two men joined him in anxious, whispered con-
sultation.

Ahia sat down again and tried to straighten her
daughter's legs. It seemed hours since she had been
doing this, but, as fast as one leg was freed, Alapai
jerked it up to her chin and Ahia pulled it straight
again. The sick girl breathed in sobbing gasps, and her
cries were less strident. Was she better, or only weaker?
Ahia could not tell. She pulled the lids down over
Alapai's half-closed eyes. Perhaps she would sleep now.

The priest, of whom they had hoped so much, looked
at the sufferer with hopeless eyes. In a storm like this,
the omens were all against Life. Tonight the round squid,
whose live body carries healing medicine and scatters

evil, would lie safe in his hole though the whole world of chiefs were dying. He made the usual incantations and gave Alapai a potion to drink, but she spewed it up. "It is a foreign spell," he declared. "Your daughter is bewitched."

Ahia nodded. Hiku had looked like that.

"If it is truly a foreign sickness, a foreigner can heal it," Kaha said heavily. "I will search out John Young at Kawaihae and bring him here."

The chiefess scowled. "Have we not had trouble enough from foreigners that you must bring one into our very house? And you cannot go! No canoe can live in this hurricane!"

Her husband tied a grass rain cape around his neck. "I can walk! John Young has never yet refused me a kindness. Son-in-law, help all you can till I return!" He went out, and the door blew to behind him.

Ahia's tears dropped on her daughter's unconscious face, as she wiped the cracked lips with a rag. "Do your utmost for her," she urged the priest.

The learned man shrugged his shoulders. He had no power against foreign spells.

Suddenly the sick woman's eyes rolled back, and Ahia bent over her. "The spirit is leaving the body. Catch it!" she commanded.

The priest snatched up an empty coconut shell, made some passes with it and clapped his thumb over the eye. "I have caught it! It is inside the coconut," he declared, and, mouthing a prayer, he forced back Alapai's great-toe nail and pressed the coconut between the nail and the flesh. The foot jerked away, and Aalapai flopped on her face and covered the mat with her life's blood.

Ahia shook her fists at the night beyond the flapping door. "Woe to the sorcerer who has brought this death upon us," she cursed. "May the Great Worm gnaw his vitals! May maggots eat his brain! Gone is my child to the kingdom of the dead! Gone in the high tide of life, forever, like a torch blown out!"

Kaha had been fighting the hurricane for hours, leaning on the wind, falling in the mud and going on until he was near exhaustion. Only a giant could walk so far on such a night, even though love winged his feet, but he was nearing his goal now. He could see the light in John Young's house and made for it, but it flickered and went out, leaving black dark in the place where it had been. This must be dawn—the hour of *ao*, the end of every torch. Kaha set his face against the blackness. It was only a little way now. He pounded on the door and almost fell as it opened and John Young helped him across the threshold.

"Kaha! What are you doing abroad in this hurricane?" He struck a light, and half a dozen people on the floor sat up and blinked at the newcomer; then, seeing that he was only a Hawaiian, rolled themselves in their tapas and lay down again.

Young set two chairs away from the sleepers. "Sit ye down," he invited. "After a shell of grog, we will talk." He poured out the drink. "Is there trouble in

Kohala?" he asked in a low voice.

"Ay, there is trouble! Alapai is sick. The priest says she is bewitched by a foreign spell and that she must die. I have come to you for help."

"Good! Your priests kill more folk than they cure, with all their howlings and purgings. What is the nature of the sickness?"

The chief made an expressive gesture. "She vomits. Her belly is swollen, but she is all bones. Her skin is black and spotted, and hangs on her like a wild dog's. The servant, who died yesterday, swore that the Britisher had put a spell on him. If my foreign son-in-law has worked me this harm . . . " his fists opened and closed.

"Your son-in-law is in Honolulu. What could he do to a man in Kohala?"

The chief hesitated. If his friend were to learn why Hiku had gone to Stone House, he might refuse to help. "The servant was in Honolulu—on private business. He came back in a tramp schooner two days ago."

Young listened intently. There was a schooner stormbound at Kawaihae now, and it was rumored that there were sick on board. Kaha's description of the mysterious trouble completed the evidence. Cholera was come to Hawaii. He covered the Hawaiian's hand with his own.

"This has nothing to do with your son-in-law. The sickness comes from the tramp ship. It can kill every man, woman and child on this island, and the only way we can fight is with tabu. If your people are frightened and run away, they will carry it with them wherever they go. No one must leave Kohala nor Kawaihae!"

"Must we all die?"

"No, not all, but the living must bury the dead."

Kaha stood up to go. "And my Alapai? Will she die?"

"Your daughter is in God's hands. God be with ye, my friend." He touched Kaha's nose with his own and opened the door.

In the leaden daylight, they could see a schooner tossing at anchor, half hidden by sheets of rain. "I will proclaim the tabu to my people," Kaha promised, and set his face to the storm. Tears were blinding him, but he needed no eyes to find the path to Kohala and to Alapai, jerking her legs in the big grass house.

Chapter XVI

·*Tattoo*

ADAM sat at the *Lucy's* cabin table, studying his homemade chart, copied on a sheet of tapa from charts belonging to other vessels, with their captains' comments written in a long column at the side. In fancy, he was already making his landfall. He could almost see the Monterey dunes with their twisted pine trees and adobe fort on the point above the harbor. There were no soundings for Monterey—he would have to take his own, and in anticipation he reached in his open sea chest and ran his hand over the lead in its coil of knotted rope. The chest had held his midshipman's dunnage on the *Discovery*. Now it contained a sextant, planisphere, medicines, and a few tools too precious to go in the carpenter's box forward. The elaborate lashings holding it to the ringbolts in the floor were a bit of native art; Hawaiians were good at ropework. Any captain might be proud of the cabin of oiled *koa* wood, with its lamp in gimbals over the table and its mat-filled bunks—his own, Kilohana's and Lucy's. The king had visited him yesterday, and had left Adam's waist belt heavy with the price of the new ship, but Adam was determined to make the schooner's cargo of coconuts and rope pay for a big share of the purchase. An English pilot, named John Har-

bottle, was sailing with him to help recondition the Spanish ship and bring the *Lucy* back to Honolulu. Adam's
mood was one of deep satisfaction. At twenty-nine he
was master of his own vessel, built in his own shipyard,
and sailing on a royal mission. He climbed the companion ladder to the deck, and laid his hands on the new
walking wheel as though bidding it good-night. This
wheel was the latest innovation known to shipbuilders
and Kilohana had wanted it inlaid with dogs' teeth, but
they had compromised on white wood. He was glad to
be getting to sea again, away from Stone House. As
far as he could tell from this distance, everyone was
quiet there now, worn out with the wailing that had
gone on all day since the news, brought by a traveler
from Kohala, of the death of Kilohana's little sister. It
was the Hawaiian custom to wail over the death of a
relative, and though Kilohana had not seen Alapai for
years, her grief was real and audible. Adam himself
hardly remembered the girl.

He returned to the cabin, locked the chest and put
the key in his pocket. This time tomorrow he would be
in open water. In the morning the *Lucy* would teem with
shouting life but tonight she was still all his, inviolate.
There was something virginal about a ship.

He slipped down the rope ladder and rowed ashore.
How quiet it was everywhere—no one passing, no one
even sleeping on the grass. Why was the place so deserted? Inside the house, he could see people moving,
and a noise, like the buzzing of a hive, drifted through

the window holes. No doubt they were packing the last few calabashes, and perhaps Kilohana was trying on one of the dresses he had bought her to wear in California. There were two, one of India muslin and one of dark blue silk, sprinkled with little nosegays; and he had been at some pains to fit her out with the stockings, heelless Spanish mules and embroidered shawl suitable to the wife of a well-to-do merchant captain in the trades. Kilohana was never tired of posturing about in her new finery. No doubt she had seen him leave the schooner and was waiting just inside the door, ready to greet him with outstretched hand, in the English fashion. "*Aloha*, Capena! Welcome to de schooner *Luki!*" she would say in her clipped English, and Adam would take take her hand and bow, after the manner of a Spanish governor paying his respects to an ambassador's wife. They had rehearsed the scene together many times.

He pulled open the door. The crowd in the room parted, and Adam saw his wife kneeling on the ffoor. Her head was thrown back, and an old man standing over her seemed to be pulling her tongue out by the roots. "Stop! What are you doing there?"

Kilohana pointed to a set of tattooing implements on the floor. "This man can make the marks of my grief last forever," she explained through her tears. "It is for Alapai."

Adam picked up the wooden block set with fishbones and dripping with blue dye, and the priest thrust himself forward. "It is quickly over," he said officiously.

"You seize the tongue, thus—" Adam struck his hand away. "Take your tools and go! My wife does not need your services." He was white with anger. Kilohana had brought her heathen claptrap into his house, into the very room where they lived as man and wife! She should suffer for this.

The tattooer picked up his instruments, and the other Hawaiians crowded after him out of the house, but Kilohana still knelt with her head thrown back, too confounded to move.

"How dare you desecrate my house with your filthy heathen claptrap?" he demanded. His hands twitched. If he touched this woman now, he would throttle her.

She stood up, and her eyes blazed level with his. "You shamed me before my people."

"Shamed you? You don't know what shame means, you God-damned black-hearted *wahine!*"

She reeled as though he had struck her. "There is no color nor creed to sorrow. Black or white, grief is the same. Grief for the dead—" her thickened tongue made her soft voice gutteral, and she fixed him with her eyes—"grief for the living when they kill something . . . here . . . " she choked and pressed her heart as if to hold it still. "I am a chief mated to a man of my own choosing, not an Englishman's slut. If I follow your gods it is because I love you, not because I believe in them. I am Hawaiian. I cannot change myself. Have a care, Adama. There is lava in my veins!"

Adam glared at this wild stranger ranting of gods

and lava, and his lips curled in passionate contempt. "Silence!"

Her nostrils quivered as if her hot breath scorched them. "If you were Hawaiian, I would have you strangled," she said between her teeth.

"Well I am not Hawaiian! I am an Englishman, so help me God, Adam Gordon, yoked to a naked savage who wants to have her tongue tattooed!"

Kilohana's eyes seemed to smoke. "You laugh at my people and scoff at my gods! What do I know of yours? Did *your* gods save you from death on Nuuanu Cliff? Did they snatch you from the jaws of the shark? Answer me!"

In a flash, Adam seemed to see his wife hemmed in by her gods—giants with owls' feathers and shark mouths, a lizard with woman's breasts. His gorge rose. "Leave my gods out of it! All I want of you is to act like a civilized human being!"

Her eyes met his squarely. "You have told me a thousand times that I am not civilized. How can I be something I do not understand?" She pointed to his wrist. "Look at that scar on your own flesh! You told me that when your mother died you slashed your wrist so that you would always remember your grief. I have often kissed the scar. *You* are civilized, Adama, have you forgotten sorrow?"

Slow red dyed Adam's face. "I was only eight years old," he muttered. "You are a woman—my wife."

"Who knows what I am to you? Our thoughts are

strangers, yet—" her voice shook—"our hearts are like the grafted fig." The words fell between them like a stone dropped into water.

He walked to the window and spoke to her over his shoulder. "The scar on my wrist was the act of a child. Must I tell you that again? I won't have my wife tattooed. It's indecent."

He could feel her stubborn, baffled eyes in his back, then she said again, "I cannot understand."

"Now that I am become a man I have put away childish things. Do you understand *that*, Kilohana?"

She looked at the ink stain on the floor, like a child trying to sense the guilt she could not comprehend. "Yes, I understand. You have become a man, and I am still a child." Her voice was so low that he could barely catch the next words. "Are you going to put me away, Adama?"

He did not look at her. Outside, in the dark, someone was chanting, and a drum throbbed like a heartbeat of the night. He might wish that he had never known her . . . yet having had her, life without her now was inconceivable. He did not try to articulate his thoughts, but answered her with her own words. "What you say about the fig tree is true."

She touched him, timidly. "You are civilized . . . what would you do . . . if someone you loved died? If you will only love me enough, I can share your thoughts, Adama."

A flood of compassion swept over him. Love her

enough! Love Kilohana, trying so valiantly to keep in step!

The air was throbbing with drumbeats now, and he turned away from the window and met her eyes, black as the Hawaiian night. Could they ever see life in the same colors as his blue ones? That was the miracle Kilohana was proposing to him. He answered her spoken question. "If someone I loved died, I should put up a stone in memory."

"A stone for love? A cold stone?" She weighed the thought and accepted it wanly. "Alapai's spirit might come there to dwell and I could feed it with lizards and butterflies."

Adam did not chide. Lizards and butterflies, or flowers, what could it matter to the dead if the living were comforted? Black eyes or blue, what did their interpretation of life matter if they understood one another's meaning?

He tried to take her in his arms, but she held him off. "Will you . . . civilize me . . . Adama?"

"My darling . . . we are like the grafted fig, you and I . . ." His lips were in her hair, but she twisted away from him.

"What is that you call me, My Darling? Is it a civilized name?"

"It means my heart's love!"

She relaxed against him, filling the depressions of his body as plaster does the mould. Her swollen lips were parted as if for kissing, and he kissed them roughly,

striking her teeth with his, and her eyelids and the warm
hollow between her breasts.

CHAPTER XVII

Cast Off!

THE *Lucy's* nose swung round and the swimmers alongside yelled, as the towrope tautened and the men in the towing canoes strained at their paddles. Outside the reef, they held her head to wind while the crew hoisted her sails and the mainsheet purred through the blocks. The swimmers dropped astern, and the canoes paddled hard to keep abreast as she gained way. "Let go!"

"All gone, sir!" The towropes splashed in the water and the first Hawaiian-built vessel was sailing for America.

Kilohana, hanging in the ratlines, climbed up another step. The higher she was, the longer she could see her friends on shore. She pulled Lucy up beside her, for the child was crying that she could not see Stone House. "Never mind, you can see Leahi, standing guard over the whole island," Kilohana comforted, wiping her own eyes. They were flying past the familiar landmarks like a dragonfly blown off shore. A cross sea struck the schooner's quarter, soaking them with spray, and Kilohana climbed down from her perch, with Lucy under her arm. The deck was falling away! It came up, and she stumbled and caught the bulwark. "The ship moves like a drunken dragonfly," she said uneasily.

Adam's eyes twinkled. "Like a sea bird, you mean. Feel her ride! I wager you and Lucy will have your sea legs in no time." The schooner tobogganed down a wave, and Kilohana tried to laugh. "Don't be afraid, Luki," she encouraged, "even the sea does Adama's bidding. Come, let's look for fish." They leaned over the rail, and Lucy promptly hid her face in her mother's skirt. "Oh, the Great Creature, the Sea Lizard coming to eat us up!"

Kilohana stroked her head. "That's a dolphin, following the ship to bring us luck."

Lucy peeked fearfully at the dolphin. Then the island of Molokai, like a half-submerged dragon, caught her eye. "Is *that* the Lizard, then?"

At sight of Lucy's fears, all Kilohana's self-possession returned. "Who has been filling your ears with tales? There are no lizards here. Come, sit down, and I'll tell you about the good-luck fish rolling around out there. He followed my canoe all the way when I first came from Hawaii."

Lucy snuggled up to her mother. She knew the story by heart. "Go on," she prompted. "You were wearing the red *pa-u* Vanacuva gave you, and Adama saved you from the bull, but he did not save the *pau-u* and it was all spoiled—begin there."

The clouds settled over Oahu, orange and crimson, and, as the light faded and darkness fell, the *Lucy's* foaming wake turned to a streak of silver. Adam looked up at the stars in deep content. There was no place like a ship! Here, the perplexities and disappointments of life ashore took on their true perspective, for everything about the sea was real, and Adam was not good at fighting phantoms.

"Shall I take the helm, sir?" John Harbottle, the pilot, asked. It was not customary for the captain of the vessel to be his own sailing master, but Adam shook his head. He would not relinquish the wheel just yet.

Hours later, he tiptoed across the deck to where Kilohana and Lucy lay curled. "Come!" he said, "Our watch below." He laid the sleeping child in the bunk and Kilohana put her hands on his shoulders. "You are the greatest chieftain of them all! You have tamed the sea and the wind," she said passionately.

He took her face in both his hands, and saw himself reflected in her eyes. Yet Kilohana was more than a mirror, she was faith itself, buttressing him against the world.

She kissed him on the mouth and lay down; but Adam, determined to keep awake, went to the table under the swinging lamp. His tired eyes fell on the chart, tracing its lines and curves, its dots of islands and columns of figures. The rush of water against the planking and Lucy's regular breathing seemed timed to a sort of tune, a hobbly tune, jumbling figures and islands together. His head dropped on his arms and he slept.

Moonlight streaming down the companionway woke

him, and he climbed on deck. He had not intended to sleep this first night on sea. He took the wheel again, and in a few minutes he had forgotten everything but the *Lucy*, slipping through the phosphorescent night.

Adam noticed that his wife was changing. On their first day at sea, she offered to eat with him in the cabin and he pretended not to notice, when, with the meal half over, she bolted from the table and finished her share in the corner with her back to the room. That night, she sat through it and Adam never heard her explanation to the Hawaiian cabin boy that, on board an English ship, English tabus superseded Hawaiian ones. Sometimes she leaned on the stern for hours, staring at the southern horizon, and afterward she would steal to Adam's side and sit brooding. The sextant always diverted her, and her comments on the antics the sun did at Adam's bidding entertained him. Then, there was the bit of scrimshaw he had begun years ago on the *Discovery*. How could he make those tiny lines with his stubby fingers? Was the lady in the helmet, whose bosom he traced with so much care, a goddess, or the portrait of a friend? He explained that it was Britannia, and later he heard her telling Lucy that it was Adama's goddess.

One day Lucy ran out of the pilot's cabin waving a wooden doll with red cheeks and china-blue eyes. "Mine! My goddess, Adama!"

John Harbottle followed, wiping his eyes and laughing. "That's a sailor, not a goddess. I made ye an 'im, not an 'er."

She held the doll up to her father's face. "She is like you, eyes and pantaloons. She is an English goddess, prettier than your Beretania. Why are Adama's eyes blue, when ours are brown?" she asked her mother.

"John Harbottle painted them blue."

"But *our* Adama's eyes, why are *they* blue?"

Kilohana pondered. "He is a child of the Sea and Sky, and we are children of Earth. You can tell by the eyes."

Lucy rocked her wooden sailor. "Child of the Sky, child of the blue, blue Sky," she crooned, looking at her father. "Now I know why your eyes are blue. Kilohana told me."

Adam laughed. Whatever these Hawaiians had of England, they gave it a native twist. In a child it was charming. "Isn't she rare?" he chuckled, and Kilohana nodded absently, for her thoughts were traveling ahead to that strange island, California. What fate awaited her there?

The weather was growing so cold that the Hawaiians could not keep warm, though they bundled themselves in tapa and rags of canvas, and even wore their sleeping mats as shawls. Several of them caught colds. So, also, did Lucy, and Adam made her a hug-me-tight from an old scarf to wear under her dress. At last the fog shut down hard, and Adam spent hours of every day covering sheets of paper with figures. One day he called the pilot, and when they had checked over the dead reckoning they went on deck and walked up and down, too restless to do anything else. A fog breeze was blowing, and the sun was trying to struggle through the mist, which moved a little now and then. Then, all at once, the fog broke, and the lookout in the cross-trees yelled.

Adam took off his hat and stood with it against his breast, in the naval salute. Ahead, so close that he could almost hear the crash of breakers, was a coast of dunes and twisted trees, and in the distance blue mountains towered. He made a trumpet of his hands. "The water is changing color, we're on soundings! Heave the lead, and keep a bright lookout for Monterey!" Through the glass he could see an adobe fort clinging to the point like a mud-wasp's nest, flying the red and yellow flag of Spain. After a month of sea, Adam had made his land-fall.

CHAPTER XVIII

Caballero

L ITTLE LUCY GORDON stood at the taffrail. By poking her head through the life lines and leaning out she could see the end of a rope ladder hanging overside, wriggling like a live thing trying to reach the water.

The sailor sitting in the tender grinned at her. "Going ashore, Luki?"

She nodded and began to climb the rail, but turned as she heard her name called and saw her father and mother coming out of the cabin. Adam was wearing a cocked hat, and his clothes were blue, with silver buttons. His face was freshly shaved and a pistol and a leather purse like a double-toed sock were thrust in his belt. Lucy ran to him and hugged his knees. "Can I go with you, Adama?"

He brushed her aside, and, before she could realize it, the tender was pulling away and Kilohana was standing on the poop, looking after him and waving. In her tightly wrapped calico *pa-u*, she looked naked and wistful.

Lucy's lower lip went out. Why had Adama pushed her away? On shipboard, she tagged him everywhere. She picked up her wooden doll and made a face at it. "You look ugly today," she scolded. "I will tell Ha-

boka to make you a cocked hat." Everyone had forgotten her, but perhaps by now Adama would be lonely
and wishing that he had taken her with him. With Lucy,
thought and action were simultaneous. She untwisted
her skirt and wrapped the doll in it.

"Stay here," she ordered, dropped down the ladder
as she had done so often in the harbor at home, and
jumped in. The cold water closed over her and she
gasped, then struck out bravely. She had never been in
the water alone before, and the schooner, towering above
her, looked mountain-high as she slid past; but though
the current was carrying her faster than she could swim
she did not seem to be gaining on the rowboat, and she
was getting tired. Suddenly she began to flounder, and
a big bird with yellow claws swooped and drooped,
almost on top of her. "Adama, come!" she screamed,
and sank. Then something inside her let go, and she
opened her eyes and shot to the surface. Oars were
creaking somewhere.

Adam dragged her over the side. "Lucy, you
damned little water-rat! If I hadn't seen that pelican
dive . . . "

He shook her in mingled anger and relief, and Lucy
shrank away from him and curled on the floor boards,
panting and shivering. Adama's rage would be soon
over. He would take her ashore and people would stare
and point at them saying, "Who is that handsome man
with the beautiful little girl?" She sighed luxuriously
and her eyes closed. The sun-baked boards felt delicious

after that awful water, and the creaking of the thole pins sounded like gulls squabbling round the *Lucy.* Then, in her dreams, she heard Adama's voice. "Take the child back to the schooner and return here."

She sat up with her fists in her eyes. The boat was thumping gently against a dock on which Adam was standing, buttoning his coat. She put out her arms to him.

"No! Manu will take care of you."

She burst into tears. "Can't I even stay in the boat and wait for you? I love you, Adama, and I want to go with you."

He looked down at her and laughed, in spite of himself. "I said, no! Someday, when you are properly clad ... " He was off, up the lane between the rows of houses.

Lucy's sobs subsided, and a sly look crept into her eyes. "Have you seen this place?" she asked the sailor.

Manu nodded. "I was here in a ship long ago, before I came to work for the Master. That is why he left the others on board and brought me—I can speak with these people." Her eyes wandered longingly over the blank fronts of the adobe houses. Behind them, men stored red wine that makes the heart brave and loving ... and in the cool dark rooms lived girls with skin like morning-glory petals.

A boy loafing in a doorway caught his eye, and Manu waved to him. The boy went into a house and came out, carrying a drinking horn. As he neared them, a drop on the end of the horn fell and splashed a little crater in the dust. Manu reached for the drink, but the boy held it high. Hawaiian sailors were not uncommon sights in Monterey, and, after a month at sea, they were fair game to the denizens of the waterfront. *"Dinero!"*

The Hawaiian felt in his loincloth and took out a pearl, small and yellowish, but worth more than all the wine in the inn, and the boy relinquished the horn.

Lucy was curious. "What is that? *Awa?*"

Manu wiped his mouth with the back of his hand. "No, *awa* is chief's drink. Here in California all drink. Bring more!" he ordered, throwing the empty horn to the boy.

Lucy licked a drop off her arm. "Do you like it?" she asked, making a face.

"It makes the slave equal with his lord."

She hugged him round the waist. "Then you can take me on shore if you are a lord. Just a little way," she wheedled.

"I am afraid of the Master."

The boy returned with another horn full of red wine, and Manu drank thoughtfully. Then he set Lucy on the dock and clambered up after her. "I am not afraid now," he bragged. "Come!"

Hand in hand they walked up the town's single street, sniffing strange smells and looking into court-yards. Now and then they glimpsed a skirt slipping out of sight, and eyes behind barred windows smiled at the bronze giant leading the naked girl child through the street of Monterey in broad daylight.

A sudden clatter of hoofs sounded round a corner, and Manu flattened himself and his charge against a wall just in time to keep from being trampled, as a horse and rider galloped down the lane and stopped short beside them.

Lucy hid her head under the sailor's arm and Manu patted her. "She is afraid," he said to the stranger, in Spanish. "She has never seen a horse before."

The *caballero* shook his bridle hand so that all the little silver bells on the reins jingled at Lucy. "Welcome to Monterey."

Lucy peeped at the horseman. There were little red balls all around the brim of his hat, and on his upper lip perched a young mustache. She put out her hand, timidly, but he swung her up to the saddle in front of him. "Where shall we go, Senorita?" he asked gaily, in Spanish.

The bantering voice pleased her and she reached up, offering him her nose in the Polynesian kiss.

Manu put his hand on the bridle. "We must go back to our ship."

The governor's son laughed, and Lucy felt his arm tighten round her as he drove his heels into the horse's ribs and they galloped downhill. This was fun, better even than riding in front of Adama on his surfboard! They stopped with a jerk that nearly threw Lucy out of the saddle, and Manu and his crowd of followers ran up. "Is that the ship?"

Lucy answered with a torrent of Hawaiian and Manu nodded, too out of breath to speak.

The *Caballero* pointed to the child. "Your *nina*?"

Manu shook his head, but Lucy stamped her foot and pointed at the schooner, riding at anchor—"Come with me! I want to show you to Kilohana. You are like a god, riding the mountain!"

Manu translated: "She wants her Mama to see you."

Esteban Sepulveda stroked the new down of his mustache. He had never seen a Hawaiian woman. No doubt she would be naked, like the man and the child, and she might be beautiful. He flung his reins over the horse's head, and jumped into the row boat. "Is your Mama pretty?" he questioned.

Lucy poked at one of the red balls on his hat brim. It bobbed and swung and she poked first at one, then another, trying to keep them all going at once. Her new friend's eyes were merry, with brown shadows in them, like ferny pools.

The boat's nose grazed the schooner's planking and John Harbottle leaned over the rail, wagging his finger at Lucy. "So ye ran away in the tender?" he called down to her. "I've been a-huntin' ye these two mortal hours. I was just about to wake yer Mother in the cabin. Why didn't ye tell a body where ye were goin', Lucy?"

She pointed to her companion. "Look!"

The pilot scowled. "I see 'um. I knows they Spaniards—all paint and no ballast." He stood as if to block the way, but Esteban pushed past him and Harbottle snatched up the child's *pa-u* and twisted it round her. "Put yer skirt afore company," he growled.

The Spaniard's long eyes were taking in the schooner. "Senorita?" he questioned.

Harbottle pulled his side whisker reflectively. "Have ye business with the Captain?" he asked, in English.

The *caballero* shrugged, and Harbottle indicated a water breaker. "Sit down!" He spoke very loud with the conviction that English, if loud enough, is intelligible to everyone, and, taking Lucy's hand, shambled off with her to the cabin.

Lucy threw herself on her sleeping mother. "On deck is a man all red and gold, with white, white hands!" she cried.

Kilohana, only half awake, sniffed and ran her hands over the child's legs, where a few horse-hairs still stuck. "Where have you been, Luki? You smell like an animal."

Harbottle interrupted. "There's a Spaniard on deck. I think he's come to see the Captain."

Kilohana sat up and swung her legs over the edge of the bunk, while the pilot unhooked a netted calabash and set it down beside her. "We'll take care o' the visitor while ye dress up in yer new finery," he volunteered.

They found the Spaniard still sitting on the water

breaker, with the native sailors crowding around him, and Lucy pulled at his coat. "Kilohana is in there," she announced waving toward the cabin, and the Spaniard rose; but the pilot's heavy hand pushed him back and he sat down again, unable to hide his irritation. She held up her wooden doll, chattering at him in Hawaiian, but when he took no notice, dropped his hands and danced to the rail. The rowboat was coming back! Adam had hardly jumped over the rail, when she was upon him. "Look, Adama," she gloated, pointing to the Spaniard. "See what I found in California!"

He made no attempt to disentangle himself, but strode across the deck, dragging Lucy with him, and put out his hand; but Esteban did not notice it, for from within the ship a woman was coming, draped in a fringed white shawl and stepping carefully, as though strange to the green velvet mules she wore. Her flowing black hair was bound with a wreath of yellow feathers, and, with a dignity that was royal, she offered her hand to the stranger. "*Aloha*, Capena. Welcome to de *Luki!*" she said in English.

Adam chuckled. This was the scene that he and Kilohana had so often rehearsed at Stone House. "All visitors are welcome to the *Lucy*," he said cordially, in Spanish. "I join my wife in greeting you."

The *caballero's* eyebrows went up. "Your wife?"

Adam's face grew suddenly hard. "Yes, this is Mistress Gordon. Will you drink a glass of rum with us in the cabin, and may we have your name?"

The Spaniard bowed. "I am Don Esteban Sepulveda, son of the Commandante of Monterey.'

Adam led the way to the cabin where he pulled out
his own chair for the visitor, and measured the drink
in three half coconut shells. "Your health, sir!" he
toasted, and all three drank.

Esteban coughed, unaccustomed to the strong
liquor. "A fine ship you have here, Senor Capitan."

To Lucy, the little cabin seemed overcrowded. The
Spaniard, in her father's chair, was taking up the whole
place. She edged nearer and leaned against him. "That
is Adama's chair."

Adam pushed her off. "Don't be tiresome, Lucy!
Run outside and play."

Adama had taken her friend for himself and he
was sitting in the Captain's chair, while her father and
mother perched on the edge of the sea chest. She could
tell by Adama's looks that he was talking about the
ship, and Kilohana was listening to him, but the Spaniard was not listening. He was looking at Kilohana.

CHAPTER XIX

Monterey

DURING the weeks at sea, Kilohana had watched Adam's restless preoccupation drop from him like an old coat; but where, on the voyage, he had been merely happy, he was now exuberant. When the fog shut down at night, marooning the schooner in a soundless world, he would wrap Lucy in his jacket and carry her out on deck, saying, "This fog will make your cheeks rosy, like a little English girl's;" and, in the morning, when the land breeze chased away the mist and the air was filled with sea gulls' clamor, he would throw back his head and shout, "Fill your lungs with it, Kilohana! This wind blows straight off the snow mountains," and Kilohana filled her lungs, and coughed. The fog chilled, and the land breeze smelt like medicine, but Adam's joy warmed her through and through. She was the quiet one of the two now, watching his every move and trying silently to fit into her new role of captain's wife.

In Honolulu, she had never been welcome at the shipyard, nor had Adam ever discussed his work with her, but here in California it was different. The governor had accepted his offer of four hundred pounds gold and the *Lucy's* cargo for the *Lily Bird,* and Adam and John Harbottle planned to careen and overhaul her in the salt grass at the head of the harbor.

"How could any sailor man let a new ship go so foul? Her bilge stinks to heaven," Adam would say, and John Harbottle would twist his whisker and grumble, "They papists spiles h'everything they touches, but the *Lily Bird's* a fine leddy just the same, Captain Gordon," and Adam would slap his leg and chuckle, "Ay, that she is, Mr. Harbottle, that she is."

At last Kilohana begged him to take her on board the *Lily Bird*, and he did so, explaining the ship to her in detail as though she were a man. As they were starting back to the schooner, he ordered the boatman to the dock. "We've lain at Monterey a week now, and it's time you set foot ashore," he said to Kilohana.

The land seemed rolling under her and she took Adam's arm to steady herself, but the Mexicans and Indians of Monterey looked not unlike Hawaiians, and she could have felt at home, except for the smells. "I like the breeze we have on the *Lucy* better," she complained.

"That's the town smell."

Her face fell. "Is it civilized?"

Adam laughed. He was always laughing of late. "That depends. Harbottle would say no. He doesn't think California is even as civilized as Hawaii."

She fell behind a little, trying to see inside the houses, and Adam halted in front of one of them, and waited for her. They went into a dark room, the floor of which was heaped with saddles, bladders of tallow and sacks of wool, but Kilohana's eyes saw only the shelves, piled with colors such as she had never dreamed—red, purple and orange.

The shopkeeper spread out his wares and she touched each new texture timidly, but, when Adam asked her to choose, she hesitated, letting her joy sink deep. "You choose for me."

He leaned on the table, fingering the Spaniard's treasures, and at last selected a length of red silk and took out his double-toed purse.

"Wait! Look, Senor Capitan. Our Lady herself has not a more shapely hand than the Senora. Does this not become her?" From his strong box he took out an Indian bracelet of pure gold, carved like a snake, with turquoise eyes, and slipped it over Kilohana's wrist.

"Would you like it, Kilohana?"

The bracelet fitted her like a fetter. "Would you like me to like it?"

Adam counted out the gold pieces. His wife should have the finest bracelet money could buy.

Out in the street, Kilohana's inquisitive eyes were everywhere. Suddenly she stopped and sniffed, and, with a cry of delight, picked up a twig on which hung a faded orange blossom. "The flower from Manini's island has followed us to California!" she cried. All the treasures of the shop had not evoked such rapture. As she stood with the twig between her lips, a woman left her barred window and came into the street, holding out a bunch of orange blossoms. She offered them to Kilohana, but her eyes were on Adam. "Will the Senora accept these?"

Kilohana buried her face in the bouquet.

"My wife wishes me to thank you."

The giver shrugged. "It is nothing; they are common flowers, but it is rare to see so fair a man as the Senor Capitan in little Monterey."

"It is long since a Senorita has made me such a pretty speech," Adam answered gallantly. The girl was white as a magnolia blossom.

She indicated a box-like structure, wedged between two houses. "There is my dwelling. Sometime, when the Senor wishes to visit Monterey, alone"—her pause was freighted with meaning,

Adam bowed, to hide his confusion. "You are kind to the stranger. *Buenas noches*, Senorita!"

Back again on the *Lucy*, Kilohana slipped off the green velvet mules and stretched her cramped toes. Her eyes were mocking. "Will you teach me to speak this Spanish, Senor Capitan?" she asked, in perfect imitation of the woman who had given the orange blossoms.

Chapter XX

Cascarron

THE PRESIDIO of Monterey was built of adobe, and within its walls were the governor's palace, barracks, and rooms enough surrounding the square courtyard to house all the gaiety of Alta California. It was the night of the Governor's ball, and women in evening dress and men in short velvet jackets sauntered through the candlelit rooms.

Adam Gordon, threading his crowded way with Kilohana on his arm, felt that all eyes were on his wife. Her piled hair, rising head and shoulders above the other women, was starred with pomegranate flowers, and her white dress moulded breast and thigh in the empire fashion, new in Monterey.

The leader of the musicians called to the *caballeros* to choose partners for the quadrille, and Esteban, the governor's son, crossed the room to Kilohana and raised her hand to his lips. "Will you do me the honor?"

She answered him hesitatingly, in Hawaiian, and Adam interpreted: "My wife and I are strangers here. She is not acquainted with your dances, and prefers to look on."

"As the Senora wishes!" The *caballero* drew her hand through his arm and swept her possessively away.

Adam felt half inclined to follow them, but his attention was caught by a girl calling *"Cascarron!"* who rapped his head lightly with something she was carrying, showering him with confetti.

A servant offered him a tray of tinted eggs. *"Cascarron,* Senor?"

He took one, wondering what to do with it, then sprang at the girl who had assailed him and cracked it on the gold pin in her hair, while everyone cried *"Cascarron,"* and the quadrille was forgotten as the guests showered each other with confetti.

Someone held up a glass, shouting, "I pledge you the Englishman," and others took it up, calling for a song while they filled his glass as fast as he could empty it. Port, Madeira and Angelica, they were all one to Adam, and he danced the hornpipe and sang, while the musicians thumped the time on the backs of their guitars.

> "Green grow the rashes, O!
> Green grow the rashes, O!
> The sweetest hours that e'er I spend
> Are spent amang the lasses, O!"

"Gringo! Gringo!" the Spaniards joined in, and Adam sang louder and capered higher with each glass of wine. At last he dropped on a chair, and the guests, mad for fresh diversion, began to call another name— La Sevillana.

A dancer stepped into the center of the floor and hesitated, while the whole room seemed to throb in time to a little pulse beating in her throat. Then the guitars twanged and she began to move lazily, dragging one foot in a rhythm that alternately rushed and held its breath.

Adam's heart missed a beat as her skirt flicked his knee, and he recognized the woman who had accosted him in the street. To his bemused senses, it seemed that he had been sitting all his life in this smoke-filled room, watching the whirl of a scarlet skirt to the twang of strings. She spun faster, singling him out of the crowd and dancing for him alone; then, like a dipping swallow, she dropped and poised on his knee, with her arm around his neck—the dance was ended. The guests applauded, and someone seized the dancer and led her to a table. Adam stood up, unsteadily. The air in the room seemed suddenly unbearable and he walked across the courtyard to a wall, jutting beyond a screen of oleanders, and laid his burning face on the adobe.

The branches parted and sprang back, and the dancer leaned over him, touching him with all her body. "I left them to find you. Ever since we first met I have been waiting," she said, and kissed him.

"I'm tipsy, and you are California wine," he laughed and clutched her awkwardly, drinking in her musky fragrance.

At last she pushed him away. "Have you no heart at all? I thought you knew how to kiss," she panted.

"I'm drunk, thass all. Too mush heart. Can't love girl right with so mush heart, I mean so mush drink . . . *you* know that."

She whirled away from him as Kilohana and Esteban came through the oleanders.

Adam caught his wife's hands. "See thish lady, Kilohana? She's Spanish dancer, thinks she can dance. Never seen you dance the *hula*, thass why. Come on, show her how to dance!" He thumped his feet and clapped a *hula* rhythm.

Kilohana giggled. Adama was funny with all that colored paper in his hair! Her audience of three waited, while she tied her shawl about her hips and lifted her arms, as if about to begin. Then—"I don't want to dance the *hula* tonight! Come, Adama, take me inside! I want to watch the Californians," she said, and pulled him after her through the shrubbery.

The guests were saying good night, and Adam and Kilohana sought out the Commandante and his lady in the mirror-lined sala. "One more glass of California angelica, Senor Capitan," he urged. "It is only on Easter Monday that we *conquistadores* may forget our exile and fancy that we are back in Spain. I pledge you the Senora Kilohana!"

Adam drank, and Kilohana made a sweeping curtsey as she had seen the ladies do that night.

The Commandante took her hand and laid it in that of his wife. "Is she not charming, my Concha?"

Dona Concha stroked her upper lip, shadowed with

a faint mustache. "What a pity she has no Spanish!" she said, emphatically. "Leave her here at the Presidio for a month, and we will teach her our ways."

A servant opened the gate and Adam and Kilohana started down the hill arm in arm. A man and woman, evidently quarreling, were walking ahead of them. "I did not bring you to Monterey to have you throw yourself at another man."

"Do you mean that English lout? Remember, I saw you with the Hawaiian woman." They let themselves into La Sevillana's house.

"I don't like Esteban," Kilohana whispered. "All the time he was pretending to show me his father's house, he was talking fool's talk. He hasn't the training of a hairless boy." They settled themselves in the rowboat, and slowly, Adam's head drooped to his wife's shoulder; then, with a sigh of content, he slid off the seat beside her and pillowed his head on her lap. Tenderly, Kilohana brushed the confetti from his hair and watched it swirl away astern in a tiny eddy of colors.

"*Cascarron*," Adam murmured in his dream.

CHAPTER XXI

Crown of Thorns

KILOHANA sat on the cabin floor, staring at the litter around her. How could all these rags and feathers ever have come out of her calabashes? She jammed a feather *lei* into one of them, and tried to fit on the cover. Why had she ever come to California? Adam was leaving her and Lucy at the fort while he went on a trip. It was unthinkable, yet the unthinkable was happening. Only this morning, he had told her of the Governor's invitation to accompany him on a hunting trip after renegade Indians. "And while we're civilizing the redskins, the ladies may be able to teach you some of their ways," he finished, patting her shoulder affectionately. He did not tell her that he had kept the governor's invitation secret until it was time to go. Adam hated scenes.

But Kilohana made a scene, begging him to take her with him, or even to leave her on the schooner. Why had he brought her to California, only to drop her like a withered *lei* at the first threshold? He retaliated bitterly, regretting his hasty decision to keep her with him, and wishing he had left her behind to go to the devil—or to her mother—it was all the same. Who

was she to spurn the chance to associate with the women
of Adam's world? She could neither act like a civilized wife, or take the consequences. He ran up the
ladder and slammed the hatchway shut.

Kilohana cried till all her mouth was salt; but Adam
did not even look to see . . . then, suddenly, she knuck-
led; Adam was master here, and the harder she fought,
the worse would be her defeat. She dragged out her
calabashes and began to pack hurriedly, crying all the
while. At the sound of running feet on deck she looked
up, but it was only Lucy, who scampered down the
companionway and rubbed her cheek on her mother's.
"Don't cry any more, Kilohana! Soon we'll be in
Monterey with *Caballero!*" Her tongue caressed the
name.

"Where is Adama?"

"On deck, cleaning his gun. You should see his
face!"

"How does he look?" Had Adama been weeping,
too?

"Funny. He's all grease, like this," She imitated
smears and Kilohana gave a dry sob.

"Time to shove off!" Adam's voice was cheery,
and his good-natured face showed no rankling memories.
"Shiver me, but this cabin looks as though the pack
rats were moving in." He dragged his wife's two dresses
from under a heap of fish line, and held them out to
her. "These are all you need, Kilohana. Which one are
you going to wear?"

She sat dumb, working a bit of string between her fingers.

"Kilohana!"

With a sidelong look at Adam, she reached for her dress. "God damn your soul to everlasting hell," she muttered into the muffling folds.

Adam wanted to pay a last visit to the *Lily Bird*, and, all the way up the harbor, Kilohana sat on the forward thwart beside Manu, the sailor, breathing through swollen lips and looking straight ahead.

The ship lay careened at the head of the inlet, with her bowsprit and spars poking up from the salt grass, and all the ropes running from her masthead to the ground. Men carrying tar buckets and wads of spun yarn crawled over her sides, and John Harbottle stood astraddle on the tumble home. "Come aboard, Sir, and stick yer knife in her planking! The *Lily's* sound as a nut," he shouted, and Adam climbed up, followed by Lucy.

Kilohana walked off to where some men were stirring tar in an iron pot over a fire. She was not interested in jubilations.

When they came down again, Harbottle held out his hand. "Good-bye, Kilohana. You and I'l be glad to see the Captain home again, eh?"

She stumbled off without answering. She was sick of the reek and talk of ships; of her tight dress, and the hairpin pulling at a single hair; but sick most of all of Adama's face, so like a stranger since they had quarreled; yet in the tender she took her own place beside him and pressed against him to show her forgiveness, but Adam's arm was like wood inside his blue sleeve, and his eyes never left the sail.

At the dock he mounted a waiting horse and took Lucy in front of him while Kilohana clambered to the pillion and Manu walked behind, carrying the dunnage. They were the last of the Governor's guests to arrive, and Adam was given a shakedown with the *cabelleros*, while the Lady Concha welcomed Kilohana and Lucy, and forgot them again in the hurly-burly of hospitality. The sala was crowded with ladies, and Kilohana took up her station at a window where she could see the courtyard. Surely Adama would see her waiting there and come? Food was passed and she tried to eat it, but Lucy cried and pushed her plate away, refusing to be pacified, until an old woman with a face like an idol's gave her a candied pear and led her off to bed.

Then the ladies said good night, kissing one another's cheeks, and the governor's wife put her arm around Kilohana, still standing in the window.

"Where is Adama?" Kilohana asked eagerly in Hawaiian, but the Spanish woman only shrugged and moved her heavy eyebrows up and down. She tried again. "Senor Capitan?"

This time the Senora's answer was voluble. The Captain would be late tonight, in fact he might not go to bed at all, and it would be better for the Senora not to wait up for him.

Kilohana kept time to her words with nods and smiles. The Governor's lady was evidently very kind, and it would never do to let her know that her conversation was beyond anything Kilohana could understand. She opened a door and showed Kilohana a room almost filled by an immense bed in which Lucy lay sleeping with the pink satin coverlet wound tightly round her neck. "This was my daughter's room. *Duerme con Dios, Nina,*" she said, and made the sign of the cross over her guest.

Left alone, Kilohana dropped her clothes on the floor and slid into bed. Her eyes fastened on a head on the wall, under which a tiny red lamp was burning. A wreath of some sort was pressed on its forehead above the half-closed eyes, and drops of blood glistened on the bearded cheeks. Was it the head of some loved one, hung to the wall for safekeeping? Hawaiians often kept such mementos of their dead. Resolving to make it a fresh wreath in the morning, she snuggled up to Lucy and fixed her eyes on the door. In a few minutes it would open very gently and Adama would come tiptoeing across the floor to her in the big bed . . .

She woke with a start. Bars of early sunlight striped the floor and Lucy was sitting up beside her, drinking from a cup.

"*Ciocolate?*" The Mexican woman, who had put Lucy to bed, held out another cup, but Kilohana shook her head. The smell sickened her. Where was Adama? Why had he not come to her in the night, she asked

over and over, dragging on her clothes, but the woman
only shrugged.

Lucy licked the spoon for the last vestiges of choco-
late. *"Caballero?"*

The nurse pointed to the courtyard, and she wriggled
out of bed and made for the door after Kilohana, but
the woman pulled her back. "Mother of God, you cannot run out naked!" she screamed.

The courtyard was swarming with men and horses,
and Kilohana backed against the wall, afraid to trust
herself in the melee. Her eyes searched the crowd for
Adama—why had he not come to her last night? He
might be sick, or even hurt.

"Will the Senora give me her flower to wear?"
Esteban touched the wilted pomegranate blossom in
her hair. He was dressed in black, and his red sash
reminded her of a *pa-u* she had worn, long ago. She
slipped the flower through the lacing of his shirt, and he
kissed it meaningly. Then, like a dazed child who senses
what is expected of it, she raised her face to his.

He rammed the flower into his pocket. "Not here!
your master is looking," he said crossly.

"Where?" Kilohana pushed past him. Through
the crowd Adama was coming to her, dressed in the
sombrero and leggings of a *cabellero*, leading a spotted
horse.

"Fancy, Kilohana, the governor has given me this
horse for my very own! Isn't he splendid? I'm going
to ship him on the *Lily* with one apiece for you and

Lucy—where is she?"

Kilohana patted the pony, trying to tune her jangled nerves to Adam's happy excitement.

"Where's Lucy? I want to tell her good-bye. We're off at last."

She wound her arms around him. "Take me with you, only let me walk beside your horse," she sobbed.

"There, there, don't cry so. I shall hardly know you when I come back, you'll be so civilized." He freed himself gently; then, with a jingle of spurs, he climbed into the saddle and galloped out of the courtyard after the others.

Kilohana watched him disappear in the dust. The strong bond that held them to one another was stretching, pulling the very heart out of her body, and she fancied that she could see it bumping along at the horse's heels, like a hat on the end of a rope.

Chapter XXII

The Sea People

To the visitors from the *ranchos*, the sojourn at Monterey meant the storing up of memories for months to come, when, back in their own adobes, built on exposed hillsides for fear of Indians, they tried a new pattern, or watched the first buds on a seedling they had brought home in a saddle pocket. They rose early and after prayers brought their work into the sala. It turned Kilohana dizzy to watch their flashing needles and their hands fluttering among the bobbins on the lace pillows. She could not understand their talk nor why they wore shells, like beetles, under their clothes.

In the courtyard, where the boy children whirled riatas all day long, she felt more at home, and planned that, if her child were a boy, he should have a riata and a red sash and a hat with little balls; but at night, with Lucy curled beside her in the big bed, she was afraid. What if some mischievous spirit should discover the empty hole she imagined within her, and enter her body as she slept? There were spirits everywhere, waiting for just such chances to gain an earthly body. Kilohana had once seen a woman so possessed, sitting at the door of her hut, nibbling at a crab shell and throwing the meat to her little dog. There must be spells to frighten away such spirits, if one only knew them. She made a *lei* of orange blossoms for the Christ on her wall and prayed to it until she found out that it was not a god, but only the image of his son, who was dead. After that she ceased praying and the wreath shriveled and drooped over one eye. Sometimes when there was music the sound filled the hole and she grew bold and joined in the singing. She learned to strum the guitar a little, and one night she improvised a dance, but the girl who was her partner drew away, ashamed, and Kilohana finished alone. "That is the *hula* of the women of Monterey," she volunteered.

Someone sniggered, and the governor's wife cleared her throat noisily, exclaiming, "God forbid!" Kilohana was sorry, for it was easy to see that none of the others could dance, except with the feet. Later, in the room next to hers, she heard smothered laughter and spied two girls in their nightgowns, trying the *hula*. She offered to show them again, but they jumped into bed and pulled the covers over their heads, and she went on, sorry that she had frightened them, to the cliff where she could sniff the night smells, and try to time her clamorous blood to the waves on the moonlit beach toward the town. Every night, on her way to bed, she looked at that strip of beach, yet she had never been down to it, for none of the women ever left the fort. The adobe parapet on the other side was so high that she could not see over it. Was the sea there, too, splashing up the shelving sand and sucking back within itself in the moonlight? She tucked her skirt into her waistband and climbed down the cliff.

There were no dwellings on this side, yet she could see folk playing on the rocks off the end of the point, diving and rolling each other over and over in the water. She could almost hear their voices. She stole nearer, keeping to the shadow, undid her dress and waited on a rock for the wave she knew would come. Surely these happy people would let her romp with them in the sea tonight! She dived, and the receding wave carried her out. A rough body pushed between her legs, and a furry muzzle came up beside her. These were not men, but Sea People! A school of flying fish skimmed the surface, and she caught one and tossed it to the seal, calling out her own sea names. Instantly the water was boiling with the fighting seals, tumbling her over and over. "I am of your kindred, don't hurt me," she gasped, and an oldster, with grey whiskers, raised his head and barked. Then, as suddenly as they had come, the seals dived and vanished.

Kilohana sat on the rocks for a long time. Then she went back to the fort.

Since she had found the Sea People, Kilohana was almost happy, and her tricks and stories, pieced out with gestures, amused the Spanish women beyond anything else in the fort.

" 'Whence come you, bold prince?' Umi held up

the King's necklace and loincloth, which his mother had given him. 'From your own royal loins, my father and King. Do you remember the hour when you gave these keepsakes to my mother, the maiden Akahia?' King Liloa's mighty laugh was like a trumpet note. 'I have sipped the honey from many a flower, but the golden Ilima of Hamakua was the sweetest of them all. Upward the face, my son!' " The ladies' eyes flashed, as Kilohana strained the invisible child to her breast. "Umi became a great king afterward," she said in an altered voice. "He was numbered among my ancestors."

They called for more, but instead, she took a piece of string from her pocket and twisted it round her fingers. "This is Umi's necklace," she said, and tossed it from one hand to the other, calling out the figures as she did so—"fish-in-a-net, the bird snare, the bride's little house." She picked up a guitar.

"I will sing you the song I have made for Adama's coming:

"Over the mottled sea, where the Sea People play in the moonshine, the spindrift whirls. Where are you my lover?

"You are as far from me as a sword, hanging between the stars. In this grey, cracked land of dust and burning skies, there is no song; my nights are only for sleeping.

"I cannot see your face. Where are you my lover?"

The strings jangled, and she put down the guitar and hurried out of the sala. She had almost forgotten the empty hole in her breast, but the song had made it suddenly unbearable, and she ran along the veranda, running to get away from the pain. Down below, tumbling in the surf with the Sea People, she might cheat the pain. She climbed down, dropping her clothes as she went, and dived off the nearest rock.

Left in the sala, the Spanish women wiped their eyes and looked meaningly at one another. *Quel amor!* It was like a novel. Yet the Senora Capitan had been happier than they had ever seen her until she tried to sing. Someone suggested that women in her condition sometimes went mad and did themselves harm, and they dropped their work and hurried after her.

She was not on the veranda, but some children, led by Lucy, were running toward the cliff. The women followed, panting with the unaccustomed exercise. Kilohana was standing on a rock at the water's edge—then a wave broke and she vanished. One woman fainted and others stood spellbound, watching the weltering foam where she had disappeared, but the Governor's Lady clutched Lucy and dragged her back from the edge. "Run!" she panted. "Get Manuel, in the kitchen! He can swim. Your mother has drowned herself."

Lucy pointed to Kilohana's head, rising and falling in the green waves beyond the surf where seals were playing. "Kilohana is not drowning, she is playing. She goes out at night, and comes back with her hair all wet. Let me go!" She tried to wriggle away, but the Senora held her tight.

Kilohana was swimming to the beach now, and the seals were leaving her. She climbed the cliff, walked up to the Governor's lady and kissed her. "The pain is done," she said sweetly. "I left it in the sea."

The Senora shook herself free. "Go and dress yourself," she said fiercely, and, still holding tight to Lucy's hand, picked up Kilohana's dress and gave it to her. What was it the child was jabbering, calling her mother by that heathenish first name of hers? "Don't scold so, Senora, don't make those awful eyebrows! Kilohana only wants to play with her kindred, down there in the sea." The Senora held Lucy at arm's length to make sure that she understood. People who played with seals and called them kindred were either demented or . . . She called to the waiting Manuel, "Ride to the Mission, and take a horse for Father Ortega to come here at once!" She pulled Lucy along, driving Kilohana in front of her. This was a matter for the Church.

It was night when the Franciscan Prior of Monterey Mission rode into the fort, and Manuel helped him to dismount. It was the custom of the Order to walk, even on errands of mercy, but as the Senora Commandante had sent a horse with her urgent message Father Ortega had broken his rule, fearing some sudden trouble in the governor's absence. The Senora herself came out to meet him and knelt to receive his blessing.

"Is anyone ill?"

She led him into the sala. "Eat, my Father. You are thirsty and hot, but we are in sore need of you here."

He munched the beans and sipped the wine set before him, while his hostess told him how the Hawaiian woman had run away from them all, jumped into the sea to play with the seals, and how she had kissed her, the governor's wife, stark naked. Later, when questioned, she had referred to the seals as her relatives, and could not be made to feel ashamed of what she had said and done. The whole thing was unchristian and smacked of evil, so the Senora had sent for the priest.

"I know her. Her husband brought her to the Mission when they first came to Monterey. She had never seen roses, fancy that!"

The Senora handed him a long iron key. "She is in her room. Shall I call her?"

"No, I will go in."

As he opened the door, Kilohana's eyes were on him and she crouched lower on the floor, as if to shield the child asleep across her lap. "Don't wake her," she whispered, "she has cried so long."

The friar made the sign of the cross over Kilohana, and sat down in the room's only chair. How should he talk to this woman with the eyes of a tortured animal? "My daughter," he began, and held out his hand to her.

Gently, she disengaged herself from Lucy and came out of her corner. This man with the furrowed face and shaved head was Adama's friend. "We are prisoners. What have we done?" Her face was swollen with weeping and her breath came and went in spent little sighs, like sobs, but her pulse beat strong and even where the veins marbled her breast at the edge of the draggled gown. Life welled in this woman like sap in spring, rising from her with the headiness of sun-warmed earth, unconscious, unbeaten—the life of Earth itself.

He spoke low, not to waken the child. "Are you happy here in Monterey?"

Her chin quivered. "Does the bird sing that is covered with a calabash?"

He put his hand over hers. "What is it you long for, my daughter?"

"To swim, and be free and naked with my—" she shut her teeth on the words.

He finished for her . . . "With your brothers, the seals?"

Kilohana eyed him. Would he, too, pry into her confidence, only to punish her as the Senora had done? "I long only for the eight seas of Hawaii," she answered dully.

"Our Holy St. Francis himself called the fish and the birds his brothers, and even preached to them."

"Who is Our-Holy-St.-Francis?" she imitated.

"He was the greatest of all our blessed saints, and he loved all earthly creatures and called them his brothers."

"Then, why"—she looked at the iron key lying on the table and two tears splashed on Father Ortega's hand. "Do the people of Monterey know him?" she asked, stormily.

"It is many years since he lived on earth. People

might not understand him at all if he were to come back today." He stopped, shocked at his own thoughts. "Tell me about your brothers, the seals."

Then Kilohana told him how, in her loneliness, she had found the Sea People, and how her play with them had eased the ache in her breast where Adam's going had pulled the strong bond and torn a hole. She told him her own sea names, and, to prove them, even whispered part of the chant of Niuhi, the Shark, which only his children know. She told him how her kinsman, the Owl, had saved Adama's life by flying in his face on the edge of a precipice, and, as she talked, she smoothed the man's rough habit till the life in her taper fingers made it crackle and thrill, like wool in thunder weather. Even so might the blessed St. Francis have talked of the fish and the birds he loved.

A scratch at the door roused him into reality, and he rose and put his hand on Kilohana's head. "Except that ye become as little children," he murmured, and a thrill ran through him as though touching this woman had charged him with life.

The Senora was waiting for him. "I grew frightened, you were in there so long," she said anxiously. "Has she been baptized?"

Father Ortega shrugged. "She is God's own child, if ever I saw one. Hearing her talk of the birds and the fish was like listening to the blessed St. Francis himself."

She crossed herself, and held her candle up to the

friar's face. If the Hawaiian woman's power over the seals were of the devil, she might bewitch even Father Ortega; but he only smiled and blinked in the candlelight, as he too crossed himself. "It was as if the blessed Saint himself were speaking," he repeated.

The Senora sighed, for a heavy weight had been lifted off her, and kindness came back into her face. "Now that I know she is not of the devil, I had better send her some food. She has been locked in since midday. Here is your candle, Father. Sleep well."

Kilohana knew no more why she was reinstated in the Senora's favor than why she had been deprived of it. After a night crouched in the corner, with Lucy asleep across her knees, she awakened the child to eat the cold tortillas a servant brought, and later, still crouching, watched the door open to admit the Senora.

Lucy flung her arms around the plump waist. "Are we free? Is the tabu lifted?"

The Senora smoothed Lucy's hair while she told Kilohana that Father Ortega had left her his blessing, and that he had started for the Mission at daybreak to welcome the returning Commandante and his gentlemen. She waited for an answer, but the Hawaiian woman's stare was more animal than human, and she went out.

Lucy put her lips to her mother's ear. "Adama is coming."

Kilohana dragged her eyes to Lucy's face. Adama was coming! She ran out of the fort into the road and looked toward the mountains, shading her eyes with her hand. The sunlight was blinding. She shut her eyes, and little rainbow suns danced inside her eyelids . . . when she opened them again, it would be easier to see the distant dust cloud; or he might even be nearer, within sight, riding his spotted horse. She felt Lucy tug at her dress.

"Hurry, Kilohana, the ladies want you to help make ready. When they come tomorrow . . . "

"*Tomorrow?*"

Lucy danced up and down. "Yes, yes. Hurry, *wiki-wiki*, there is so much to do."

With a gulping sob, Kilohana followed Lucy back into the house. Tomorrow!

CHAPTER XXIII

Senor Ossa

ON the Rancho de Los Palos Verdes the Governor's nephew, Don Juan Sepulveda, had collected the Indian guides who were to help hunt down their renegade tribesmen, and the Governor and his party reached the *rancho* the evening of their departure from Monterey. The ground around the fort-like adobe dwelling was trampled by the cattle that were feeding all around as for as the eye could reach, and inside the house the smell of burning wood and cooking food made the travelers' eyes smart and their mouths water. After supper, Adam and the other young men rolled themselves in their serapes, and, with their saddles as pillows, lay down on the earthen floor to sleep. The night was vibrant with sounds: the bark of a ranch dog, cattle cropping, the throaty twitter of a mocking bird guarding its mate on the nest, and the howling of distant coyotes—Adam fell asleep counting them on his fingers.

At daylight, a crowd of servants came in to mend the fire and squabble over their master's gear, and Adam joined a group of men talking in the courtyard.

"What a pity," one of them was saying.

Juan Sepulveda, the manager of the ranch, shrugged. *"Es costombre.* Will you help us wreak vengeance

on the murderer, Senor Gringo? See what he has done!"
He pointed to a dead cow, ripped from lungs to tail.
"Senor Ossa must have been disturbed at his kill or we
should have lost more," he remarked.

Adam examined the footprints on the bloody grass.
They were like a man's but with claw tips. "Who is
Senor Ossa?"

The Californian slapped him on the shoulder. "Sen-
or Bear. You must learn to throw the rope my friend."

The party made for the mountains and pitched
camp in a spruce forest on the edge of a lake. They
hunted Indians, guided by mission converts only less
wretched than their starveling quarries, driving them,
like cattle, into enclosures like cattle pens; and they lay
in ambush for grizzlies, which they roped and dispatched
with lances.

It was Adam's dream to kill a bear. He set up a post
on which to practice roping whenever he was in camp,
and tried his aim on every bush he passed while hunting.
At last his chance came. He was riding ahead of a small
party of hunters, when, thirty feet below, on a patch of
bare rock, he saw a grizzly. It raised its nose and
sniffed him upwind. then sat upon its hind legs and
rocked back and forth, beckoning him with its ridiculous
fore paws. Adam whirled his riata and threw, and the
bear toppled with the loop around its neck. Then, with
a vicious growl, it got up on all fours and began to pull.
The bear was full-grown—what a prize for his first
catch! He drove the spurs into his horse but the animal

stood stiff-legged, then reared. The bear was pulling
in earnest now. What if the rope should part and Adam
lose his prize? He leaned forward and dug in his spurs
for the third time, and the frightened horse plunged
ahead as Adam took in the slack rope. Sweat streamed
down the horse's sides. The bear was master now—
must he cut the rope at the saddle horn and let his prize
get away? He had made a mistake ever to rope it round
the neck. The bear turned on them with a roar, and,
with one rake of its paw, laid open the horse's side.
Adam pulled out his knife and slid from the saddle.
"Come on, you swab," he yelled in English. "Come on
and I'll rip your belly for you, or you'll rip mine!"

A lariat whirred overhead and the bear fell sidewise,
with its front paws roped together. "Stay where you
are, *Cabellero!* We must truss your captive properly
before we venture too near!" a voice called, as another
noose caught the bear's hind paws.

Tears of mortification stood in Adam's eyes as he
saw the bear dispatched, but Juan Sepulveda put an arm
round his shoulder. "You could have cut the rope and
let go. You are a game fighter, my friend!"

Adam lay with his feet to the fire, drying his boots.
He had been wading in the lake all day and returned to
camp at sundown, carrying a string of pink-meated
trout. Around him lay men on blankets throwing dice,
smoking, or cleaning their bark plates of the last spoon-

fuls of stew. Now and then someone threw an armful
of sticks on the fire, which blazed up and showed the
hobbled horses nibbling the grass, and men, in other
circles, lying around other fires.

A coyote barked and was answered by other animal
voices, dwindling to distant howls, as the noise was
taken up farther and farther away. After the quiet of
the Hawaiian forest, what a world of life there was in
these California mountains! It seemed years since his
first set-to with a grizzly—he had roped and killed
several, and was even gentling a cub for Lucy—he smiled, thinking of her. It was only since the cub's capture
that he had thought of Lucy or Kilohana at all, for he
had been wholly engrossed in hunting and in the almost
forgotten pleasure of association with white men of his
own class. With his quiet gift for friendship, Adam
understood these men of the second generation of
Spaniards in California who called themselves not
Spaniards, but Californians. Brave in danger and fatal-
istic in misfortune, they were carving themselves a New
Spain in the Californian wilderness, and Adam's association with them had freed, not only his tongue, but
his thoughts. Some men playing cards on a blanket
called to him and he sat down beside Don Ramon Yorba,
who offered him a bag of gold dust from his own pile.

Adam waved it away. "No thanks! Your Commandante has given me enough dust already to put me
in his debt for life."

Don Ramon laughed. "Still the Gringo, talking of

debts! You will never be able to pay a Californian save with hospitality, my friend."

Adam laid down his cards. "I should like to pay it that way best of all," he said seriously. "I want some of you to come out to the Sandwich Islands to live."

"Thank you, but here in California there is room for all! Your Sandwich Islands are too far away."

Adam looked round the circle of faces, his own face suddenly intent. "You're wrong, Don Ramon. California is separated from the rest of the world by a continent. You're bottled up here. You cram your storehouses with hides and furs and wine that you can't sell, except to passing ships at their captains' own price. Can't you see that a world market is at your door, with the trades to blow you there. The *Lily Bird* is going to carry the first cargo of Californian goods to Honolulu, and soon there will be more ships and other cargoes, until a steady line is formed between the Sandwich Islands and California. Yankee whalers from round the Horn always touch at Hawaii before they come here, and East Indiamen will make it a regular port of call if we can supply their needs."

"We Californians are landsmen—we have no ships."

Adam's face glowed. "I will furnish the ships, if you supply the cargoes. Store them in warehouses in Monterey, and keep agents there and in Honolulu. Have every vessel afloat on the Pacific laden with Californian goods in bottoms flying the Union Jack, with Honolulu as the central port of call!"

"Bravo! So might the old sea lords of Spain have spoken!" No one had seen the Governor come up behind the circle, and they all rose respectfully.

Adam flushed with pleasure. His dream had rushed him into the longest speech of his life.

"Tell us still more, Senor Gringo," Esteban drawled. "Are there beautiful native women in your islands—enough for all?" The words held a veiled insult.

"I spoke of trade, not women," Adam answered curtly. There was that about the governor's young popinjay that made one want to thrash him.

Juan Sepulveda laid a steadying hand over Adam's. "Give us time, my friend. Someday we may do as you ask, but we are still too busy civilizing the Indians."

"Why not leave that to the padres and sail back with me on the *Lily Bird?*"

The governor laughed. "You are like the Yankees, Senor Gringo, always in a hurry! Next year I will build a warehouse and when you come again I promise you it will be stocked to the roof. And now, my friends, it is a month since we left Monterey. These poor Indians—" he made the sign of the cross, "must be returned to the fold. I have decided to start back tomorrow."

They broke camp early. Men with *machetes* walked ahead of the cavalcade, chopping chunks from the trees on either side to mark the trail. Then came the twenty gentlemen, each with a bear cub strapped to his saddle, and the retinue of pack horses and captives followed. Wreaths of blue tobacco smoke floated above the gentlemen's heads as they laughed and sang, and if a wail from the rear of the column occasionally interrupted their talk, what the *vaqueros* did to their charges was no concern of the gentlemen.

Adam rode silently, with slack reins, taking no notice of the country through which they passed. As a child with a sea shell to its ear conjures up the sound of waves, Adam was building his dream, peopling the harbor of Honolulu with ships deep in cargo, ready to girdle the world.

CHAPTER XXIV

Fiesta

MONTEREY was in fiesta. The Commandante had returned from his hunting trip with eighty Indians and a bear cub for each gentleman of his party, and had ordered horse races and a fandango to celebrate the occasion. The roofs of the one-story houses were hung with serapes, and along the town's single street friars and *vaqueros*, Indians and shawled women with herds of dogs and children milled ankle-deep in dust. Their unhurried progress was toward a field above the fort where the horse races were to be held and where the bear cubs were on show. With the crowd drifted John Harbottle. His round face wore its holiday look, and he winked at the girls shuffling past in their heelless slippers and jingled the money in his pocket in anticipation of the races. Thank God, he was not bothered with women any more, but there was one woman he meant to see today and he knew she would be at the races. How had she fared at the fort? He had thought of her often during the Captain's absence and once he had even put on his best blues to go and see her, but at the landing his heart failed him and he rowed back to the schooner and sat until dark looking at the fort through the spyglass. He had not been to town since, but now with the horse races and the fandango coming on and the Captain back in Monterey, he felt ready to enjoy himself. In the field, Indians with flat baskets of grapes and pears on their heads were calling their wares, boys carrying dripping wine skins jostled friars with looped-up gowns, while *caballeros* in black hats and fringed leggings spurred their horses through the crowd shouting orders no one seemed to hear. He fell in behind a mountebank, who was whirling his riata and jumping through it shouting that he was now a deer, now a grizzly or a billy goat, and calling to the people to throw coins for him to catch in the air. The Englishman could not understand his jabber, but the man seemed to know his way about and Harbottle followed him to where four race horses stood behind a rope between two flags. Everything that could be loaded on their backs was there, silver-mounted saddles, massive stirrups, and bridles heavy with little bells. The riders' clothes were stiff with bullion. In Harbottle's opinion, one little half-pint jockey in silks could clean up the lot of them.

The starting pistol fired and the horses tore past with a brown mare in the lead laboring already, the specky grey who had started second passing her and nosing out ahead, the dun who had been third moving up to second. They were coming around the field again, the horses punished with whip and spur, and, as they passed, the crowd yelled, the yell following them in a wave round the big field. Harbottle craned his neck. The grey was a game one, for all her mangy hide, but

the dun had got the pole of her and was coming up inside
next to the flag. Now they were on the last lap together,
his nose to her quarter, and the grey's rider leaned out
of the saddle and struck the dun in the face with his
whip. The dun faltered and the grew drew out ahead.
Men stretched a rope across the track and the winning
grey galloped into it and stopped, while the crowd pulled
the rider from the saddle. The grey mare stood drooping
and forgotten and Harbottle patted her. It was not her
fault that the jockey was a swab.

A sailor from the *Lucy* passed with his arm around
an Indian girl and Harbottle sauntered along behind
them. There would be a good bit of time to kill before
the next race.

Someone clutched his sleeve, and he turned and
stood face to face with Kilohana, standing on a bench.
She pressed a bag of gold dust into his hand and her
eyes glistened with all the Hawaiian's passion for
gambling. "Adama is riding in the *Caballeros'* race. I
want to bet on his horse."

Harbottle hefted the bag cautiously. "Shall I halve
it?"

"Put it all on Adama! Hurry! He told me to stay
here with the ladies." She indicated the other end of
the bench on which some older women sat fanning themselves.

The pilot eyed her mildy. She was handsomer than
ever in crimson, with that snake bracelet on her arm and
the waxy red flowers in her hair. "There's no hurry.

The Spaniards may not start the next race till *manana*. How've ye ben, you and Lucy, and how's the Captain after his huntin' trip? Don't ye knew I ain't seen ye for a solid month?"

Kilohana tapped her foot impatiently. "Adama is happy to be back in Monterey. Luki is—" She looked round apprehensively. "She was here a minute ago. She must have run back to her bear cub."

"To her what . . . ?"

"The funniest creature. Adama found it out hunting and brought it home. It's in a corral back there." Characteristically, she did not mention the prizes of the nineteen other hunters.

He elbowed his way to a corral inside which twenty bear cubs were mauling one another and rocking back and forth on their splay feet. Lucy stood inside the fence holding out a cake.

Harbottle swooped after her. "For tuppence I'd trounce ye! They bears could eat ye up in two bites."

She threw her arms around him. "Haboka, I love you! I thought you had forgotten me."

He lifted her over the fence. "Come along o' me, away from they wild beasts," he said affectionately. "Maybe we can find ye some jimcracks to hang round yer neck." He bought a string of shells from an Indian woman and steered Lucy to the bench. "Here's yer child, Kilohana. Take care of her while I place your bet."

Kilohana took Lucy's hand, with her eyes on the

horses prancing between the flags. "Hurry!" was all she said.

There was no time to lose, and he felt in his pocket for the bag of gold dust. It was gone. What should he do? He hurried back to Kilohana. "I've ben robbed. I've no money on me, or I would of bet my own for yer," he said desperately.

She ripped off her gold bracelet. "Bet this!"

He fingered it doubtfully. In his slow-witted way he felt it was not the thing to do, yet Kilohana was game.

She gave him a push, and for the second time he made his way toward the line. Near the flags betters were shouting, holding up their fingers and plunking silver pieces, nuggets and bags of dust on a blanket on the ground. Harbottle waited in vain for some familiar word, for he knew the names of neither horses nor riders, but the people were moving off and the horses were ready to go. In a voice that made the betters notice him, he roared, "I give ye Captain Adam Gordon" and threw Kilohana's bracelet on the pile.

The horses were off. Five of them almost abreast and fighting for the pole. "There goes the captain on his piebald, crowding for third place, and the youngster on the black with the cut mouth is dropping astern. Way enough there, Captain Gordon, these coves are bound to blow themselves out, second time round. Steady on, now, easy does it; that's right! Nose up on that grey so's he can't get too much of a lead. The black is out of it . . . no more need to worry about 'im, sir."

They were coming round again. "Second time round will show 'em where the wind is," he bawled at Adam's back flashing past. "Look out for that grey, he's tryin' to get to weather of ye. Sneak up on 'im now while he ain't lookin'. Sneak up and blanket 'im. That's it, drive 'im and nose 'im out. *Now* let 'im 'ave it! By God ye've passed him! Now keep 'im there in yer stern wave. Give 'im yer deadwater, Captain Gordon!" He ran down the track as Adam's horse burst through the rope, and the frantic crowd seized his bridle.

Adam waved his hat. "A great-hearted horse," he panted, and slipped from the saddle.

The Commandante kissed him on both cheeks. "A great-hearted Gringo! That was a sweepstake, my friend. Winner takes all." He motioned to a soldier with a bag on his back and the man poured out the contents: silver, copper, nuggets and bags of gold dust; and a twisted snake of a bracelet with turquoise eyes. Adam had never imagined so much wealth outside the Bank of England.

Kilohana fought her way to him. "Did I not tell you we should win?"

Harbottle seized Adam's hand and pumped it up and down. "Ye're the grandest jockey that ever stepped in shoe leather, sir."

Two men raised Adam on their shoulders, and carried him away through the crowd, and Harbottle pressed something hard into Kilohana's hand. "Here's yer bracelet. I stole it off the pile. Don't ever bet it again,

Kilohana! And don't let Lucy stray away in this crowd. T'would make the Captain wild against ye."

She pointed to Lucy jumping up and down on the bench. "All right, then, I'll leave ye. This has been a great day and it's goin' to end with a great celebration." He turned away and joined the crowd on its way to the fandango.

Chapter XXV

Gringo

A S THE TIME for the *Lily Bird* to sail drew near, Adam became a familiar figure on the trails, riding at the head of his pack train. He was putting all his own money and what was left of Kamehameha's into wine and hides, tallow, nails and horses, with some silk shawls thrown in for the queens, and he expected to make a good thing out of the cargo in Honolulu.

Then, one day at high tide men righted the ship, and with logs under her keel rolled her into shallow water and warped her down the inlet winding between the sand dunes. They towed her out into the harbor and dropped anchor while the red pennant which signifies that a ship is homeward bound was run to the masthead.

Homeward bound! Adam stepped into the captain's cabin, still bare save for his homemade chart nailed to the wall. Taking a needle from his lapel, he pricked an anchor on the indentation marked Monterey, making each fluke carefully with the initials L. B. between them; thus marking forever the *Lily Bird's* first anchorage. Across the chart ran a black line notched with marks dividing it into sections, one for each day's run. We would mark the voyage Home in red, like the pennant. Home! A sudden picture leapt to his eyes: mist on the Solent and the bumboats crowding round to ferry Jack ashore . . . then the foam of breakers and Stone House with its flagpole and the Union Jack whipping aloft.

The moment passed and he sensed the slapping of bare feet on deck, rope ladders creaking and voices calling to one another in Spanish. With his bronzed face still colored with feeling, Adam stepped out to meet his guests. He was eager to show his friends the ship and even made them climb down into the hold, waiting black and empty for its first California cargo. "Only smell," he exulted. "She's almost as sweet as a new ship already, but when I get to Honolulu and can fill her bilges with salt, I wager that people will be trying to stow away down here."

The landsmen laughed and clapped him on the back while they made for the upper air. They were more interested in the cabins; the captain's under the poop deck, with glazed quarter galleries as big as windows clear across the stern, and the mate's and supercargo's forward. Even on the eve of sailing, Adam still hoped that he might take one of his California friends back to Honolulu. "I have no supercargo. Shall I fit up the cabin for you, Ramon, or Don Juan?" he invited, but the Californians shook their heads. Another time, perhaps. Adam was glad that it was easier to get a crew than a supercargo. Monterey was filled with men eager to try their fortunes in Hawaii and he had picked twenty of the best to serve under Manu as mate in the *Lily Bird* while Harbottle was to take the *Lucy* with the other eight Hawaiians who had come out in her. The two ships were to race to Honolulu, and odds were heavy on the *Lily* as the bigger ship, but Harbottle was confident of the schooner. "No, Captain Gordon, the *Lucy* don't want no handicap, just give 'er a head wind and we'll show these papists what a Hawaiian-built fore-and-after can do. Why, with our stout sails—."

"Don't talk about sails, Mr. Harbottle. The *Lily* could lug canvas, too, if she only had it, but with these damned rat-gnawed rags she's got aloft, I'll have to take it easy, that's all. Curse these Spanish wasters! But the ship's a bargain at that, and the cargoes will sell for more than enough to outfit her with the best canvas money can buy. As it is, the lack of sails will make the race more equal. The *Lily's* got bulk and spread before the wind, and the *Lucy's* got handiness and sails that can carry a bellyfull. It's a race between the old and the new, Mr. Harbottle, that's what it is." He turned to join his guests and the pilot's eyes followed him with admiration. The old against the new. The Captain had put the whole thing in a nutshell. Well he, John Harbottle, was for the new.

They spread the picnic on deck—tongue-scorching tamales wrapped in cornhusks, beans with meat and cheese, tortillas and spiced candied pears washed down with wine. When they had eaten, guitars were brought out, and everyone sang.

Esteban played with the fringe of Kilohana's shawl.
"Why do you sing straight from the lips?" he asked.
"Your voice is more like a boy's than a woman's."

Kilohana laughed. She had often noticed that the
Spanish women sang as if their heads were hollow.
"It is the Hawaiian way. It comes from the heart."

He stroked her arm under the red shawl. "That's
why I love it, and why I love—."

"You're full of love, Esteban, so young, yet so full,
full, full of love." She moved her hips a little as if
dancing. "I wish you knew my little bull calf, Esteban.
I used to feed him like this"—she dipped two fingers
into a cup of wine and held them up for him to suck.
"I shall name my very next bull calf for you, Esteban."
There was a general titter, and he snatched up a glass.
"*Salud!* I drink to the Senora, and her bull calf," he
said angrily, and dropped it overboard.

Someone picked up a guitar. There were shouts of
"Gringo," and Adam sang "Green Grow the Rashes
O," over and over, while the guests pledged him and
Kilohana, and the *Lily Bird*. At last they began to say
good night and the women kissed Kilohana and begged
her to go ashore with them, but Adam had chosen to
spend this first night on board. One by one they climbed
down the ladder until he and Kilohana stood at the rail
alone. An odd thought thrust itself into his mind. "I
forgot to bring any blankets aboard, Kilohana. I ought
to take you ashore."

She looked at him long and deep, filling her eyes

with his image. The bond that held them together was tightening, drawing them so close that she could hardly breathe.

Two days later the last of the cargo was brought aboard and Adam, his wife and Lucy took up their quarters in the captain's cabin. Now that Kilohana was leaving them, the foreign ways seemed to her infinitely desirable and she felt real grief at parting from the Commandante and his wife. They visited the ship daily, bringing last presents of oranges, olives pickled in brine, hair ribbons for Lucy and even little seedling trees wrapped in sacking, and Kilohana gave the Lady Concha her *mamo* feather *lei* as a remembrance. The *Lily's* deck presented a fantastic appearance. Horses and burros, four on a side, stood in stalls amidships, flanked with sheep and goats, and the jolly boat aft of the stalls was filled with chicken crates. A pet kid with a blue bow on its neck bleated on a tether, and the rigging was hung with sacks of oranges, strings of peppers and maize, and strips of jerked meat. In the boat over the stern, young trees were growing.

Adam looked at the *Lucy* sitting low in the water, deep-bellied with cargo: a home made thing with bulgy lines and sides like a fat duck, yet she was his. He had set every plank in her and knew every treenail holding her together. Someday he might build handsomer vessels, but he could never build a stauncher one. But

Kamehameha would be pleased with his big new ship. Funny, how he had almost forgotten Kamehameha, he had been his own master so long.

"The tide has turned, sir."

Adam snapped out of his reverie. "All right. Dip the ensign."

Manu shouted an order, and the flag dipped and was answered by the *Lucy*. Smoke puffed from the fort cannon, and the crowd on shore changed to a waving mob, as Adam roared, "Heave round!"

"Anchors aweigh, sir! All gone, sir," the boatswain shouted back.

The Skippers' Race was on.

CHAPTER XXVI

Cholera

THE YEAR 1804 is recorded in Hawaiian annals as the year of *ahulau*, the vomiting sickness. Cholera raged. The dead were everywhere—in houses, under overturned canoes and sprawled in muddy lanes where the living kicked them aside. Outside the temples people herded, staring at the smoke of the sacrifice fires and listening to the mouthing of oracles in their wicker towers. The temple drums throbbed day and night.

In Kawaihae John Young was fighting the general scourge with the only weapons he knew. Every day his crews towed long strings of corpses out to sea but the terrified Kanakas often failed to tie the weights securely and the bodies washed ashore again. The sharks were glutted. John Young could not fail to see that the priests went out of their way to avoid him; and the rumor that the cholera was a spell cast by foreigners was common talk.

One morning he sighted a schooner flying the royal *kahili* at the masthead. While she was still beating around the point, a canoe put off from her and John Young forgot his own trouble as he saw Kamehameha at the prow. Men were already straggling out of the houses to watch the landing and Young jumped into a canoe and ordered them to paddle him out. "Shove off, Sire! You can't land here! We have cholera in Kawaihae!"

"I know! I am not afraid!" the king shouted in answer.

Young went back to the beach to wait for his royal master. How had the news of Hawaii's desperate plight reached Kamehameha over one hundred and eighty miles of open ocean?

The king waded ashore alone. "John Young, you know why I have come."

"Is there sickness on Oahu?" Young asked in new concern.

Kamehameha groaned. "Aye, sickness everywhere. At Waikiki the fishermen die hauling their nets. In Manoa they drop in the mud of the *taro* patches and the birds peck out their living eyes. Last night I lay at Hana. The whole island of Maui is in panic. The priests say that this is a curse which the foreigner has put on the Eight Islands." He waited in a silence fraught with suspicion.

Young shrugged. He felt tired to death. "'Tis the cholera. 'Tis no respecter of persons," he said indifferently.

The king's eyes were like gimlets as he put his next question. "You are the only foreigner on this island. Why have you not sickened?"

"I've had the cholera. Those who live through it once never have it again. It was years ago, on the Yalu river. When the Chinese came on board to loot I was the only one left alive."

"What cured you?"

"It burnt itself out. That's what the Chinese woman that nursed me said."

The King pondered. "If you can find a cure, it will be well. I don't need to tell you that if I die, you die, too."

Young's grey eyes met his steadily. "Of course. I know your people all hate me, but I can't help that. When the cholera first broke out I tried to tabu Kawaihae to prevent it spreading. Kaha trusted me and would have helped, but he died. Now, all I can do is to get rid of the corpses and I can't do even that much longer. The priests want to make burnt offerings of them."

Kamehameha scowled. So Kaha was dead. "Does Ahia, his wife, still live?"

"Yes, the damned old trouble maker! 'Tis she started all this talk of cholera being a foreign spell. She won't let her people stop praying even to bury the dead and she herself is closeted with her priests day and night." He opened the door of his house and a half-grown boy lying on the floor rose, then dropped and covered his face as he recognized the royal visitor.

Young pointed to his son. "The cholera has left me but two out of all my brood," he said bitterly as he poured some spirits into a coconut shell and offered it to his guest.

The king drank with his eyes on Young's face.

Above all men he trusted this common sailor by whose help he had risen from the rank of a minor chief to that of Conqueror. The subject chiefs of his own race hated and feared Kamehameha; but this man was neither afraid of him, nor of the others, nor of death by cholera; and he spoke the truth. With swift decision Kamehameha took the Englishman's hand. "You are a faithful servant, Olohana; we will fight this cholera together. My people are children."

Under the shaggy brows, Young's eyes glowed. "Then you must drive the people away from the temples and set them to work! No one works any more. Unless they do, those who survive the cholera will die of famine. And you must bury the dead! Cholera breeds from its own stench."

"We will do all that." The king beckoned the boy from his corner and handed him his spear. "Take this to my temple and summon my chief priest."

The boy went out and the two men fell silent, each occupied with his own thoughts. Soon there was a scratch at the door and the king cried, "Enter!" A priest dropped on his face on the threshold.

Kamehameha spoke without giving the customary permission to rise. "Send my royal spear to every temple on the Island of Hawaii with this message: 'I have within this hour set my Governor, John Young, over all other priests and chiefs of this island. He orders the people to go to work and the living to bury the dead.' Now go!"

Kamehameha looked at the English boatswain he had first kidnapped, then honored, and whom he had just made second only to himself in the kingdom. Save for a slight trembling of the hands, Young was impassive. Kamehameha stood up and his head touched the rafters. "I am going to Ahia at Pololu."

Young sprang to his feet. "God, no! Don't go to that hell-hole! It's terrible. You don't know the woman!"

The king chuckled. "Yes, I do. Ahia is one of the old people, fond of the old ways. She hates innovations, that's all. But she's the most powerful of all my kinsmen. I am going there now to win her to—an idea—" he stared at his minister and a slow smile lit his black eyes.

Young shrugged. "You'll be wasting your time, Sire."

"The woman needs a husband," Kamehameha answered brusquely. "With all the rank I've just given you, you can handle her easily. The marriage can take place at once."

"If ye wed me to that harridan, I'll murder her!"

The King glared at his newly made governor. This shoulder-high Englishman whose life hung by a thread, dared to oppose him! Then, at the sudden picture of the wedded pair, he burst out laughing. "Go your ways alone then, Olohana. Make your bed where you will and we will find Ahia another husband. Let all the deaths be from cholera!" Still laughing, he ran down the beach and jumped into his canoe,

John Young watched him go. As he turned back into the house, he looked up at his coffin swinging under the eaves. Less than two hours ago he had avoided looking at it. He had gone out to warn Kamehameha away from plague-stricken Kawaihae and had come back Governor of Hawaii . . . well, he was safe for a while. If the king caught cholera and died, the priests would never take John Young alive.

He pried a loose stone from the wall behind his bed, revealing a cubbyhole in which a small calabash was hidden, set it on the table and took from it a quill, a cowrie shell caked with dried black paint and a sheet of stained tapa which he spread out carefully. Bugs had eaten away the edges and the creases were broken, but the writing on it was firm and legible. It was his life's record. He read it aloud, as men do who live much alone.

"This 10th day of March 1790 kidnapped from the snow *Elenor*, Captain Metcalf. 14th . . . from this place in the mountains where they have taken me, I can hear guns. With the help of God, I may yet be retaken from these savages." There followed crude accounts, scattered bits from the Book of Common Prayer, Bible verses and snatches of hymns set down at random, as though the exile were afraid of forgetting them. The next dated entry was ten years later. "Tamehameha appointed me Superintendent of Taxes of Island of Hawaii. Building my stone house at Towaihae. Established harbour dues to increase Tamehameha's revenue." He moistened the dried paint with the drop of liquor left from his drink and wrote slowly, making heavy black marks. "November, 1804. Cholera raging. This day Tamehameha appointed me Governor of Hawaii. God save the King."

Chapter XXVII

Pololu

IT TOOK all night for the King's little schooner to beat
up the coast. Sometimes she drifted in irons with
flapping canvas. Then a puff struck her and she wal-
lowed on her beam-ends scarcely able to right herself.
Now, at dawn, she lay off Pololu, deepest of all the
cloud-filled valleys of the Kohala coast. Save for one
mighty landslide, where a cliff had toppled into the
sea, Kamehameha's native valley looked just as he
had seen it last. Behind the rampart of beach wedged
between rock walls the valley was brimming with clouds.
As the sun rose they stirred and one by one flew up to
stay till nightfall, plastered on the sky. As they lifted,
the misty land took on daytime colors—green coconut
crowns; a column of smoke above the temple; and inland, on the rising floor of the valley, figures, like ants,
moving among the breadfruit trees. Still higher, where
a rain cloud was spending itself, a rainbow formed and
arched across the cliffs. It was a good omen.

A man's head appeared over the parapet of beach,
then his body, and a procession of priests carrying a
feather god filed down to the water's edge and stood
up to their knees in the surf. As the king's canoe ground-
ed they fell on their faces and the Conqueror stared

into the god's pearlshell eyes. "Rise!"

They stood up and their young leader made the formal speech of welcome. "Where is my kinswoman, Ahia?" the king asked.

"Sire, Ahia is shut in her house with the high priest, seeking a way to lift the heavy curse that has fallen upon Kohala."

"The sickness is in all the other islands. Kohala is no worse off than another place."

The priest raised his eyebrows. "Sire, that is news. Ahia told us that the Englishman put this spell on us because he was angry at her for trying to take the child."

The king grunted. Something of importance had evidently happened in Kohala about which he was ignorant. "Let us go to the temple. There I will eat and rest from the sea."

He led the way up the steep, gravelly beach. In the palm grove below stood the temple dotted with huts and towers which his ancestors had built, standing in long lines and passing the black lava and white coral from hand to hand while their slaves laid it up in the solid rectangle ordered by the gods. He entered his own grass house. Idol posts with carved heads grinned at him on each side of the low door, and the bones of his forebears wrapped in tapa and tied with sennit swung from the crossbeams within. The place was dark and smelt of decay . . . he blew his nose. So, Kohala was under a special curse because of some child!

The young priest entered with a carved dish holding a roast puppy, and Kamehameha tore off a leg and chewed noisily. "You are not starving here in Pololu!"

The priest wrung his hands. "Sire, there is hardly anyone left alive to supply the temple with offerings. They fall and die wherever the Curse overtakes them."

"Who buries the dead?"

"Of what use is it to bury them? They rise again and steal up behind the living and push them down. Sire,"—his eyes were hot—"why should the Englishman's curse fall on us? No one in Pololu knew of Ahia's plan to steal the child. Must we all die to keep the death from taking her?"

Kamehameha wiped his mouth with the back of his hand. "I am going to Ahia now. My people will wait for me in the ship. This place is tabu."

As he walked through the village a few Kanakas ran and hid in the already tumble-down houses. Hogs rooted in the fence corners and under the house walls, and a swollen corpse lay with its feet in the stream. The tabu staffs at the entrance to Ahia's compound guarded houses whose roofs had fallen in. He stepped round a body huddled against a broken taro dyke. The creature must have fallen while trying to stop a leak with the stone she still clutched.

The valley was growing narrower. Waterfalls turned to rainbow spray halfway down the cliffs and the giant tree ferns were laced together with creepers. The valley was well named Pololu, a spear thrust deep in the island's heart. Spatters of rain fell, and now and then a wild dog's muzzle poked through the undergrowth. There on the left was the familiar cave piled with dried fern where the wild pigs bred. In such a shelter he himself had been born on a night of hurricane, to eat the eyes of kings.

The path ended at a cluster of empty huts whose doors banged in the wind, but in the long house behind them he heard chanting and he pulled open the door. The floor was covered with people sitting and lying down, all intent on a man and woman in the center of the room. They were scooping up handfuls of ashes and rubbing them into their bloodshot eyes, while behind them in a half circle some old women kept time with drums and rattles, following their motions with guttural interjections. Suddenly the crowd fell on their faces and Kamehameha saw his foster sister lying on the dais.

Save for her eyes he would not have recognized the once corpulent Ahia in this gaunt creature. Her jaws were cavernous, like idol-jaws, and her grey wool was matted with dirt and bits of straw. He crossed the room and touched his nose to her cheek, rough and chilly as a shark's.

"So you have come at last, Paiea."

Kamehameha scowled at the crowd peeking at him through their fingers. Ahia's folk would be quick to notice her lack of respect due the Conqueror of all Hawaii. No one but Ahia would dare to call him by his familiar name. "Send these people away."

She sat up. "Go outside and ring this house with your incantations," she ordered, and to Kamehameha, "The chanting never ceases day nor night."

He watched them push through the doorway; priests, beldames and sweating men whose eyes burned with fever, skeleton women with babies, or puppies, or little pigs at their breast.

Ahia waved at their departing backs. "They are all the cursed Englishman has left his mother-in-law," she cried hoarsely and began to wail.

Kamehameha joined her perfunctorily until the wailing spent itself.

"So you have come at last," she repeated. "I knew the Curse would spread. The gods are angry. Mountains have fallen. Boiling water rises in the sea and kills the very fish in the nets and wild hogs have rooted up all the awa patches." She took a long drink from her bowl, and shuddered. "This is the last of the awa. After today there will be no more forgetfulness, only remembering."

Kamehameha made a face behind the bowl. Why must the woman stick to awa when there was English brandy to be had? Yet Ahia was so terribly changed that he could not help feeling sorry for her.

"What of the child?" he asked suddenly.

Ahia wrung her hands. What indeed? Instead of Kilohana's child, the slave had brought the English-man's curse and had spewed it out at her feet. It had killed Kaha and Alapai and all but a handful of her people. She rolled her loose skin between her fingers. "It has left even Ahia, high chiefess of all Kohala and Waimea no better than a starveling dog; but it could not kill me. My spells are too powerful. Kill all the foreigners! Burn their houses and desecrate their flesh! Nail John Young up in his own coffin and set him adrift!" she screeched.

Kamehameha buried his face in the *awa*. It was better to drink than to watch the trickle of slime at the corner of Ahia's mouth. "There are those who do not think the foreigner is to blame for this sickness. I have not had it."

She spat into her spit bowl set with human teeth. "The foreigner is not ready for you to die yet, Paiea. You are too useful to him. Your time will come."

The contempt in her voice made him squirm. Here in his native valley he was only Paiea, the upstart, wearing a red cloth jacket and worshiping foreign ways. The guns which had won him the name of Conqueror throughout the eight islands had not re-echoed in Pololu. Unconsciously he repeated John Young's words: "This sickness is cholera. It spreads by its own stench. Make your people bury the dead if you want to save the living. Then it will burn itself out."

Ahia did not answer. She was listening to the growing din outside and a single name chanted over and over. O Pele! O Pele!" Softly she repeated the name.

The color drained from Kamehameha's face, as he

remembered the dancing man and woman smeared with ashes. "You are not invoking—Her?" Even the Conqueror dared not name Pele, dread goddess of volcanoes.

"Why not? Better the fiery death for all than this slow creeping doom for us Hawaiians. Let the lava stream over the eight islands till they sink beneath the sea!"

He jerked away and ran toward the door. He must stop this mad invocation—at any moment Pele might hear and answer with showers of stones and red hot lava, or the earth under the very house might open and swallow them all. The whole valley echoed with her name.

"Stop. Here *I* am chief!"

"But you're mad, Ahia! Suppose—"

She laughed. "There's a cloud like a mushroom hanging over Mauna Loa even now. It will not be long, Paiea, until my dead are avenged."

His fists clenched, but Ahia was tabu, even to him. Nevertheless, he must stop this madness at any cost. He veered to a new attack. "Come away with me in the ship to Waikiki. We will tabu this place and let the houses rot. I cannot forget that you and I have nursed at the same breast," he muttered, trying not to look at her.

Painfully Ahia gathered herself and stood up. Her legs trembled under her and her slack belly pouched over her ragged skirt, but her mad eyes were level with his own. "You have ever been jealous of me. If the Curse had carried me off, you would be chief now. But you must wait a little longer, Paiea. You have queens enough without me. Go, hide your head in Kaahumanu's fat bosom and then beat her because she has seen your shame! Better had you died with your brains dashed out like a slave child than to have brought this Curse on us all!"

Kamehameha ground his teeth. "You lie," he muttered. "I am no slave. I eat the eyes of kings."

She pointed to the door. "And you came to quarrel with me, your milk-sister, Paiea, slayer of chiefs? Go —and the Curse go with you!"

He fled, overturning the drums and pushing the dancers aside—down the trail, tripping over vines and rocks, running as if Pele herself were after him. Folk dragged themselves to their doors and the priests crowded the temple walls as he jumped into the surf and struck out for his canoe. Pololu should never see his face again while Ahia lived.

Chapter XXVIII

The Skippers' Race

THE BETTING on the race had been heavy. The day was clear, with an offshore wind and the *Lily Bird* moved out ahead of the *Lucy*, breaking out her stuns'ls like little white puffs at the end of the yards as she left the point. Her red home pennant blew ahead almost to her main-top, and she passed the *Lucy* to leeward, followed by a screaming flock of gulls.

Night found the two vessels becalmed off the channel islands and the crew of the *Lily Bird* saw Harbottle point to his own drooping pennant and then to that of the ship, and laugh. In the morning the schooner was gone on the breeze too light to fill the *Lily's* sails.

Gradually the islands drifted astern, the gulls disappeared, a low mist hid the shore line and the *Lily Bird* was alone on the open ocean. There followed days of slop with light, contrary winds; and then a period of showers, sometimes as many as six in sight at once, and puffy clouds began to dot the horizon—rising to overcast the sky at dark.

On the tenth night from land, Kilohana wakened and sat up, tingling all over. Water was purring past the planking, timed to the regular roll of the ship, and she could hear the drumming of reef points on canvas above the banging of fall blocks and the glug of tanks. Adam was not in his bunk and she ran on deck. He was leaning on the binnacle box, writing in his book by the light of the lamp. The ship had changed her course. They were in the trades, and morning broke, sparkling, with a brown gonie, dweller of the open sea, swooping in their wake.

Adam was well satisfied with the ship. He felt at home on her roomy deck and her tall spars brought back his midshipman days. Only the sails were a disappointment. They had been stored so long that they were pitted with ratholes and the patches tore away from the rotten canvas almost as fast as the men could mend it. With new canvas aloft the *Lily* would be a match for any ship of her tonnage in the Pacific. Yet ships must go. As sure as Adam was a shipbuilder, the new fore-and-aft rig would one day push the square rig to the wall. Then there would be no more waiting in harbor for a fair tide and no more delays miles off shore waiting for a fair wind into port. He reached for the spyglass and scanned the horizon for a trace of the *Lucy*, but a school of blackfish breaching several miles away was the only sign of life on the oily sea. The afternoon was breathless and the sun a dim yellow ball drawing water. Clouds were making up in the north. Adam lit his pipe and watched the smoke curl straight up. There was no wind yet. A long swell like the rippling of a leviathan moved the horizon and rolled across the water and the *Lily* pitched and creaked. If there were another ship in sight now she would stand above the water like a mirage. He gave the order to Manu, the mate, to shorten sail, and both watches came on deck and scrambled, some to the gear and some aloft. There was wind in the cloud bank, but the squall would come up against it from a double header piling up in the south, with a light inside it like the inside of a copper bowl.

The coppery light went out behind a mist filled with gentle hissings and the ship shivered on the crest of a swell and plunged into the trough, a ship on a treadmill moving in a circle of mist. A horse neighed and stamped in his stall and was answered by the other horses. Then, suddenly, the sea was lashed white with rain bouncing off it like bullets, blotting out everything but the streaming deck, and the rigging whined in the onset of the gale.

There was a sound like a cannon shot aloft and a man dropped at Adam's feet and lay still, quite dead, with his eyes flicked out by a rope's end. The others came down sucking their torn hands and two of them wedged the body in the scuppers to wait for burial until the weather cleared. The main topsail had parted as they were clewing it up, and the slat of the sail must have thrown the sailor off the yard.

It was night when Adam heard a crash forward followed by the neighing and stamping of frightened animals and the Hawaiian mate came aft, clinging to the life line. "Seas are breaking over the stalls. What must I do, Master?" he yelled above the noise, and

Adam shouted back, "Set up the lashings and save what you can." Adam wiped off the streaming binnacle and looked at the compass card. The wind in the rigging was howling like a banshee but the ship was taking the waves on her bows gallantly. Damned if he would shorten sail again tonight! He gave the order to shift the course to the northward and signed to the helmsman that he was going to the cabin to look at the glass.

A small lantern, rocking in gimbals, filled the cabin with moving shadows that made it hard to see, but Adam soon found what he had anticipated—the glass was so low that there was almost no water in the spout. There would be no immediate change in the weather. After the buffeting wind the cabin seemed stuffy and comparatively quiet. Kilohana and Lucy were sitting in a corner of the floor and he dropped on his bunk to rest a minute before going on deck again.

Kilohana made as if to pull off his boots.

"No! I'm going on deck directly—" his eyelids drooped and closed. Adam was asleep.

Lucy scrutinized her father. "What are those purple marks under his eyes?"

"Sh-h! He has conquered the wind and the sea and he is tired. The jealous gods must not catch him sleeping." She squatted beside him, on guard. In these foreign seas danger lurked everywhere. Yet even here Niuhi, the shark whose eyes are fire, might find her if he would and smooth the waves around their ship so that Adama might rest.

She whispered a prayer and, as if in answer, Adam's hand uncurled and he sighed like a child in its first sleep. Then, in a breath, he was awake again, brushing the crusted salt from his eyes with the old knitted comforter he wore. "She's a grand ship, Kilohana, steady as a rock," he cried, and went on deck.

On the fourth day the storm cleared and left the ship rolling high on sparkling seas. It had blown her well off her course but the glass was high and Adam went about with his lips pursed in a soundless whistle, taking stock of the damage done. The main topsail was gone and one of the crew dead. An injured horse had been shot and the small animals and most of the plants had been washed overboard, but except for the loss of some of the water breakers there was no serious damage. He cut the daily water ration and went about the business of setting up the rigging, reeving new lanyards for those that had carried away and overhauling and restowing what he could of the cargo.

It was not until the fifth day of clear weather that he noticed the strange behavior of the crew. They were at it everywhere, whispering at the gunwales and in the forepeak. The lookout in the crosstrees shook his head and put his finger to his lips whenever the relief came and the Mexican helmsman crossed himself and made horns against the evil eye every time he turned the glass. A shark was following the *Lily Bird*, swimming like a prisoned shadow in the shadow of the tumble home.

Adam was worried. There could be but two reasons

for a shark to follow a vessel—either there was a Jonah on board or someone was about to die. He spoke about it to Manu, the mate, but the Hawaiian's answer was noncommittal. Everyone on the ship was in good health and there was no trouble among the men. Adam resolved to kill it; with the shark out of the way, the ship would be right as rain. He left the poop with a light heart and passed Kilohana sitting cross-legged in the lee of the house, busy with a lapful of colored rags. "Making something?"

"Yes, a *lei*."

Adam laughed good-naturedly. A *lei* made of colored rags, in mid-ocean! It was like one of Kilohana's fancies.

"Who is it for?" he asked, to humor her.

She stared past him at the ocean. "I wonder."

When he passed her again with the baited hook and line she was so intent on her work that she did not see him. The shark was in plain sight, rolling along in the wake. In a minute, or an hour, he would smell the bait and strike, never to let go.

"Seven bells!" The hail passed around the ship. It was time to take the midday sun and for the moment the shark was forgotten. Adam made his observations and wrote them in the log. With this favoring wind and sea the *Lily Bird* would soon be home. He made his noon rounds and found all snug among the animals and the vaquero in charge of them placidly plucking his guitar. Only the sailors standing at attention turned their eyes away from him as he went to look at his shark line. There was something hooked on it and he hauled it in. The bait was gone and the hook tangled in a bunch of colored rags. He hacked them off with his knife and called for a piece of meat. No one answered him, yet the helmsman with his back turned so squarely must have heard, and there was Kilohana, too. "Fetch me some bait, will you? Bait, Kilohana," he bawled.

"What for?"

"For that shark, you ninny! I'm going to catch him and cut him up with a strip for every man aboard. Somehow this *lei* of yours got caught on the hook." He pointed to the sodden mess at his feet.

She gathered it up and held it out, all dripping. "I made the *lei* for him—for Niuhi—it is an offering."

"WHAT?"

She smiled and nodded vigorously, in the quick way she had. "When you were so tired and slept in the storm I prayed and Niuhi, whose eyes are fire, left the Eight Seas and came to smooth the sea around our ship. For five days and nights he has guarded us. I made the *lei* for him."

Adam's face was terrible. "Bring me the bait. Your brother or whoever he is, got away once, but I'll catch him this time if I have to stand here all night. Serve you right if I made you bait the hook yourself for this God-damned—"

She touched the hook. "You didn't try to catch—?"

"Yes, and I got this contraption of yours instead,"

he snapped.

Everything was clear to her now. The shark's kindness had been met with treachery and he had thown
back the *lei* in defiance of her and her foreign husband.
"Put your hook away, Adama. Niuhi will not trouble
you any more," she said and began to wail as if for the
dead.

Adam looked over the rail. The shark had vanished.

All the rest of that day, Kilohana sat huddled
against the poop rail. It was no use to look for her shark,
to throw the *lei* to him with an invocation; Niuhi was
gone back to his home and Kilohana's in the heart of
the Eight Seas. And Adam? Adam had derided her
gods. Someday they would seek revenge and his fight
against the strong unseen things would be the pounding
of a child's fists against the wind. From now on his
life at sea would be in constant peril, yet he would never
understand.

That night in his bunk with the ship's noises deaden-
ing every lesser sound, Adam cried. Everywhere, even
on his own ship, heathenism and savagery were weaving him round; and Kilohana was the worst of all. She
would never understand, and he had always known it,
even while he tried to cheat himself with her pretty
ways. What a fool he had been to believe that she could
ever be different, she who identified herself with the
earth and the birds and even fish! Adam was England,
he was Civilization. If he toppled, the whole world must

fall; and in that moment he knew he would fight the unseen enemy to his last breath for, like the shark, he could never let go.

Next morning as he came on deck something blew towards him and he stood stock still staring at the long shred of crimson winding itself around his trouser leg. He called a sailor and ordered him to pick it off. "Throw it overboard. I cannot bear the touch of . . . silk." He spoke thickly and his hands shook like those of a man who had been drunk the night before. It was lucky that there was plenty of work to be done, unimportant things enough to fill a week, or a year, or even a man's life, and every day at noon the sun recorded so much time passed. At mealtimes he ate standing wherever he happened to be, and at night he doused the lantern after Kilohana and Lucy had turned in, without looking to see it his wife's eyes were watching him in the dark.

The *Lily Bird* was romping full on her course again with all her patched canvas spread. According to Adam's figures they were on Latitude 22 and if his reckoning was correct they should see the Southern Cross soon after nightfall. He felt both anxiety and confidence as the first star rose above the horizon followed by the others until four stars formed a constellation like a kite lying on its side. Instinctively he doffed his hat and stood bareheaded before the symbol of success. He had navigated his first ship alone halfway across the Pacific ocean.

"I have watched for them, too." Kilohana's voice was the incarnation of the night.

He did not look at her as they stood side by side watching the brief glory of the constellation. When the last star dropped below the horizon he realized that she had gone. The sky was spangled with stars, small, pale worlds to eyes dazzled by the Southern Cross. He lay down on the deck and looked up at them, conning over those he knew: the Dog Star, Aldebaran, and Arcturus by which he steered, dripping with all the colors of the Northern Lights. These same stars would be shining on Stone House now, gilding the thatch and making black and silver patterns under the arbor. All the grass around Stone House would be silver tonight, and the fishermen on the rocks would flash their torches in the empty window holes as they passed on their night's work. Adam slept, and dew fell and morning dawned before he woke.

Adam saw it first—a steel-white peak set in moving clouds. Then one by one the clouds separated and Mauna Kea's snow-covered top stood out above the island of Hawaii, shouldering to the ocean. They were in the Eight Seas! He shifted the course to northwest, steering for the channel between Oahu and Molokai, and the ship raced along with the wind behind her while the blue islands turned to green and black and red hemmed with breakers that beat against the cliffs. It was hard to believe that this show of spouting waterfalls and cloud-filled valleys over which the rainbows arched in pairs had been going on during all the six months of Adam's absence. He had left them sinking into the sea; now it was as if some fairy wand had raised them and touched them into life at his return. They sailed up the windward coast of Maui and Molokai and beyond Kalaupapa's long point Oahu hove in sight. Kilohana sang one of her passionate, tuneless chants while Lucy chattered and skipped until he ordered them both to be quiet. The island looked greener and the mountains bigger than he remembered.

"Sail ho!"

Adam swung his glass in the direction of the lookout's pointing arm and saw a schooner rounding Makapuu Point ahead. The sunlight glanced on her red hull and he grinned ruefully. Every rag of canvas the *Lily* owned was already set.

The Mexican sailors grumbled and pointed to the *Lucy* slipping along in the calm belt close to shore. They had bet heavily on their own ship, but it was plain that the *Lily Bird* was unlucky.

The cabin boy took away Adam's victuals untasted as he paced up and down, or took the wheel to get even ever so little more out of the ship than could the helmsman. She was sailing fast with the following wind, but she had more distance to cover than the schooner hugging the shore, and Adam could only hope that the wind would hold. If it held for an hour more, the ship's greater momentum would sweep her past her rival in the calm belt and through the reef channel in the surf. They were off Waikiki now and Adam fancied he could see the *Lucy's* canvas flapping. The ship's mizzen royal shivered, anticipating the dropping of the wind, though her courses still bellied bravely.

There was a faint sound behind him and he noticed Kilohana, and realized that she had been waiting to speak to him for some time. "There is no one on shore. No canoes are putting out to meet us. Look!" She handed him the glass, and he swept the empty shore with it. It was probably a tabu day and all the people were shut up in their houses.

"I'm afraid the *Lucy's* beating us," he said indifferently. Since the night when he had cried, life seemed all one to Adam.

Kilohana smiled, glad to be noticed again. "Of course she is, she's a better boat! Foolish Kamehameha, ever to buy a vessel not built by Captain Gordon!"

They were nearly up with the *Lucy* now, hitching ahead on little offshore puffs which did not affect the ship's steady advance. In another five minutes they would blanket her.

Adam hailed, and someone on the schooner answered. Then a gust blowing out of the valley hit her and she veered and struck in through the reef. The Skippers' Race was won!

CHAPTER XXIX

Keep the Flag Flying

THE *Lily Bird* was anchored off Waikiki and Kilohana stood in the bow watching the shore. Figures
like shadows were stirring under the coco plams and
here and there she could see the smoke of an oven, but
there were no canoes in the water, and no one fishing
along the reef. Even the waves rolling up on Waikiki
beach were empty of surf riders. The island must be under a terrible tabu when no one came out to welcome
the *Lily Bird*.

A rain cloud gathered and spent itself over Manoa
Valley and the rainbow, which is Manoa's guardian
spirit, flung its arch across. Sudden fog rose from the
valley floor, the rainbow feet faded and Kilohana knew
that the shark Kauhi of Manoa was creeping inland under cover of the mist. "I am your blood, Kauhi," she
shivered. The mist blew over the water, hiding the shore
and whispering around the *Lily Bird*, and Kilohana
peered down into the eddies. Darkness fell and stars
came out, big and soft as the light from Adam's lantern,
but she still looked down, trying to pierce the secret of
the eddies in the mist. "I am of your blood, Kauhi, I am
your sister," she whispered over and over. All the ter-
rors which she thought had dropped away from her at

sight of the Eight Seas were clamoring at her again. Kauhi, the shark was below there, waiting, swimming round and round Adama's ship. The dip of a paddle roused her as a canoe slid past the bow.

"*Lily Bird*, ahoy!"

Adam's voice answered from amidships. "That you Mr. Harbottle? Congratulations. I'm proud of the *Lucy*. Shove along a little and I'll throw you a ladder."

The ladder slapped against the planking, followed by a steady creaking, and the pilot's head and body came in sight. "She's all snug in 'er berth, sir. We had a good vy'ge," he reported.

"Did you get the gale?"

"No, sir. We saw summat to the suth'ard, but it didn't bother us none."

Adam slapped his leg. "That proves it! Schooner's the only rig, Mr. Harbottle. Why I had to sail right through the damned thing! We lost a sailor and a horse, and on top of that you beat me in."

The pilot's face was a study of mingled pride and sympathy. "That's not the 'alf of it, sir. The question is now, how're we goin' to get ye in now ye are here? There's not one of our old men left to man the towing canoes. They've had cholera here since we left and it's killed off nearly everybody in the place."

In the shadow of the gunwale Kilohana drew a sharp breath and the two men looked up.

Harbottle glanced warningly at his chief. "God bless ye, Kilohana, ye fair startled me," he said, pump-

ing her hand. "The king's sending out a double canoe
to fetch ye all in first thing in the morning."

Adam saw his wife's anxious face. "You'd better
tell her, Mr. Harbottle. She's bound to hear it."

Harbottle's voice was sober as he told them how
cholera had swept the islands. Whole provinces had
been depopulated, and Honolulu was filled with strangers, living in deserted houses, while Adam's own people
had died or fled, God knew where. The shipyard and
Stone House were ruinous from neglect but, due to
Adam's well-known tabus, they had not been tampered
with.

Kilohana plied the pilot with questions. Were her
father and mother alive? Had Hewahewa and the
king escaped the sickness, and had cholera killed all the
dogs and pigs as well as the people? But Harbottle
could only repeat what he had heard, that the scourge
had burnt itself out and that it was safe to land. When
at last he said good night they heard him wake the sailor
lying in the bottom of the canoe. Cholera had robbed
the natives even of curiosity. Times were changed, indeed.

Adam was up before daybreak, dressed in his blue
trousers and his coat with the silver buttons. Nothing
could be more different than the triumphant home coming he had expected, yet as he stood at the rail waiting
for the big double canoe putting out from Waikiki, he
was content. He had been beaten in the race by a
handier vessel, but he was bringing Kamehameha an

able ship and a rich cargo.

It was a long paddle from the anchorage to Waikiki and Lucy screamed with delight when the spray wet her dress, but Adam and Kilohana sat without speaking, thinking of the cholera. Kilohana was dressed in her bravest finery—the crimson shawl, strings of beads almost hiding the snake bracelet on her arm and the small round mirror, which was her greatest treasure, dangling at her neck. But her troubled eyes shifted from Adam to the shore and back again, trying to read in his face the meaning of the grief her heart foretold. Half the folk in the island were dead!

The knot of people on the beach parted silently as Adam waded ashore and made his way to the king, standing with his suite apart from the others. "There she is, Sire! The sturdiest ship afloat! Will you come aboard?"

Kamehameha touched his nose to Adam's. He was greyer and there were pouches under his eyes. "This has been a long year, my friend. There are not many of us left to welcome you—" The rest was lost in a howl from the crowd pressing round Kilohana. "The cholera has carried off half Hawaii," he finished, with his mouth to Adam's ear, and joined the general lament.

Adam listened while the names of whole families who had gone down into the Twilight of *Po* were called and the crowd repeated their virtues. His eyes searched the mourners for his friends—the giant Keeaumoku,

Hewahewa and John Young. Where were Lani, the bodyservant whom he had left in charge of Stone House, and Mawoa, his one-legged spar finisher? There was no one he could ask. He began to pick out men with his eyes—that gaunt fellow with the braided beard looked strong; and there were others who could do a day's work at the shipyard with less waste of energy than they were using in their wailing for the dead. No doubt, with their chiefs gone, these people had quit work and were living on bananas and coconut water. With decent food they might be able to take the dead men's places. At last the wailing dwindled to whispers with only an occasional outburst, as if the mourners were too weary to go on. Adam took the king's hand. "Sire," he gulped, and two tears splashed on Kamehameha's brown fist.

Kamehameha patted his shoulder. "I understand. It is so new to you. Well, if it were not for John Young, we should all have died. Even Hewahewa with all his spells could not fight it."

"Is Hewahewa—?"

"No, my friend. He is getting well. Now go to Stone House and we will visit the *Lily Bird* tomorrow."

The wailing broke out again, more faintly as their canoemen drew away from the shore, and Adam asked his wife a question.

She answered through swollen lips, 'No, not all of them. Ahia still lives."

They rounded the point in silence and Lucy

clutched at his trouser leg and pointed. There was Stone House and the arbor just as he had left them, and the Union Jack was flying!

John Harbottle ran down the hill straight into the water, up to his knees. "I ran the old flag up to welcome ye, sir!" he greeted Adam and turned to the others. "Here, give me yer hand, Kilohana, ye don't want to wet them fine velvet slippers of yourn . . . and Lucy, my poppet!" He pranced off with her up the path and a little dog ran out and jumped on her. "Don't screech so, that's yer own little bitch I brought ye from Californy," they heard him admonish.

Left in the rear of the procession, Adam was thinking that Stone House looked smaller than he remembered it, when Kilohana stumbled and fell. With a shocked look at her face, he knelt down on the grass. "Put up your foot and let me take off your shoes. You must be worn out with all that awful keening," he said, and kissed the mark of the shoe on her brown instep.

CHAPTER XXX

White Blood

THEN the child cannot be born at Kukaniloko?"
"Certainly not."

"But all the chiefs of Oahu are born there."

"Don't talk about it any more, Kilohana. The child is English and will be born at home like other English children."

Adam fixed his eyes on the toggle he was splicing as if to shut out the rest of the room. His midshipman's chest and the chair in which he sat seemed to belong to it far less than the surfboards and fish spears along the wall and the feather *leis* dangling from the roof. The carved bed which had looked so grand in California was heaped with native sleeping mats. He spoke loud, as if to convince himself. "The child is English. Remember that."

Kilohana's hands unclenched and she shrugged despairingly. "As you will, Adama. The child is yours." It was hard to give up her dream of Kukaniloko, the sacred birthing place where the old chiefs, standing each on his own rock, welcomed the new chief into the world while sharkskin drums beat and shell trumpets bawled the news; but she would bear it for Adama's sake for

this child would be an *ehu* child, fair, with blue eyes. In
any case it would not be born with the indecent lack of
ceremony which had marked Lucy's birth, for Kilohana
had secretly arranged with Hewahewa to be present.
The child might even be born before Adam came back
from Pearl River, where he was going now. Since their
return from California he was hardly ever at Stone
House any more, but spent his time traveling over his
domain. The survivors of the cholera were apathetic
and afraid, crying that they could not pay their over-
due tithes; that their canoes were stove in, and their
nets in holes; there were no more fish within the broken
fish-pond walls. Adam remitted the tithes and set the
people to rebuilding their tumble-down huts.

Kilohana begged him to take her with him on these
journeys of rehabilitation, but he always put her off,
saying that there was no room for her in the canoe, or
that he was going on horseback, and now that it was
too near her time.

He was going to visit the Spaniard, Marin, in Pearl
River, taking him some trees he had brought from California. The soil around Stone House was poor and
though Adam had planted oranges and pears he had
little hope of their thriving; but the Spaniard could raise
a whole orchard provided he was still alive.

"Take me with you," she begged.

Adam pushed open the pine door he had bought
in California. "Look there, Kilohana! Why should you
want to go traveling when you can see half the popu-

lation of Oahu right in that pasture? All they need is a fence to lean on!"

She smiled in spite of herself at the ever-changing crowd of natives who followed Adam's five horses around the pasture, while Lucy charged up and down on a sixth whirling and throwing a lariat which the good-natured by-standers caught and recoiled for her.

"Don't let Lucy stray off too far while I'm gone. She's so mad to ride."

Kilohana laughed, all her good humor back again. "What is 'too far?' She can go faster than I can, with all this . . . ," she pointed to her middle.

Adam was amused. His wife was certainly in no condition to run after Lucy and the pony on whose back she spent her waking hours.

He took a boatswain's whistle from his pocket and blew, and at the shrill blast Lucy clattered across the field and stopped short. "That's the way we stop them in California."

Adam picked a burr from the pony's matted tail. "A Yankee would say that you and that piebald were 'pardners!' "

Lucy tossed the hair out of her eyes. "His name is Jesus," she announced. "Paniolo says that is the best of all names."

Adam changed the subject. The differences in his own religious training and that of the Mexican *vaquero* were too intricate to explain. "Well, take good care of your Mother, Chickie."

Lucy eyed Kilohana's stodgy body. Take care of *her?*

There was small love between these two.

Kilohana shot a warning look at the girl. "With you away, Adama, one day will be as like another as seeds on a string."

Adam walked to the water with his hand on the pony's neck and Kilohana followed. It was odd how he and Lucy both loved the horses. Kilohana herself was afraid of them.

The two canoes, filled with trees, looked like little burgeoning islands. Two goats bleated in the bottom of one of them and Kilohana patted their soft lips and fed them bits of green through the slats of their crate, while Adam ran his practised hands over the lashings.

They shoved off and Lucy galloped to the flagpole to wave as long as she could see Adam waving in answer. Then, slapping her pony with the end of the rope bridle she shouted, "Vamos!" They scampered off and Kilohana, following heavily on foot, turned toward Stone House. Somewhere in the bottom of one of her calabashes she had a string of *wiliwili* seeds. She would hang them on the bed now and count off one each day until Adama's return.

Since the cholera, people were too weak or too busy with their own affairs to visit. Kilohana saw even Harbottle only occasionally and the servants were glum and listless. Then one morning, the harbor came to life again. Kilohana ran up the Union Jack, people seeped out of their huts to the beach, and canoes loaded with coconuts and bananas put out to the brig coming into port. The hails of the sailors in the crosstrees and the answering shouts from the towing canoes as their cables tautened and they pointed her into the channel were like old times! Kilohana watched it all from the arbor with Adam's spyglass; there was no need to trundle her heavy body any further. When it was too dark to see any more she sat down in his chair under the *hau* tree and stretched her cramped legs. What a day it had been! How Adama would have loved the excitement, and to visit the brig and talk with her captain about the voyage. Perhaps he might be back before she left port: Kilohana had already counted many days on her *wiliwili* seeds.

The sound of galloping broke her reverie and Lucy rode up and slid off her horse. Her hair was wet and her long calico dress was off and twisted round her hips like a native *pa-u*. She held out a folded paper covered with writing. "Here."

Kilohana examined it in the failing light. "Where did you get this?"

"On the ship. A man gave it to me. I swam out with the women. There were ever so many of us and the sailors gave us presents." She held out her arm to show a glass bracelet.

Kilohana scowled. She was thinking of Adama's

anger . . . English people were different about these things; yet it was the English sailors who were the worst.

Lucy was talking again. "I had to wait a long time before they gave me anything. All the other women went off with the sailors but they laughed at me and said I was too young. Then a man gave me the bracelet and this," she pointed to the letter, "and rowed me ashore in a regular boat, not a canoe. Why did he say I was too young?" Lucy's eyes filled with tears and her lip quivered.

Kilohana's scowl deepened. "You are different from the others."

Lucy smirked. "That's what the man who gave me the bracelet said. He said, 'Give 'er another five years and she'll outstrip all these blackamoors. She's got more than one drop o' white blood in 'er, that young 'un.'" Her imitation of the cockney sailor was perfection.

Kilohana turned the letter over and over in her hands. Why was it that Adama never allowed her even to go to the dock when there was a ship in port? Perhaps he would explain to Lucy himself when he returned. "This must be for Adama," she said absently, and went into the house to put the letter away.

Lucy sat down in the chair her mother had vacated. In the last rays of the afterglow her bracelet was green and red with lights deep down in it like fish turning under water. It was smooth, like goats' eyes and the eyes of the big man who had given it to her when she cried that his buttons hurt. She longed to go back to the ship. The man had said something about her English blood . . . that must be it—white blood calling to white. She could even hear it calling, high and soft like the song of the rigging on a gay day, with a throb in it like a drum. White blood calling to white. Of course Kilohana could never understand that. Lucy smiled her small secret smile.

CHAPTER XXXI

Mark

T HE BRIG had been gone two weeks when a canoe of the heavy sort used for traffic between the islands dropped its matting sail at Adam's landing and a young Englishman waded ashore, walked up to Stone House and banged on the door.

A woman's voice answered in English, "Welcome, Captain." She came towards him through the patched shadow of the arbor, holding out her hand.

"I seek Captain Adam Gordon. Can you tell me where he lives?"

"He lives here at Stone House, but he is gone on a journey."

Mark Gordon flushed with disappointment. To have voyaged all the way to the Sandwich Islands and then sailed two days in a native craft only to find Adam from home was too much.

"I'm the Captain's brother. Can you tell me where I can find him?"

Kilohana's look of faint surprise changed to one of eagerness. She dragged him to the flagpole and pointed north. Adama had gone north to Pearl River, but he would soon be home, and in the meantime . . . "

"Are you Mistress Gordon?"

She nodded and her outspread hands seemed to offer him herself, the arbor, even the earth on which they stood. "How old are you?" she asked abruptly.

Mark burst out laughing at the unexpected question. He could not know that this brown woman, big with his brother's child, was seeing in him her young lover of the cattle feast, stripped of all the years. So this was Stone House, Adam's Little England. The house itself looked just like the tool house at Windycross with some native huts crowded behind it, yet there was steadfastness in its homely square, set in coco palms, and the arbor at one side had an English look. Across the point on the harbor side were the dock and warehouses Adam had described in his letters; buildings at the edge of a tangle of vines and trees that seemed to cloak the land clear to the distant hills. He indicated his canoe. "I must pay those fellows off."

"No! You are my guest. Come!" With an order to a servant lolling in the shade, she pushed open the door and gave him the room with a gesture. "All that I have is yours. Lie down and rest from the sea and soon you shall eat, Adama's brother."

Left alone, Mark examined the place. It was dark after the brightness outside and sunlight filtering through the arbor made shifting leaf patterns on the Indian blankets covering the floor. A huge carved bedstead with a sea chest at the foot, a tall stand hung with calabashes and a homemade table and chair made up the furniture of the room; a fowling piece hung against the wall and strings of red and yellow feathers dangled side by side with bunches of red peppers, garlic and long vanilla beans from the rafters, above which the roof sloped into peaked darkness. He sat down in his brother's chair, took out his sketchbook and began to draw what he saw from the window. The book was a sort of diary filled with his impressions and as he penciled in the long flat warehouse and the jetty of sawed-off coconut stems, he projected himself into his brother's life. He had not seen Adam for years and had built his brother's dimly remembered personality into that of a sort of king, lord of uncounted acres and master of native tribes, building ships to carry his name and cargoes to the ends of the earth. The light faded from the window holes, the room darkened and Mark pocketed his pencil and sat musing, There was a scratch at the door and Kilohana entered, followed by a little girl and a procession of servants carrying food.

Kilohana put the girl's hand in his. "This is Lucy," she pronounced carefully.

Mark held her at arm's length, somehow, he had expected Adam's child to be English. "Well, Lucy, this is your Uncle Mark," he said at length, half ashamed.

Kilohana pointed to the ship's lantern being brought in by a servant. "That is Adama's lantern. It's eye pierces the darkest night and even the wettest rain cannot douse it. Listen!" Suddenly tropic rain was splashing on the thatch and spraying through the window holes, till the Indian blankets underfoot bristled with moisture, and tiny bubbles of it stood in Kilohana's hair. She dragged the sea chest to the table and sat down on it. "Tell me about Beretania."

Mark laughed. These natives were all alike, mad for stories; but it was easier to ask questions than to answer them. "Tell me about my brother," he countered with his mouth full. "I haven't seen him since I was a regular shaver."

The door flew open. The lantern flickered and brightened in the sudden gust and Adam stood outlined in the doorway, crossed by slanting blades of rain. He strode into the room and stood shaking himself and staring at his wife and Mark in the lamp-lit circle.

Mark held out his hand. "Adam, it's Mark. Don't you know me?"

Dark blood mounted in Adam's sunburned face and while a man could count fifty he stared at Mark's outstretched hand. Then, taking him by the shoulders, he turned his brother's face to the light. "How many years has it been, Marky?"

Mark swallowed. Somehow the forgotten pet name seemed to link him to this stranger.

"Fifteen years. I'm twenty-two. You must be thirty."

Adam felt suddenly old, as one who is surprised by a birthday. No one took much account of the passage of time out here. "How did you come?" he demanded.

"On my ship the *Sea Witch* out of Bristol. Zounds!" he rubbed his stomach. "Your victuals are tasty after two days of dried *poi* and coconut water."

"What's your service, Marky?"

"Tea and silks. I wanted to see the world and Captain Penhallow gave me a berth on account of his friendship with the Pater. He's got the ship careened at Lahaina and I'm on leave."

"Well, he ought to know better than to lay up at Lahaina!" Adam exploded. "I've got the only decent overhauling gear in the islands right here in Honolulu. However, we'll not talk business now. Tell me the news —begin at the beginning." He pressed his younger brother into his own chair and stood over him like a kindly watchdog.

Mark fished a gold turnip watch from his money belt and laid it in Adam's hand. "There's this. He wanted you to have it—" Mark hesitated. "Didn't you get Rose's letter?"

"No. I haven't had a letter for five years."

At the word letter Kilohana got up and began to rummage in one of her calabashes. "Is this a letter?"

Adam snatched it from her. "How long have you had *that* hidden away?" he snapped.

Kilohana's eyes filled. "Four times four days. A ship left it while you were away from home."

"Yes, a ship left it," Lucy echoed with a guilty look at her mother.

But Adam was already deep in the letter which told of his father's death. "He wanted you to have his watch. It is the only bit of England we can send you so far away, and Mark will bring it to you," Rose ended.

Adam fingered the square seal. All the jagged little wheels at the back of the watch were still turning, though the gentleman warming his coattails at the fire was still and dead, buried beside the mother Adam scarcely remembered. He fitted the watch key to its hole and wound slowly. The little wheels would still be turning when he himself was dead.

The lamp wavered and burnt out, and Kilohana and Lucy tipped away, leaving the brothers talking in the dark, of the Pater's last illness and the bloodletting that failed to cure; of Hugh's inheritance of Windycross; of Honora and her parson husband, and Rose who would keep house for Hugh until he married. The little sister was an old maid of twenty-eight whose letters were Adam's only link with Home; but so few of them ever reached him that he had long ago given up trying to keep any connected picture of life at Windycross. Now Marky had come to set it right again, little Marky, grown a man. Adam put his hand over his brother's lying on the table. "I'm glad you came," he said huskily. "I need a bit of England."

CHAPTER XXXII

·Half Gods

T HE BLOOD of the Awini is strong, the kindred of the
Awini is woven together like the strands of
a strong mat. Kelahuna, child of the tropic bird, look
upon us from the blue cliffs of the Jumping Off Place
of Souls!" Hewahewa circled chanting around the
breadfruit tree, right, left; left, right, and the branches
creaking in the night wind swayed with his measured
dance as he called on the half gods of the Awini clan.
"Kahalaopuna, soul of the trembling rainbow, Mano Ai,
whose fishy sire gave him a shark's mouth, and thou,
O Kilawahine, beautiful lizard woman whose red hair
spins the sunbeams of a perfect day, we offer you this
Little One." The invocation ended and the high priest
stood with face and palms upturned to the moonlit sky.

Adam swayed a little, still hypnotized by the rhythm
and the sound of a drum beating somewhere . . . or
was it the pulse in his own ears? His eyes were glued
to the bundle in the crotch of the breadfruit tree while
something in him kept repeating passionately to another shadowy Adam standing apart, that this creature
which he and the priest had wrapped in tapa and set in
the tree was none of his begetting. Yet, if the wind
were to blow ever so little harder . . . Adam shut his

eyes. He could not see it fall. He opened them again warily. The bundle was still there and a shred of white tapa wrapping fluttered from it like a little pennant or a tiny, waving hand. Suddenly he realized that Hewahewa was speaking to him.

"The darling Hiiaka herself was an egg in Pele's bosom until the Goddess warmed her to life and she became the Soul. This is a sign from the Gods. It is a twin?"

"Yes, there is also a baby girl."

"I see. One for you and Kilohana to keep and one for the Gods of the Awini clan. The blood of the Awini is strong, the roots of the Awini strike deep. At sunrise they will have claimed their own. Come away."

Adam plodded behind the earthbrown giant. This moonlit pasture where his horses cropped the grass without raising their heads to watch the strange procession; these rocks he called his own lapped by the waves he loved; Stone House casting it angular shadow like a beacon; all these were Adam's bit of England. Yet tonight Hawaii was mistress here and lizard women and bird men watched in the creaking trees.

At the canoe landing, Hewahewa touched his nose to the Englishman's. "We Hawaiians are children of earth. In us the shapes of our half gods, our forefathers the birds and the beasts still sometimes quicken into life. Kilohana has brought forth the likeness of a god, and I have given it back to the gods. That is all. You are a different breed who have forgotten your beginnings. Good night and love to you, my friend . . ." He raised his hand and Adam bent to receive the blessing.

Adam watched the canoe until it was a speck on the dappled water. Then he turned to the breadfruit tree bowing and swaying in the wind. Half way up was a white blot from which something fluttered. "I have paid my sop to you, Awini," he said out loud. "Go in peace."

Noiselessly he let himself into Stone House and un-hooked his ship's lantern from the wall. For a long minute his eyes followed its ringed shadows on the floor as if loath to leave them. Then he lifted the light high above his head and looked at his sleeping wife. She lay on her side with her face hidden and one brown arm round a bundle of tapa, topped by a baby's fuzzy hair. Her own hair, still matted with the sweat of her agony veiled the leaf poultice binding her breast and she frown-ed a little and sighed in her sleep. Kilohana had borne him twins, one of which was a monster and Hewahewa had wrapped it in his own mantle and laid it in the bread-fruit tree, as an offering to the half gods of his race. In the morning it would be gone. Perhaps Kilohana would die now. Women often died in childbed, and if she died he would give up the shipyard and take Lucy and the girl twin Home to England. But suppose she lived? Adam's mouth thinned to a hard line as he set the lamp back on its hook. Kilohana would not die. It was Adam himself who must forget.

Adam dropped in his chair by the window, drowsily watching the bees pushing in and out of the *hau* blossoms.

"Adama, come and look at her again. In this dark corner I cannot tell if she is fair."

He dragged himself back to consciousness. Why had he sent Kilohana's women away? The desire to keep Stone House tabu to natives even at such a time as this, had been too strong for him. Wearily he crossed to the bed and peered at the little face under its tuft of down. "I cannot tell, either, Kilohana. Her eyes might be blue," he answered patiently.

A spasm of pain like summer lightning flashed over Kilohana, and she stirred uneasily. "They will be blue. My Darling must have blue eyes."

Adam stumbled back to his chair. He felt worn out from the birth of these—of this girl child. If he could only sleep a little he might shake off the sense of calamity that was dogging him. He dozed and dreamed that he was in his canoe lifting, falling, stroking to the rhythm of a single repeated word, Adama, Adama. Something had hold of his sleeve—he jerked free and opened his eyes while the room swirled and settled into place.

"Adama, wake up! A ship is coming in!"

Still drunk with sleep, he stared at Lucy. "Then— a ship is coming in? Hoist the Union Jack." He was himself again, Captain Adam Gordon, on the alert.

Kilohana sensed his unspoken wish. "Go and see

what ship it is." He did not see her face twist in sudden agony as he went out.

Off the point, a small schooner was making for the shore before the wind. In a minute at most she would hit the reef. The pilot, putting out in his canoe could never reach her in time! Adam clenched his fists. That Captain, whoever he was, was deliberately running his vessel ashore! Her nose touched the rim of breakers and she shot round forty-five degrees and stopped in the wind with her sails shaking. God! She was quivering like a race horse and her skipper was a hardy one too, for all that bunch of red feathers flying at his masthead where the pennant ought to be. The schooner evidently belonged to some native chief from one of the other islands. Well, it was a jolly thing to have a strange vessel in port just now, if only to show young Mark what these island skippers were like.

"Adama! Come! Hurry!"

He turned back, cursing his foolishness for sending Kilohana's women away. "What's up? What do you want now?" After the blinding sunlight outside, the room was dark, and he slipped and caught the bed rail to keep from falling.

Kilohana ran her tongue over dry lips. "See . . . your boot . . ."

He held up his foot. It was slimy with blood and he was standing in a red puddle. He ripped off the tapa sheet. Blood was welling up around Kilohana and trickling down onto the floor.

"The crimson tide of Life . . ." she spoke as though her tongue were swollen and her teeth showed big and white between her stretched lips.

Adam grabbed his coat from the peg and shoved it under her knees. "Hold hard, Kilohana, steady on. This must stop directly."

How long had she been bleeding like this, and where were the women? He ran to the window and called, but no one answered.

"Water."

He held the cup to her mouth but the water dribbled away and he dipped his fingers and pushed them between her lips as one feeds a new-born calf.

"Hold me. I don't want to leave you . . ."

He climbed on the bed and cradled her in his arms, watching the pinched look that comes on the faces of the dying spread round her nostrils. "Please, God, don't let her go. Take anything else, only leave my Kilohana to me. Steady on, look at me, Kilohana," he begged, but she lay inert, frowning slightly, with half-closed eyes. Tense as a spring, Adam sat watching the slow drip from the bed and murmuring his formula over and over. "Please God . . ." there could be no life without Kilohana—their two lives were grown together like tree roots mingled under ground. Without Kilohana there would be no meaning in the day. "Please, God, take anything, anything . . ." It was nothing to him that the room was suddenly swarming with people pushing toward the bed, so long as they let Kilohana be. He gathered her closer. She was his alone, wherever she was drifting. Whoever these people were, they should not come between him and Kilohana now.

"Get away!" His fist shot out at a gaunt creature rummaging in the bed. No witch should touch Kilohana. The hand reached for the baby lying in its mother's blood and Adam drew aside. Let her care for the child, so she left the mother to him. Any one of those quick shallow breaths might be the last. He shut his eyes to shut out the crowd.

When he opened them he was alone with Kilohana again. His arms and legs throbbed with agony, but he held her carefully, not daring to move lest the hemmorhage start afresh, for glaze was forming on the puddles on the floor and there were no more red spurts quickening the dark stains on the bed. At last he laid her down and tucked a blanket round her chilly body. She was breathing more quietly now, almost as though she were asleep. Doctors always gave port after a bloodletting, and he must get hold of someone who could bring him a cask of his California wine. He tiptoed to the door, opened it and fell over Mark, sprawled across the threshold.

"How is she?"

"Better, I think. Can you get me some port to give her when she wakes? You'll find it behind the hides in the *mauka* warehouse. Here's the key."

Mark nodded. "I thought she was dying and you wanted to be alone with her. I've been sitting here for hours, keeping your people away. They wouldn't help me fight that old gorgon, but they were ready enough to shove in and tell you about it afterwards."

"I don't understand. Has there been a fight?"

Mark showed a bloody patch on his wrist. "There's the mark of her teeth. I thought they were coming out in my arm. God! How she stunk!"

"Who are you talking about?"

"How should I know? One of your native relatives, I imagine. She was in a hell of a hurry to get away with the baby, anyhow." He pointed to the schooner scudding up the channel under her bunch of red feathers.

Adam stared after the departing vessel. "I don't know what you mean—where are they all?" Then—"Puka! Hoku!" he shouted between his hands.

Mark shrugged. "No use calling. I've frightened them off. They won't be back for hours."

Adam stumbled back into the house and sat down on the floor with his head against the bed rail, too dazed even to try to puzzle out what his brother had told him. It didn't matter, really, so that Kilohana was better . . . his head drooped and he nodded.

Her fingers in his hair brought him back to consciousness and he slid carefully onto the bed beside her.

"Take anything, only leave my Kilohana to me," she muttered.

He nestled his cheek to hers. "Don't try to talk. Go to sleep. I won't leave you."

"When I was dead I heard you talking to your God.

'Take anything'—then I came back to you."

He put his arm around her carefully, so as not to jostle her, but his voice was tense with love. "Nothing else matters."

Her free hand groped for the baby. "What did Ahia do with My Darling?"

Ahia! The gaunt arm rummaging in the bed. . . .

Adam clutched the bed rail. My Darling was scudding up the Alenuihaha channel, kidnapped, under a bunch of red feathers . . . it was all clear to him now. God had answered his prayer in the very instant of asking, and his own child was the price. He steadied his voice with effort. "Go to sleep, Kilohana, and dream that I'm loving you. The child is right as rain."

The ghost of her old smile lit Kilohana's face though she did not open her eyes. "Right as rain," she mimicked. "I wonder! What makes you say such funny things, Adama?"

CHAPTER XXXIII

Halemaumau

IN THE MONTHS that followed, Mark readily became part of the life at Stone House. Since the night of his arrival when he and Adam had sat until daylight asking and answering questions, they had shut the door on the past and plunged into the life of everyday. Adam was magnificent, a virtual feudal lord with God only knew how many thousand acres and men belonging to him; friend and counsellor of the king who could beat the chiefs at their own sports of boxing and spear catching, yet even with a native wife and half-breed child, he was still more English than even Mark himself with his daily ceremony of shaving and his clothes, made for him in China from English patterns. Adam was as rigidly outside the native life as his own flagpole. One day Mark spoke to him about it and Adam, always inarticulate, tried to explain that aspect of his life to his younger brother. "I have to be. Those men who mix it up with natives, especially women, lose something out of themselves."

Mark understood. Everywhere in the South Seas were derelicts of manhood living on *awa* and alternately worshipped and beaten by their native harems; yet there was no need to be a prig, for all that. The pages of

Mark's sketch book were crowded with drawings of plump, bent knees, ripe breasts and wide, inviting smiles.

Lying on his mats in the grass house Adam had assigned to him, Mark watched the first daylight seeping through the wall. He had spent the night torch fishing on the reef and at moonset had gone home with some girls. He smiled reminiscently. "*Aurea prima aetas . . .*" well, there was no need to say it in Latin. Out here, everything breathed of it. His brother was a man to be worshipped, not copied. He snuggled back into his blanket, but the sun was growing hot and the mildewed smell of the grass walls tickled his nose. He sneezed and opened his eyes as he heard a covert snicker behind his head. "Who's there?"

There was no answer.

Thoroughly roused now, he sat up to blast the intruder and saw Lucy sitting in the corner. "How long have *you* been here?"

She raised her eyebrows. "I wonder! Do that again. You look funny." She crept across the matting and snuggled up to him like an affectionate puppy.

"Why did you wake me? Where've you been?" he grumbled, pushing away her wet hair.

"Swimming. Kilohana says too much loving in the night makes you tired in the morning. Come swim with me!"

Mark laughed ruefully. He could still taste the *awa* he had drunk last night and his legs felt silly. "All right, youngster. Go on and I'll follow you."

"Kiss me first. I love you!"

"Luki! Marki! Where are you? Adama says if you want to send that letter you must take it to him *wiki-wiki!*" Kilohana pushed the door curtain aside and sat down on the floor. The art of handwriting was beautiful to watch—little black marks scampering over the paper with nothing to guide them, yet coming out at the end in a design finer than any she could make with her choicest printing sticks. As she sat watching him a thought which had been forming in her mind crystallized and she spoke to Lucy, low and in Hawaiian, "You wish to marry him?"

Lucy shook her head. "No, only to love. Time enough"—she waved inclusively—"for all this."

Kilohana sighed. The girl had been reared in the English manner, without her mother's tabus, and it would be wise to plant her securely under the English tabus before she could repeat her adventure of the glass bracelet. She resolved to speak about it to Adam.

Mark took out his unfinished letter to his sister and conned it over, shaping the words soundlessly with his lips. "The girl, Lucy, is named for our mother and is pretty, but very forward, and Adam is more of a prig than ever. He runs his affairs like a king and even his wife, who is a princess or something in her own right, takes orders from him. He is fitting out his schooner for a trip to the volcanoes. He says it is business but I suspect that it is to show me more of the islands, as he is inordinately proud of this country of his adoption.

Why he makes business the excuse for everything he does I do not know, for in these tropic isles Father Time seems never to have ventured."

Kilohana and Lucy watched him heat the sealing wax over his tinder box and stamp the letter with the ring on his little finger.

Adam was on the dock, directing some workmen who were loading a canoe. He looked up and waved. "Make haste, Marky, we're going on board. This day is too fine to be drowsing it away."

So the letter was only a ruse to get him up, after all! Well, he was feeling better already, in spite of himself. As they paddled out to the *Lucy*, Mark felt for his pocket sketchbook. What a cartoon he could make of her, squatting in the water like a fat duck!

"What are you laughing at?"

Mark stifled the rising gust of laughter. One could never tell how Adam might relish a joke on his precious, homemade tub. "Nothing. Just a thought I had."

Adam grasped the rope ladder flapping down the schooner's tumble-home. "Well, here's something real to make you smile. Did you ever see a tidier vessel than my *Lucy?* And the high tide tomorrow morning will show you that she's as handy and able as she is fair." He went up the ladder and Mark in the canoe saw him stroke the *Lucy's* fat side for all the world as though she were a woman.

That night, lying close to Adam in the dark, Kilohana outlined her plan to marry Mark and Lucy. She was amazed at his ferocity. Was not the boy's blood as good as his own? Was not the highest marriage among chieftains that of brother and sister? It was none too soon to think of marriage for a girl whose buds were swelling, but after the first outburst when he had leapt out of bed like a man scorched with fire, he had not answered her arguments. Dragging on his clothes, he strode out of the house and slammed the door behind him

They did not lunch at Lahaina where Mark's ship was careened, but drifted along the South coast of Maui under the broken peak of Haleakala to Makena for a load of rope, and thence to Hina. Adam pointed across the Hawaii channel to where a column of smoke rose from the black rocks of the shore. "There's the temple where I was married, Marky. There's a man-idol twice as tall as I am with a bird's head and a round hat atop of it standing on the point."

Mark smiled at the picture of his brother dancing his wedding hula in the shadow of the man-bird; but Adam was talking again. "Round there is Kawaihae, where we're heading if we ever get get away from Hana. John Young lives there."

"The man the natives say started the cholera?"

"Yes, and stopped it too, I'll warrant. He's governor of Hawaii now, risen from a common seaman. Kamehameha kidnapped him from the *Elenor*, nobody knows how many years ago."

They sweltered at Hana for four days, trading with

the villagers for rope and mats and waiting for the wind, and on the fifth day put out with a fluky offshore breeze.

Kawaihae was even more desolate than Adam re- membered it. The coco palms were parched and yellow, and dust devils danced on the lava slopes above.

John Young was on the beach to meet them. He looked more dried-up than ever and his hands trembled, but he smiled wryly as he indicated the great coffin swinging under the eaves of his house. "Yon will have to wait a bit yet, in spite of your mother-in-law, Adam. Even the cholera couldn't kill me or that old harpy."

"What's she about now?"

"I ain't seen her for a long time. Gossip says she's got some halfbreed child up there in Pololu, teaching it devilment against the furriners, but I'll never trouble her so long as she keeps herself to herself. The king don't collect taxes from Kohala, so I never go there."

Mark watched his brother narrowly. Adam had never mentioned Ahia since the day she had sailed away with his newborn child; and he wondered now, looking at his brother's stolid face, if he could have dreamt it all; but the next day, sailing out of Kawaihae, Adam waved his hand at the blue cliffs to the north. "That's Kohala, where *she* lives," he said bitterly. "Kilohana's the only good thing that ever came out of that damned place."

"Aren't you going to try—"

"No," Adam cut him short.

Several days later while making camp in a forest on

the slope of Mauna Loa Adam himself brought up the subject. They were chopping fern shoots for supper while their two bearers hunted dry wood. "The Awini clan are like these giant ferns: hew them down and they spring up from the fallen trunks stronger than ever. Sometimes I almost believe what Kilohana says— that they're related to the birds and animals and get their strength from the earth. Ahia tried to kidnap Lucy; now that she's got one of Kilohana's children she may let us alone for awhile." He gave the fern a vicious dig.

"But Adam, isn't she your child, too? Shouldn't you try to save her? I should think—"

"It wouldn't be any use, Marky. The Awini get what they want in the end." He could not tell even his brother of his bargain with God and the price he had paid for Kilohana's life.

After they had eaten their supper of fern shoots and roasted breadfruit, Mark lit his pipe and stretched himself on the moss. "Adam."

"Well?"

"I want to leave my ship. I want to stay out here with you in the Islands. I've been thinking about it for months. I want to make something of myself the way you have." In the pipe glow his face was like a little boy's.

Adam stopped whittling and stared at the knife in his hands while his florid face grew white in the effort of self-control. "I'm afraid you can't do that, Marky."

"Why not?"

He shaved a thin slice from the stick and curled it carefully round his thumb. It would never do to let the boy see how he wanted him; he hadn't even dreamed it himself until a minute ago. "You'd better go back to your ship. They'd have you married to some native chiefess before you knew it, if you stayed."

"Well, what of that? You did it, didn't you?"

There was an uncomfortable silence and Adam cleared his throat. "That's just it. I know what I'm talking about. It's fight, fight day and night to keep English; and you never know if you're losing, things are so different out here. Why even your own children . . ." Adam shut his mouth hard.

"Well, then, suppose I' don't marry?"

"You can't do it, Marky. One way or t'other these islands'll get you if you stay. I didn't believe that once, but now . . ." he picked up the stick and began to whittle, and Mark knew that the subject was closed.

In the morning they left the fern forest and started across the dry lava beds for the volcano of Kilauea and Mark marvelled how the native bearers could tread the hot rocks barefoot while his own good boots were cut to pieces. They passed ancient craters so deep that the crowns of the *lehua* trees on the bottom looked a thousand feet below; craters edged with *ohelo* berry bushes and filled with lava hardened to wrinkled scum; steam cracks nauseous with sulphur smoke and lava which had cooled in tortured human shapes. At last the bearers refused to go any farther, pointing to a cloud of smoke ahead.

Adam and Mark took their water bottles and walked on, while the smoke swooped down and shut away everything but the rocks underfoot. Coughing and rubbing their eyes they clung to one another while the wind snatched up the cloud again and Adam cried, "Get back!" They were standing on the brink of a boiling lake whose lava waves surged and broke against black rock islands, real waves in a real sea. Invisible avalanches thundered round them while showers of rocks flew up and fell back into the firepit with a noise like cannon. He picked up a strand of volcanic glass and held it in front of Mark's eyes shouting, "Here's a lock of Pele's hair for your locket, Marky! She loves handsome boys like you."

Mark pointed to a platform covered with wicker towers tottering at the edge of the fire pit. "What the devil place is that?"

Adam scowled at Pele's temple through the smoke. "That's where most of the devilment in these islands starts. If the priests catch sight of us, they'll probably make Pele an offering by throwing us in."

They crept into a sheltering steam crack and hid. Then under cover of darkness, they crawled back to the edge of the pit. Moon and stars rose silver-cold and Mark shivered even while he shielded his face from the glare of Halemaumau. Lying on his stomach and staring into it, he fancied that it reminded him of something . . . now he had it . . . Adam's face yesterday, when he was whittling the stick.

By daybreak the brothers were back in the forest again, throwing water on themselves for coolness and drying themselves in the soft moss. Mark slept all that day while Adam lay and watched him, shaping a purpose in his mind. He would leave the boy with Captain Penhallow at Lahaina. Marky must never go back to Stone House.

CHAPTER XXXIV

The Net

AHIA sat alone in her great grass house, weaving. She could not clearly remember when she had left Pololu, but a long time ago most of her people had died and been eaten by hogs that in their turn had died; then when there was nothing more to eat and the wind up the valley was foul with the stench of dead things, a priest had taken her to Mahukona where there were still servants alive to wait on her and feed her pet owl and its brood; for as long as the guardian owl nested under Ahia's eaves she was safe, though evil and danger were abroad everywhere. Since she had lived at Mahukona the owl had hatched many broods.

There were always foreign ships coming in to Mahukona and Ahia at first contented herself with cursing them and gloating as she watched them sail away with death in their vitals; but that soon ceased to satisfy. She must know what manner of deaths they died, these people of the ships. Then, in a dream she saw the Net stretching across Hahukona mouth, with long fronds like the squid's tentacles and meshes strong enough to hold a whole ship in its clutch. With such a net, ship after ship would be dragged down to make a feast of white flesh for the shark. In the old days a chiefess could have had one hundred slaves twist her a net, but now there was no one she could trust. The slaves she sent into the forest for olona bark with which to make rope ran away, and even her own schooner captain cheated her, swearing that the price of rope had doubled in the other islands; but the child was worst of all. She had not been an hour old when nine years ago Ahia wrapped her in the chief's cape and snatched her away from under the Englishman's very nose. She had put her to nurse with a chiefess of only slightly lower rank than her own and had named her Kelahuna after her favorite ancestress; yet when Ahia called she ran away and hid, and she never smiled save at her own dead-leaf eyes in the water. Ahia might as well be grandmother to a shark—yes, the child was worst of all. A tear of self-pity streaked her cheek and she wiped it away crossly. Ahia was still strong enough to bring forth her burden alone. She blew on the smouldering torch beside her and it flared, blackening the shadows and lighting up the coils of rope piled to the ceiling.

Night was the best time to work at the Net, for when the grudging snivelers who served her were asleep, Others came. At night she had only to look up and see them all around her—men with bird's claws and beaks, women with glittering scales, and lizards like dragons conjured from the twilight of Po. She heaved at a knot and tightened it with her cracked teeth. The meshes were crooked and the holes of monstrous size, but what of that? Monstrous fish were the prize. She laughed, and echoes cackled in the corners.

A platter beside her holding a roast dog caught her eye, and she scooped out the guts and crammed them into her mouth, then tore off a piece of meat and held it out to a half-wild pig rooting in the floor. "Come, sweet Alapai. This is a tender morsel, even to one in the kingdom of the dead. Eat well, and soon the fat spirits of the foreigners shall fill your pretty belly. Spirits of foreigners, I suck your marrow! I swallow your pale eyes!" she croaked.

The torch flickered and shadows writhed and curved, making the room alive with darkness, and Ahia's voice rose in the name song of the Awini passing before her mad eyes in the moving shadows—here a gleam catching a single feather of a cloak; there a hot, smooth curve of dark flesh stirring; the rustle of a *malo* and the swish of a chief's long cape like the whisper of leaves; the click of a dog-tooth anklet, like the knocking together of a pig's tiny split hooves. The shadowy procession was endless and Ahia's voice beat on in the chant that was part of herself, calling their names as they passed before her, fierce eyes glittering, dark unseen faces glaring. These were her people, sons of the Shark and the Lizard, bred of Water and Fire.

Outside, an owl hooted and Ahia heard the name chant change as though another were singing it, calling on the Old Gods by their forbidden names. A priest

would have trembled there, but in her madness Ahia
was unafraid. The names of Pele surged round her like
tongues of fire and as if in answer, the torch leapt and
died in a whorl of black smoke and cinders like little
evil eyes. The warning owl cried again, but Ahia scream-
on, fed by he rown frenzy, until her voice was gone and
only her laboring breath spewed out the names with
her eyes fixed on the embers of the torch; eyes veiled
with skinny lids as the ash glowed and fell away; drow-
sy eyes, holding Ahia's fast.

The door banged open. The coals flickered and
were gone, but Ahia still blinked and stared at the puls-
ing ashes with their centers of greenish heat—reptilian
eyes. As though the last warmth in the world had
vanished with the dying torch, sea fog swirled into the
room, mounting in the corners, whirling around a core
of cold she felt but could not see. She pulled up her
cloak of draggled feathers and coughed. That tall man
muffled in the fog must slam the door and shut out
this creeping cold! She screamed at him, but her voice
seemed to drop at her feet. Saliva spangled her lips
as she cursed and struck out at the still figure and
toppled, with her fist doubled under her. With a grunt
of pain she hitched herself up and tried to recognize
him, but the skull rising above the fog wore no feather
helmet nor tossing mane. In it was no gleam of eye-
balls, only a deader darkness in the face stretching
from temple to temple. The breath she was saving for
more curses whistled empty away and she drooped

before the Thing she could not know, yet knew—that was her will and yet above her will, emotionless, undiverted, implacable as the ocean tides. One greater even than Pele had answered her call. "Eyes that see in the night, Eyes that pierce the ocean depths, I called and You have come . . . "

Across the jaw there stirred a gash, crescent-shaped, and Ahia saw the rows of inward-raking teeth. Whimpering and sucking her bruised knuckles, she fell on her face. "I am ready. Is it tonight?" she croaked.

The answering wave of cold struck her vitals.

She got up shakily and dragged at the net. Sweat streamed into her eyes and streaked her flanks as she pushed and pulled it toward the door, tripping and falling and scrambling up again, but never looking back, for the smell of ocean slime filled her nostrils and in her ears was the swish of a great tail.

At last the door! She pinned it back and screamed as something struck her face and fluttered to her feet. It was only an owlet and she picked it up and studied it, trying to remember something. Now she knew! The owl was an interfering creature, but he should not learn Ahia's secret, not he. She wrung its neck and crushed it under her bare foot.

The net moved more easily along the ground, but Ahia was growing tired. She kept falling and her head was light while her feet were as though wrapped around with a robber's thong and stone. At last she reached a canoe and sank down on it, trembling. "The names

of the Awini are great, like a strong mat, woven together . . . " she panted. Where were the Awini? She
tried again: "Oh, Thou, whose eyes pierce the ocean
depths . . . " She felt stronger now, almost strong
enough to launch the canoe. But first, she must get
the net on board . . . she heaved on it with her utmost
strength.

When she came to, she was lying half under the
net in the bottom of the canoe, listening to the grating
of the outrigger on pebbles. The fog was so dense that
she could hardly see the bow, but she needed no guide
in this harbor. The tide was going out and the net
would lie quietly on its mooring stakes, waiting to be
fed. Her breath came in gasps as she tried to paddle.
"Oh, Thou, whose eyes pierce even the darkest
night . . . " The mooring stake loomed ahead and she
threw the guy rope over it and pulled on the free end
till the outrigger flew up and the net started over the
opposite side. "You Net, my beautiful Net, I spread
you now for their ships, for their feet, for their souls,"
she crooned, telling off the buoys of yellow *wiliwili*
wood on her fingers as the net slipped away and spread
slowly in the dark. So great was this net that it must
surely cover the whole harbor mouth, reaching out its
tentacles catch the ships, like the net of her dream. Her
hands relaxed on the gunwale as she sensed the buoys
bobbing away from her. Each one had been set with
a curse. Yes, the net was good. But what now? The
work of vengeance for which she had existed was

finished, yet whoever struggled to his death because of her could not bring back the old days, nor Kaha, nor Alapai. The gods were cowards. Ahia was in rags, and splendor and reverence were gone forever from the world. She laid her head on the gunwale and wept.

The canoe drifted slowly in the night breeze and Ahia dozed and whimpered in her sleep. She dreamed that she was lying on the grass watching a little girl and a boy whose head was shaved to look like a chief's helmet, scuffling over a *lei*. Another child, dressed in a feather cape and carrying a spear threw it at them, and the children fled, while the little chiefess mocked them with scornful, dead-leaf eyes. The frightened girl crawled into Ahia's lap and she knew that it was Alapai. Poor Alapai! She had been sick and weak, even in those days. Ahia picked a tidbit from the platter beside her, chewed it fine and put it in her child's mouth. She had ever loved Alapai the best. The child in the feather cape laughed and Ahia moaned in her dream, "Mouse-eyes! Woe to the day I stole you from your foreign father!"

A savage sense of something strange made her open her eyes. Something was coming, sliding through the water with the sound of a dog lapping. She saw it high overhead, great snout poking through the fog; sleek sides dripping black; a muffled voice speaking in an unknown tongue. She bent double lest she see It face to face. The voice spoke again followed by the hissing of a line uncoiling and something splashed in the water. Another voice answered, and still Ahia hid her face. "O Thou Father of my Fathers, Thou Water Thing . . ." a block creaked and she looked up sharply. The Thing coming to her in the dark was a ship! She could almost touch its planking with her paddle and two white men were staring at her from the rail. One of them held a coil of lead line in his hand.

Ahia clambered to the bow of the canoe. "You ship," she shrieked. "You white man's ship, come! Follow me! Follow me into the Net!" She paddled with frenzy, stopping to wave and point, trying to get ahead of the vessel. "Come, a feast! A great feast on shore! Pig, and *awa*, and women . . . " She tried to *hula* as she had seen the young *wahines* do and fell sprawling. The men laughed and she scrambled up again with a look of insane cunning. "I am but one come out to entice you," she wheedled. "The shore is lined with them, young and fresh and sweet, like Aalapai—waiting only for you!" Mist wraiths drifted between her and the moving faces. The ship was passing her. She must stop it at all costs—drive it if she could not lead it, into the Net! She thrust in her paddle and the canoe swerved and struck the ship with a crash. The outrigger splintered and the canoe, robbed of its balance, rolled over and over.

She came up gasping and clutched at it but it rolled away from her as though trying to elude her. At last she caught it with one hand—but where were her legs? She ran her free hand down her thigh to make sure.

It was there to her hand though the thigh itself felt no pressure and she could see her legs trailing after her in the water. Well, whatever had happened to her she could still flatten herself along the log and paddle as babies do. She shook her fist at the departing stern. "Into my Net with you!" she screeched and gagged a mouthful of water. The log was alive and wriggling away from her. "O Thou Log Thing, Thou Water Thing," she begged, and wriggled after it through a sea alive with little bobbing creatures. Her hand caught at something under water and the yellow bobbles around her dipped and rose again. Something was holding her —seaweed perhaps, or—her flesh crept as she tried to remember the prayer to Squid. But one must have a cowrie shell for that prayer, and who was Ahia to pray to such as Squid? "My Father's Fathers," she mouthed, and vomited sea water. The Thing was wrapping her round like a net. With her last strength she flung herself clear and dropped flat, as sunfish drop, and the buoys of yellow *wiliwili* wood quivered and drew together beneath her weight.

CHAPTER XXXV

Blood of the Shark

T HE NEWS of Ahia's death reached Adam through the king himself, who with Hewahewa had come to inspect the new stone fort building under Adam's direction. She had disappeared one night and fishermen had found her body tangled in a net at the mouth of Mahukona harbor.

Adam grunted. So the old gorgon was dead at last! But how had even a net contrived to drown a Hawaiian, and why had she not been eaten by sharks?

Kamehameha shrugged. There were rumors that the net was a magic one, but Ahia was old and mad. She might have fallen in the water from weakness. As for the sharks, they would respect even a dead Awini. "We are of the blood of the shark," he reminded Adam, and the Englishman made a face in spite of himself.

"The child Kelahuna will be confirmed by the college of chiefs unless I order otherwise. It would be a good thing for Hawaii to clean out that sow's wallow. How would Kilohana take it?"

Adam jerked himself out of his brown study. Nine years ago he had chosen to forget this child of his—My Darling, her mother had called her. Now she was a full-fledged chiefess bearing the name of that ancestor who had been sired by a red-tailed tropic bird. He would never leave Stone House and his shipyard to go to Kohala and spend his life watching Kilohana revert to savagery. He answered with studied indifference. "I am more useful here, Sire. I couldn't do anything in Kohala."

Kamehameha's eyes twinkled. "I am not offering *you* the chiefhood, my friend. The Awini are far too wild to tolerate a foreigner, and besides, I need you here. If Kilohana goes to Kohala, I myself will find you a younger wife."

Adam laughed. He was happy today and could relish a joke.

Hewahewa interrupted. "The place is ridden with evil. Death-praying wizards infest it and the priests at Puuepa tell me that even the fish they draw from the sea are poison. Ahia was—" he shuddered and broke off—"but Kilohana will change all that. The child is overyoung to rule."

The smile left Adam's face, and for one bitter instant he pitied himself. He had hoisted his Union Jack to the flagpole in front of Stone House daily for years, yet to the two Hawaiians confronting him he was no more than a faithful servant ready to build ships, or forts, or to take a new wife at their bidding, "I am what I am," he said out loud. "I cannot change."

The King raised his eyebrows. "I wonder," he mocked, and only then did Adam realize that he had spoken.

Hewahewa put his arm over Adam's shoulder. "The priests have put Mahukona under tabu until I can exorcise the place. Take me there in your schooner and we will talk over this matter of the succession."

The King laughed. "You were ever a diplomat, Hewahewa. Had I need to win any man, you should be my ambassador."

Adam and the high priest left the fort together and that evening, at Stone House, they told Kilohana of her mother's death and of their plan to go to Kohala.

Kilohana's half-hearted wailing stopped. "Then we shall see My Darling!"

The two men exchanged glances. "We are going alone."

"You cannot keep me back!"

"Better take her, Adama, lest she swim," Hewahewa laughed.

"But we may be gone for weeks. Who will care for Lucy? She is too old to be left with the servants."

Kilohana threw back her head and opened her arms. "Oh, My Darling, I am coming to you in Kohala. You are the snow on the mountain. The ranting wind cannot melt you, but the sun of love will warm you and turn you to tears of joy. Where the tropic bird sired our foremother by the black Mahukona cliffs, there will I come to you, My Darling."

Lucy watched her mother as one would watch the antics of a dancing bear. "What is this claptrap of old names and places? I will stay at Stone House," she declared.

Adam patted her shoulder, firm and young under the orange riding dress. Lucy was intoxicating, like the orange blossoms she wore around her neck. Besides, he rather liked her not wanting to go to Kohala. What English girl in her right mind would choose to go to *that* God-forsaken place? "Take care of yourself when you ride abroad, Chickie."

She thrust a booted foot into her father's lap and a clink, like fairy bells, came from the spur. All her good humor was back now and she fondled his head and laughed. "Since you strung these nuggets on my spurs, I am like an old belled cow," she said, and kissed his mouth.

Kilohana had made many trips with Adam to the other islands, but he had purposely never taken her to Hawaii; at first because of her mother and later, because he intended them both to forget this child whom they had never known. Now, her excitement was pitiful. She chattered and sang until he put his fingers in his ears. She was like a woman fey.

They had been out two days when above the early morning clouds they saw Mauna Kea's snow peak and beside it Mauna Loa, violet in the distance, shaped like a woman's breast. Kilohana stood waiting, pressed against the rail. The sun touched the nearer clouds and one by one they drifted up the mountainside; then all at once they parted and Hualalai reared its black head into the sky. Kilohana fell on her face on the deck. "Oh Thou Mighty One, thou Hualalai, hold thy fires from My Darling," she prayed. As if in answer, a puff of smoke rose from its tip and Kilohana threatened it with her fist. "Look at thy neighbor Haleakala, across the channel! He was so angry that he burst and now his belly is empty and his fires are cold. Hold back they fires from My Darling! Look to thyself, Hualalai!"

Adam swept the shore with his spyglass for signs of life, but there were no canoes abroad and no people stirring on the beach. A column of yellow smoke rose from the temple. He handed the glass to Hewahewa.

"The place is under tabu," the priest said. "Dogs are muzzled, fowls are hidden under calabashes and the people are shut up in the houses. Hoist the royal *kahili*, Adama. My coming will be the signal to raise the tabu." The yellow plumes were run to the masthead and almost at once a man appeared on the temple wall and put a shell trumpet to his mouth. There was a faint blast and people came running.

Kilohana seized the spyglass. "Kohala, my Kohala," she cried. "See Adama, there is the little house where I waited for the bridegroom! It is falling to pieces. There have been no brides there in years," She flung herself into the canoe beside him. "I am landing where you landed, I shall step where you stepped. Oh, we were happy then!"

Adam slid her hand into his. "Do you remember I saved your hair?" he asked shyly. "I wouldn't let the old woman cut it off, and then we ran away."

A priest carrying a feather god appeared in front of the temple followed by a procession of priests and spear men, who halted and re-formed in close ranks, while the villagers fell on their faces. Hewahewa was the first to step ashore, and as the other priest advanced to meet him the spearmen fell back and Adam and Kilohana saw the girl seated in a litter carried by two men. She wore a red feather helmet and shoulder cape and one hand dangled a short spear. "Who are these people? Why do they not fall in the dust before me?"

Kilohana stretched out her arms. "My Darling!"

The little chiefess balanced her javelin on two fingers. "One step more, and I throw!"

Kilohana fell back. "Tell her, Hewahewa."

The high priest spoke low and earnestly but the girl screeched, " I will not have it! My mother is dead! My sire is a rusty owl! You lie!"

Kilohana's face twisted with sudden fury. "I am Kilohana, child of Kaha and Ahia, whose grandmother was Kelahuna of the Rosy Comb!" Priests and people drew aside as she came on step by step, chanting her names and kindred at the challenger; almost near enough to touch the girl fingering the spear. "The eyes!" She crumpled and the spear flew over her head.

Adam leapt to meet it, caught it in mid-air and drew back his arm. In another instant he would transfix this chattering thing holding him at bay with its dead-leaf eyes. But his English hand would not close on the spear. "Get out of here," he roared. "Get out!" and threw it into the bushes.

The child seemed to stare through him. "She dared to speak of my eyes. Carry me hence."

Adam watched the procession straggle out of sight while Hewahewa rocked with laughter. "There goes a true Awini. She's the old woman all over again except for the eyes. *They* were strange."

"They were grey," Adam answered huskily.

Hewahewa wiped his own eyes with the tail of his robe. "Well, whatever they were, it was a battle worth seeing, but this matter of the succession is something for me to settle with the priests. Take Kilohana on board the schooner and come back for me in three days."

Adam sat alone on deck in the dark and his fingers still clenched and loosened on an imaginary spear while the hot blood-waves flowed over him. Someone should rid the world of that little monster as of a rat, yet because he had begotten those pale eyes in the weasel face, he could not throw the spear. He wished that he might hear of the death of this child that Kilohana had called My Darling. He shut his eyes against the picture of Kilohana's frenzy, chanting her savage names and kindred while the people stared. No wonder she was snoring now like a drunken woman in the bunk where he had laid her. There was nothing for it but to put in to Kawaihae and lie there until time to go back for Hewahewa. He thought with distaste of John Young. Everything that his countryman had told him that night on Diamond Head twenty years ago had come true and Adam hated him for it; yet Adam's life had been outwardly one of success. He had his ships, while John Young had but a polished coffin under the eaves. Adam's work would live, for it was England.

He got up and looked over the rail. Gleams of phosphorescence twinkled in the wave curling away from the *Lucy's* side, growing paler as the black water turned to lead—harbinger of dawn. The schooner was barely moving.

A fin cut the water in a triangular ripple and as he watched it, all Adam's fury and humiliation concentrated on the shark below. The blood of the shark had colored his life just as the creature hidden in the shadow of the ship was the incarnation of the unseen savagery that dogged him everywhere. Blood of the shark! Love held him to Kilohana in spite of it, but who could tell if somehow, through the bond that held them together, he had not been tainted with it, too? The shark itself must answer for that. Adam Gordon would fight shadows no longer.

He took out his knife and dived overboard.

Kilohana roused from her sleep. She had been dreaming of that other child, whom, long ago, Adam had laid in the crotch of a breadfruit tree, ordering her never to speak of it again. She dreamt of it often lately and the little newborn thing, changeless in a world of change, comforted her. In her dream she watched it loosen the binding tapa and crawl to and fro in the moonlight, twittering and crying. Then the crying was lost in men's hoarse voices and the clattering of feet on deck.

She stretched herself and gathered her hair away from the little pools of saliva where she had drooled in her heavy sleep. Something was surely happening to Adama. . . . She rolled out of her bunk and ran up the ladder.

A Hawaiian sailor held her back. "Don't interfere or you may die, too."

"Stand away!"

Adam lay hunched on his side in the scuppers with his blue trousers in shreds. The blood spurting from his torn leg was timed by the beat of his heart.

She dropped down beside him and tore off her skirt for a bandage.

"It's no use. I'm *pau*. Just—stay with me, Kilohana." His voice was muffled as though it came from far off.

She took his head in her lap and stroked it. "What happened?"

A sailor pushed forward. "Who knows? When I came on deck the Captain was in the water and the shark was dead. We pulled him out but—" there was no need to tell more.

"Water."

They poured it over him and it ran out of his mouth and down his neck. Kilohana wiped it away and set a moist rag between his lips. Adam had always been so neat.

He looked at her as though he would draw her with him into the Land of Shadows. "Give me an English burial. Don't keep any part of me, please. I remember—" his voice trailed off and Kilohana bent double to hear it but the words were disjointed—shark, Kilohana, and again tabu. He seemed to be asleep now and she nursed his head in her lap while the sailors watched.

Suddenly Adam sat up and looked about wildly, searching for something, and his eyes fastened on Kilohana. "The ship—"

She bent and stiffened with his weight. There was a queer noise in his throat and a vein in his temple was beating. Kilohana counted the strokes, one, two, three, four, the column of blood in the vein ebbing lower with every count. The loud breathing stopped and Adam shivered and lay still.

She drooped over him. Then—"Where is the shark? He shall follow Adama into the Land of the Dead!"

The sailors looked at one another. "He has gone before," one answered.

Kilohana gathered the dead head to her breast. "No one shall have you now. You shall never leave me, Adama," she crooned. "The strange white woman of California and Lucy will love living men, but you are mine for always, never to share. They would have taken you away from me but now—" she kissed the mouth and wiped the damp forehead with her hair.

The sailors put back to Mahukona and Hewahewa came on board. Then Kilohana wailed in earnest, chanting Adam's fame and deeds for those on shore to hear. A black tapa was run to the masthead and Hewahewa ordered the *Lucy* into Kawaihae. "We must see John Young about this," he told Kilohana, who sobbed her consent.

At Kawaihae John Young came off to the vessel. "I saw the black tapa and knew summat 'ad 'appened," he explained as he stood with the tears running down his cheeks before Adam's body lying in its bunk. "Yon was a good man, Kilohana. He would want an English burial."

They buried him in John Young's polished coffin weighted with rocks and strapped with iron; and as it slid off the planks into the deep water outside the reef, three prayers went up: John Young's to Jehovah, God of David and King George; and Hewahewa's to the Life-Taker whom none had dare name; but Kilohana prayed to Adam, for she knew that his spirit had become a god.

CHAPTER XXXVII

Aloha

THERE was a feast at Stone House and the ground under the arbor was spread with fern and covered with *poi*-filled calabashes. Steam rose from platters heaped with lumps of pig and fish wrapped in leaves, and crabs and mounds of pink salt dotted the spread, down the center of which were piled oranges strewn with orange blossoms. Torches flared in the wind, lighting the leaping shadows and the faces of the guests. How Adama would have loved it! The name Adam Gordon was on every lip tonight. Kilohana fingered the broad red ribbon slanting from her shoulder to her hip where the King of England's medal dangled. The King's own admiral had put it there with a speech of thanks from King George himself for the present of the schooner *Adam Gordon*, the first Hawaiian-built vessel in the English fleet. She turned to the Admiral with the question which she asked every Englishman she met. "Tell me about Beretania."

"You are Britannia herself, Madam." This Hawaiian woman who spoke English with such precision reminded him of a figurehead, with her straight glance and queenly carriage. In spite of her size he could still see that she had been beautiful.

The officer on her left was slim and fair, like Adam. "Do you like our eight islands?" she asked him.

"Yes, but you're too civilized. I've heard all sorts of stories about Hawaii, but one might as well be in England for all that I can see. This arbor, now—"

Kilohana's white teeth flashed. The arbor *was* English, Adama had said so; and Stone House was an English home. She pronounced it home-ay, making the English word into a Hawaiian one, and he smiled.

"But it must have been utterly uncivilized when your husband came here with Lord Vancouver. Tell me about the life then."

Kilohana's eyes seemed to fling a wall between them as she rose unhurriedly and went to Adam's chair, on either side of which a giant plumed standard stood guard. The young officer followed her. "I don't remember that it was so very different then," she answered and gave the sign for the *hulas* to begin. As she grew older, Kilohana felt nearer to the old times and more jealous of sharing them with strangers.

The guests crowded around the *hula* mat as the dancing started. The dancers were all young, with only the cantor with the gourd old and fat like herself, for Kilohana knew her foreigners. They danced for an hour while the brandy passed from hand to hand.

At last she ordered them to stop and stepped onto the mat herself. "Would you like to hear an English song?" she asked and began Adam's hunting song. "Tantivy, tantivy, tantivy, a-hunting we will go!"

The Englishmen joined her, keeping time with their glasses and stamping their feet as she led them from one song to another in her clear child's voice.

The admiral raised his glass. "I drink to Mistress Adam Gordon, who knows more English songs than all the Royal Navy put together," he cried.

The ribbon on Kilohana's breast shimmered in the torchlight. "Adama taught me them."

But the admiral was not to be quenched while the brandy lasted. "Mistress Gordon, you are really English! Come back to England where you belong."

She took a coconut shell half full of brandy and drained it. "Thank you. I shall never leave Hawaii."

"But there is nothing here to keep you! You have no children. . . ."

"Ah, but I have."

Kilohana uttered a low, throaty call and a tiny lizard peeped out from under the ferns and stood blinking in the glare of the torches while she dipped her forefinger in the brandy and flipped a drop on its darting tongue.

"Brandy is a pleasant drink for all people," she smiled, "come, drink and be happy with us tonight, Little Son."

Glossary

Ahulau—Cholera.

Aikane—A companion of the same sex.

Aloha—Greeting.

Ao—The hour of dawn

Auwe—Alas!

Awa—Intoxicating drink made from the root of Piper methysticum.

Ehu—Blond.

Hala—Pandanus odoratissimus.

Halemaumau—Fire pit of the volcano Kilauea.

Hau—Paritium tiliaceum.

Hawaii Nei—All Hawaii.

Holua—Sled.

Hookupu—A tribute.

Huhu—Angry.

Hula—Hawaian dance.

Io—God of Light, above all gods.

Kahili—Plumed standard.

Kamani—Terminalia catappa linneaus.

Kane—"Lord and Giver of Life."

Kauhi—Legendary shark of Oahu.

Kekualapa and Kekupohi—Two cloth jackets given to King Kamehameha by Vancouver.

Kihei—Tapa mantle.

Kioloa—Racing canoe.

Koa—Acacia koa, Hawaiian mahogany.

Konane—Hawaiian game of checkers.

Ku—First god of the Hawaiian pantheon.

Kukailimoku — Kamehameha's personal war god.

Leahi—Diamond Head.

Lehua—Metrosideros polymorpha.

Lei—Garland.

Lomilomi—Massage.

Maikai—Good.

Makahiki—Five-day festival of ancient Hawaii.

Malo—Loincloth.

Mamo—Drepanis pacifica.

Manele—Litter.

Mauka—Toward the mountains.

Menehune—Gnome.

Moo—Legendary dragon or giant lizard.

Naupaka—Scoevola mollis.

Niuhi—Legendary shark of the Eight Seas of Hawaii.

Noho—Keep away!

Ohelo—Vaccinum reticulatum.

Olona—Touchardia latifolia, from whose bark is made the finest rope.

Pakiki—Stubborn.

Paiai—Pounded dried taro root, the food of travelers.

Pali—Cliff.

Pau—Finished.

Pa-u—Tapa skirt.

Pele—Hawaiian goddess of volcanoes.

Pikoi—Stone and thong used by robbers to fell their victims.

Poi—Pounded taro root, the Hawaiian bread.

Popolo—Solanum nodiflorum Jacq.; a medicinal herb.

Pu—Gun.

Taro—Colocasia esculenta. The root (cooked) is pounded to make poi.

The Twilight of Po—The Twilight of Antiquity.

Ti—Cordyline terminalis.

Ukanipo—Legendary shark of Hawaii.

Wahine—Woman.

Wikiwiki!—Hurry!

Wiliwili—Erythrina monosperma, a tree whose wood, lighter than cork, is used for making buoys and floats.

According to Andrews' Hawaiian Dictionary, published in Honolulu in 1865, Hawaiian is pronounced as follows:

Vowels: A as in arch, ask, etc.

E as a in irate, late, etc.

I as in pique.

O as in note.

U as in coo.

Consonants are pronounced as in English.